'Lacing everyday life with menace is Sam Carrington's greatest strength as a storyteller.'
The Times

'A, compelling read, full of twists and turns with well-drawn, unreliable characters that kept me guessing!'
Sarah Pearse

'A kick-ass page turner . . . I was knocked senseless by the awesome twist.'
John Marrs

'Sam Carrington has done it again . . . A twisty, gripping read. I loved it.'
Cass Green

xpertly written . . . with plentiful twists and unforgettable characters. An insightful and unnerving read.'
Caroline Mitchell

austrophobic psychological thriller that had me double checking my doors and windows were locked!'
Vicki Bradley

'I devoured this story in one sitting!'
Louise Jensen

Tense, convincing and complex, it kept me guessing (wrongly!).'
Caz Frear

Sam Carrington lives in Devon with her husband, two border terriers and a cat. She has three adult children and a grandson. She worked for the NHS for 15 years, during which time she qualified as a nurse. Following the completion of a psychology degree she went to work for the prison service as an Offending Behaviour Programme Facilitator. Her experiences within this field inspired her writing. She left the service to spend time with her family and to follow her dream of being a novelist.

Readers can find out more at samcarringtonauthor.com and can follow Sam on Twitter @sam_carrington1.

BY THE SAME AUTHOR

THE
COUPLE
ON MAPLE
DRIVE

SAM CARRINGTON

avon.

Published by AVON
A division of HarperCollins*Publishers*
1 London Bridge Street
London SE1 9GF

www.harpercollins.co.uk

HarperCollins*Publishers*
1st Floor, Watermarque Building, Ringsend Road
Dublin 4, Ireland

A Paperback Original 2021
1

First published in Great Britain by HarperCollins*Publishers* 2021

A catalogue copy of this book is available from the British Library.

ISBN: 978-00-08436-38-4

This novel is entirely a work of fiction. The names, characters
and incidents portrayed in it are the work of the author's imagination.
Any resemblance to actual persons, living or dead, events or
localities is entirely coincidental.

Typeset in Minion by Palimpsest Book Production Ltd, Falkirk, Stirlingshire
Printed and Bound in the UK using 100% Renewable Electricity
at CPI Group (UK) Ltd

MIX
Paper from
responsible sources
FSC™ C007454

This book is produced from independently certified FSC™ paper
to ensure responsible forest management.

For more information visit: www.harpercollins.co.uk/green

The Couple on Maple Drive is dedicated to one of my favourite couples – J and San. Good friends and excellent plotting accomplices!

Chapter One

Christie's Crime Addicts – True Crime Podcast

Live stream:

[DOUG] It's all happening in the bay, listeners! Just after we hit the stop button on today's recording, we had news of a developing situation right here in our English Riviera – I reckon Agatha Christie herself would be following along if she could. We thought we'd tag this on to the end of the usual podcast to let you know the armchair detectives are all over it! I've got Ed on the phone from the scene. [Crackling noise] So, Ed – bring us up to speed – what's happening in Torquay right now?

[ED] Well, there's a heavy police presence in the Wellswood area, Doug. One of our regular podcast listeners gave us the heads-up and we got ourselves straight here.

[DOUG] Any specifics yet?

[ED] Sketchy at the moment. We're down a team member today, too, so it's just Christie doing the behind-the-scenes searching while we're live on air . . . Oh, hang on, Christie's here now.

[CHRISTIE] Hey. This incident is working its way through the usual social media channels – I see Devon Live has just posted something . . .

1

[DOUG] We'll do our own research, eh?

[CHRISTIE] Hah! Yep, sure thing.

[DOUG] Some onlookers are messaging me saying there's some movement outside a house. Can you see anything?

[CHRISTIE] A body perhaps . . . I'm trying to get closer. Looks like police are bringing someone out.

[DOUG] Do you guys think it could be a murder?

[ED] Forensics are on scene. Maybe. I'll leave you with Christie while I see if I can find a credible source.

[DOUG] Well, true-crime fans, looks like we might have a serious one on our doorstep. As this is early news, we'll keep digging and bring you more tomorrow following our planned podcast. As ever, let us know if you've any information to share. We'll be live again just after ten a.m. In the meantime, Christie's Crime Addicts wish you a safe day in the bay.

Chapter Two

Isla gingerly shifted sideways and stretched her good arm down between the sofa and wall, her hand feeling for the TV remote. She lifted it back up, together with an empty Galaxy wrapper. Wrinkling her nose, she un-balled it to check if any shards of chocolate remained. Disappointed it was completely void of even one crumb, she screwed it back up again, launching it towards the waste-paper bin – which it missed by a foot – realigned the cushions snugly behind her back, and returned her attention to the telly.

The hundredth rerun of *Murder She Wrote* played on the screen. It didn't matter how many times she'd seen the episodes, they made a great distraction. Good old Jessica Fletcher – she always found the culprit. The show was a childhood favourite, one she'd always watched during 'The Good Days' with her parents and older brother back in Scotland. It was her go-to cosy crime programme when she was feeling low. Glum. Bored. Depressed. Lonely.

Scared.

Isla shook off the feeling. Her home was her safe space. She had to slow the thoughts in her head, make them go from fearful to positive – that's what the online therapy course had encouraged her to do. Or, something like that. It was positive, anyway. No more dwelling on what had happened, what she couldn't change – she must focus on the measures she could take to help herself, *not* on her reactions to the event. Not on feeling helpless.

'Look forward to where you are heading, not back to where you've come from,' the middle-aged, mothering voice of Dr Emile Forrester told her.

Easier said than done. And it's why she'd slammed down her laptop screen and diverted her attention to fiction instead. All that talk of optimism, the psychobabble nonsense, was giving her a headache. Of course, when Zach returned home from work later, she'd tell him she'd completed the day's online workshop – filled in her therapy journal as instructed. Everything she'd promised Zach she'd keep doing. It's not as though he'd check up on her, was it?

What he didn't know couldn't hurt him.

Isla felt a flash of guilt. He was only trying his best, ensuring she had a fighting chance of recovering mentally as well as physically. Although the bruising was slowly fading, the fractured wrist bone mending, her mind was failing to heal as quickly – her confidence had been knocked, her vulnerability brought into sharp focus. Zach intended to rectify that. His idea to move in had been a life-saving act in her eyes. Although, their relationship hadn't quite been *there* yet, if she were being honest. They were work colleagues, of sorts. She'd known of him since she first started as an intern at his father's financial company, but they hadn't become an item until three months ago. Isla had put off agreeing to a date with the boss's son for numerous reasons – some more obvious than others.

They'd bypassed a lot of moving-in-together chat once it became clear she would need extra support following the attack. And Zach had been only too keen to offer himself up as housemate potential. It made sense, he'd said. And he'd been right – Isla had needed him. Probably still needed him.

The end credits rolled impossibly quickly up the screen, and Isla immediately flicked to Netflix and began scrolling through the dozens of programmes in her 'continue watching' list. All true-life crime documentaries, or crime series. She clicked on *Unsolved Mysteries* and picked up where she'd left off yesterday. She didn't watch these programmes while Zach was home, and luckily for her, he rarely switched to Netflix – he was more into current affairs, news channels and stuff on Sky. He'd be unlikely to uncover her daily crime-fix obsession.

It'd become worse since the attack. She felt compelled to watch everything relating to crime – to delve into the minds of criminals, figure out their motivation, the reasons they gave for what they'd done. It wasn't because she thought it was helping her – in fact most people would be against her habit, telling her not to think too hard about perpetrators of crime, of the bad people out in the world. But for Isla, understanding the underlying factors, having knowledge of the *why*s, was something she needed in order to help her recognise dangerous people and situations in the future.

'You shouldn't have been walking on your own.'

She'd heard those words a dozen times since it happened – both from the accusatory voice in her head and from well-meaning family, friends and colleagues. Together with: 'You put yourself in such a risky situation, Isla.' But why? *Why* shouldn't she have been out on her own in the town she lived in? How come walking in the street alone at night is classed as putting yourself at risk? As far as she was concerned, she had every right to do that and shouldn't be in fear of her life – fearful of what someone else might do to her – if she didn't adhere to the unwritten rules of being a woman.

Isla *was* fearful, though. As much as she argued against the

5

reasoning, she couldn't shake the anxiety created by the person who mugged her. He'd taken away her right to feel safe. He'd not only stolen her mobile phone and handbag, he'd stolen her confidence. Forced her to put up a protective wall. And with each day, tucked away from the real world, cocooned within her own four walls, she was becoming something less.

She'd lost control of her life through the actions of someone else. And despite the therapy suggesting she would be able to take it back, her mind had yet to believe the claim. She knew she had to focus on herself, on the steps she could take, but for now, she was obsessing far more about the actions *he'd* taken.

And whether he would strike again.

Chapter Three

As Zach approached Isla's rented, semi-detached house, he noted that the curtains to the front-room bay window were drawn again. It wasn't even dark, yet she'd already shut herself off to the outside world. In fact, he doubted they'd been pulled back at all and she'd likely been cooped up in there, the heavy, grey blackout material obliterating natural light, for the entire day.

He gave a furtive glance towards the adjoining house as he climbed the steps, wondering if they'd noticed the closed curtains day in, day out. Probably not, he concluded. He'd never even met the couple next door. Isla said they weren't the type of neighbours who popped in for a coffee and a chinwag. He paused as he reached the top step, his gaze fixed on the chrome number five on the door and fingers gripping the key, as he contemplated the scene about to greet him.

Isla would be on the large, bottle-green-coloured sofa, legs sprawled to the side of her, remote control in hand when he walked inside. The position he'd found her in on each of the previous evenings spanning the last two weeks. He was trying to be supportive and understanding. She'd experienced a traumatic event, physically and psychologically – of course it would affect her badly. But he wished she would show signs of progression. Something positive, however little, in the right direction. He'd organised online therapy sessions, texted or rung throughout the day, made sure she had a phone to receive messages from her family and friends, and was being as patient as possible with her when he got home from work.

There was only so much he could do to help her, though, and he was running out of ideas. He didn't want to come across as pushy, and he didn't want to rush her – as that was the last thing she needed. He was there, by her side. Maybe that was all that mattered for now. She'd said she felt safer with him living there, so that was his current role. Like her, he needed to take it one day at a time.

Zach inhaled deeply, turned the key, and pushed the door open. 'Hello, my gorgeous lady, how are you?' he called. He dropped his briefcase beside the round antique-wood hall table, carried on down the hallway to the lounge and approached the sofa, bending over to kiss the top of Isla's head. A musty odour mixed with a sour scent wafted upwards. She had the same pyjamas on as when he left her this morning – a pale-blue top with her initials embroidered on, and black chequered bottoms. The same ones she'd been wearing for at least a week. Had she even washed today?

'Fine, thanks. How was work?' Isla slowly swung her legs off the sofa and pushed herself up with her good arm, turning to face him. She winced with the movement – the bruising was obviously still causing her some discomfort. Zach almost winced himself as he noted Isla's colourless complexion. Her skin looked practically translucent. He decided not to comment on it, aware it was an observation he should keep to himself. He'd have to keep a closer eye on her, make sure she was eating properly.

'I'll tell you over dinner.' Zach sighed, widening his eyes. 'I've had a bastard of a day!'

'Oh, no. I'm sorry. Is it because you're one down? Has your father not brought someone in to take up the slack while I'm off?'

No. His father had *not* drafted in any support, deciding it wasn't required yet. Basically, Zach had assumed he'd rather save the money and merely share out Isla's work among the executives. Kenneth Biggins was what was commonly known as tight as a duck's arse – it's how he made his money in the first place, he'd often told Zach. He called himself frugal. His employees called him Scrooge. Not *Mr Big*, like he thought. Zach had never had the heart – no, the *guts* – to inform him otherwise.

'Don't worry yourself over it, babe.' Zach batted her concern away with a flick of his wrist. 'Have you spoken with your mum today?'

'Of course,' Isla said.

There was a hint of weariness to her voice and he wasn't sure if it was because he'd asked, or because she was tired of her mother's daily phone calls. Living at the other end of the UK was taking its toll on Isla's mum; she'd made no bones about the fact she would rather be at Isla's side during this time, but due to her own health concerns she'd had to make do with checking up on her daughter via telephone. Zach had also reassured her she was being well looked after, so not to worry about putting her health at risk to travel such a long distance.

'She needs to check in with you, that's all,' he said.

'I don't have anything new to tell her, though. We end up talking about Fraser and what he's up to. I swear my brother stopped growing up once he hit eighteen, you know.'

'You'll have more to talk about when you're back to work.' Zach kissed her again then headed for the kitchen before his words sank in. 'Fancy a Chinese tonight?' he called. There was

9

a pause before she responded, and Zach imagined she was debating whether to say anything about his comment. He knew she didn't feel ready to return to the office, and he couldn't rush her. He was keen to get an indication, though, as in theory she was physically able to conduct her role at the business now, and he was acutely aware his father put the needs of the business before those of his employees. Even his family came second to his blessed company.

'Sure,' Isla shouted finally.

Zach rolled his head and pushed his shoulders down, attempting to relieve the built-up tension. The muscles in his neck were rigid, like a slab of stone. A hot shower with the water jets all hammering his back would be just the ticket. He found the takeaway menu and called up, placing an order to be delivered. He tidied away the breakfast bowl Isla had left on the worktop, wiped down the granite surfaces and then put out the plates and cutlery ready for the food. After taking two glasses from the cupboard, he filled one with chilled sauvignon blanc and the other with a pre-mixed G&T. He didn't see the attraction in the cans Isla stocked in the fridge – he was sure they had barely any alcohol content. May as well drink fizzy pop. Although maybe that was the point. That, and their convenience, was probably the appeal and as long Isla was happy, that was all well and good.

He walked back into the lounge. 'Here you go,' he said, handing the highball glass to Isla. 'I'm going to hop in the shower. The cash is on the hall table, just in case.'

'Oh.' Isla sat upright, a look of horror passing over her face. 'Can't you just wait until we've eaten?'

'I'll be quick. I promise,' Zach said. 'I'm sure it won't get here within the next ten minutes – it'll take them that long to cook it, babe.' He smiled, but underneath, his concern mounted. Isla hadn't left the house since returning from the hospital. Not once. It was partly his fault, he knew, because he'd been so keen to help out – be her knight in shining armour – that he'd pretty much taken over her house; her life. He wanted to make it all better. But in fact, he'd made her more dependent on him. And now, it was becoming increasingly difficult to pull back, stop being quite so eager to step in and do the things she should be doing herself. Now, he felt like he was forcing her to face up to reality against her will.

'Don't be longer than five minutes, then,' Isla said.

Zach frowned. 'Didn't realise I'd have to be timed,' he said a little too sarcastically.

'Well, it was your idea to order it.'

He nodded.

Pick your battles.

Chapter Four

THEN – *The night of*

'No thanks,' Isla said, pushing her hand across to cover the glass. 'Really, I've had more than enough celebration for one evening and you *know* I can't handle wine.'

'Oh, come on! It's not every day you get the promotion you should've got two years ago. It calls for more than your usual G&T, Isla.'

'Wow, Nicci – don't pull any punches, will you?'

'Well, you know what I mean. You've worked there since you graduated, for Christ's sake. You deserved this long ago.'

'I've got it now – that's all that matters.'

'Hence the *party*,' Nicci said, dramatically sweeping an arm towards the gathered group. Her heavily made-up, wide-set eyes scanned the lounge and kitchen and when she returned her attention to Isla, there was an expression in them that Isla couldn't quite read. Nicci was like that – often her eyes would tell a different story to the words she spoke, and even though they'd been friends for the best part of two years, Isla still hadn't learned to decipher their meaning. It had made it difficult for Isla to fully trust her, the disparity a bit unnerving. It's how her father used to be, too – and he'd managed to let everyone down. Maybe that was another reason she couldn't allow Nicci into her life as fully as she'd have liked. She wanted a best friend, needed one – and on most counts, Nicci was it.

It was just those eyes.

Isla tore her gaze away from Nicci and, reluctantly, took a swig of wine. She groaned inwardly as another Ed Sheeran song began playing. 'Ugh,' she said. 'Excuse me one moment.' She walked to the sound system, giving Alex a gentle nudge out of the way. 'Come on, Al – you're killing me, mate.'

'What? Doesn't everyone like Mr Sheeran?'

Isla shook her head, her honey-brown curls bobbing like springs around her face. She'd decided that night would be the one she experimented with her new spiral curling wand and she'd overdone it. By tomorrow morning they'd probably look perfect. 'How about something a little . . . *livelier*. The Weeknd? Dua Lipa? It *is* my party . . .'

'Hey! I'm only playing what my Danny-boy requested. Don't get all gobby with me, pal!' He put on a terrible Scottish accent to mock Isla, undeterred by the fact she'd completely lost her Glaswegian inflection and sounded more Devonshire than him. He flicked his hair, throwing his head to one side, pretending to be offended. But Alex was never offended by anything; his skin had grown too thick for that during the years of bullying and abuse he'd received growing up a gay man in a sleepy Devon village. 'What about John Legend—'

'No, Alex! Jeez.'

'What's wrong with a bit of lurve? Thought you'd be well into that at the moment, given you're bonking the boss's son.'

'Do people *say* bonking anymore?' Isla said. 'And just because I'm dating again, doesn't mean I'm going all-in for the romantic, trashy slush that goes with it.'

Alex backed away, his hands raised in submission. 'Go on, then – take over the deck, Miss McKenzie – you're in charge now.'

'I'm not actually staying for much longer . . .'

'Really? You make all the fuss, then you're going to leave early. From your own party?'

'I'm sure you guys can continue the celebration without me.' Isla gave an exaggerated eyebrow raise.

'Always, darling!' Alex reached out an arm and grabbed Danny's wrist. 'Come on, hon – it's up to us to keep the party going. Miss I've-Been-Promoted-Above-You is a right party pooper.' Alex spun Danny round in the middle of the lounge, people parting quickly so they didn't become casualties of the couple's overly dramatic moves.

Captured in their moment, Isla watched them dance. She couldn't help being a little envious. It would've been nice to have Zach here – she would stay for the duration if he was with her, dancing the evening away. She sighed, unconsciously. It was a big deal getting the promotion, and he wasn't here sharing in her celebration. Typically, his old man was making him work late so there wasn't much Isla could do about it. She'd adopted her best powers of persuasion but in the end, she'd been left disappointed. He was going to make it up to her, he said – and his surprise would be 'far better than some loud, drunken party'.

Tearing her gaze away, she began fiddling with the sound system, before realising it was linked to Nicci's iPhone. She picked it up and began to scroll, accidentally accessing her contacts. Isla noted a few unfamiliar names – some were clearly nicknames – and wondered if they were new men on the scene she hadn't been told about. Maybe she'd drop that into the conversation in a minute. She located Nicci's Spotify playlist and smiled as she found some upbeat songs in her 'good vibes folder'. She clicked on it and 'Blinding Lights' by The Weeknd started up. That was more like it.

Isla turned to face the room of people. It wasn't a huge

15

crowd – they were mainly from work, and although Biggins & Co had expanded a fair bit since she'd started there, it was still small enough that you knew everyone. Mingling with the work crowd, somewhat awkwardly, were a few of Nicci's neighbours. She always invited them to things so they would feel less inclined to complain about any noise. Much like the road Isla lived in, Nicci's neighbourhood was a quiet one. Isla danced between the people, back to Nicci, who immediately picked up the conversation from where it was left. She had an uncanny knack for being able to do that. No thread of conversation was ever lost with Nicci.

'So, I couldn't let this momentous occasion go without some serious recognition.'

'And I appreciate it. It's been great to mark the event with friends,' Isla said, her smile wide. 'But it's late, and I want to give my mam a call before I'm incapable of coherent speech.'

'You haven't told her yet?'

'No. I hadn't even mentioned it was in the pipeline – call it superstition – you know, just in case something went wrong and someone else got the promotion instead.' Isla shrugged. 'Scrooge can be a little . . . well, let's say . . . un—'

'A bit of a dick,' Nicci cut in, her cornflower-blue eyes squinting as her face contorted into a sarcastic expression.

'I was going to say unpredictable.' Isla laughed. 'But we could go with dick.'

'He certainly comes across as a man's man. Since I started there, he's barely uttered a word to me. I'm lucky if I get a curt nod of the head if he passes by me in the office.'

'Give him another two years – you might get a *hello* then.'

'I didn't think misogynistic employers were still in existence.'

Isla frowned. 'I'm too drunk to tell if that's sarcasm.' She remembered the unknown contacts in Nicci's phone. 'By the way, do you have anything you want to tell me?' She raised one brow, smiling coyly. As Nicci frowned, opening her mouth about to speak, someone shouted from across the room.

'Hey, Isla. Finally joining the elite, then?' Graham Vaughan bellowed as he moved purposefully through the group clogging the kitchen and joined them in the lounge. A sheen of sweat clung to his forehead, which he swiped at with the back of a hand, exposing a damp patch blotting the underarm of his off-white shirt sleeve. He hadn't changed out of what he'd worn all day at the office, so clearly he'd headed straight to the party from there.

'Yes, Graham. I've finally earned my place in the circle of trust.' Isla gave a tight-lipped smile.

'I'll be seeing more of you in the glass dome, then.' His tone was abrupt, just like his phone voice when he spoke to clients. Isla had always wanted to say something to him, wondering if anyone else had ever pulled him up on it. Ultimately, she hadn't felt it was her place, and no doubt because of his status within the company, it wouldn't be received well. Now, though, maybe she shouldn't be so concerned about creating the odd wave. 'Will be good to get some new blood up there, if I'm honest,' he continued. 'Seriously could do with an injection of youth.'

Isla didn't have much energy left to converse with Graham, who, at fifty-two was still single and seemingly didn't have a life outside of the company. He'd been with Kenneth Biggins since the beginning and was his second in command as he liked to tell everyone on a daily basis. It'd never been clear to Isla whether the boss actually considered Graham as highly as he considered himself. As much as she'd been desperate to be promoted, she wasn't as keen on the prospect of moving to the 'glass dome' – as the execs called the top-floor office containing the 'elite' staff – as people might think. It meant being away from the colleagues she'd come to think of as her friends – particularly Nicci and Alex – and instead, being closer to Zach.

She knew that was weird, given they'd been dating now for almost three months, but she was keen to keep her romantic life separate from work this time. Especially when her new boyfriend was the boss's son. It made life a little more awkward. Before her promotion she knew she could gossip with the people in her office and it was unlikely Zach would ever hear what she said about Scrooge. Who didn't slag off their boss on the odd occasion? That was part and parcel of employment, wasn't it? But now she'd have to curtail vocalising her annoyances – and self-editing had always been one of her weaker skills.

Still. She'd earned the rung up on the career ladder; she wouldn't let something so minor ruin her enjoyment of it. She'd deal with problems as they arose, not create them from nothing. And she already had one burning issue that would require her attention, one that was more important than being unable to openly talk shit about the boss. Her first day as marketing and budget manager was going to entail beginning an awkward conversation and possibly ruffling a few tail feathers. Graham's in particular.

'You off already?' Graham caught hold of her elbow as she squeezed past him to escape into the hallway. 'I hoped me and you could have a little chat.' He tapped the side of his nose.

'Yeah, well, I'm not exactly one to burn the midnight oil,' Isla said.

'I thought you youngsters were all party-party,' he said, jiggling his hips in a creepy, bizarre way, which she assumed was to symbolise dancing. Something told Isla he hadn't been to a club in his adult life. It was far more likely it was at an Eighties disco where he last wiggled those hips. She suppressed a smile.

'I'm not exactly a teenager, Graham. Those days have gone

for me, too.' She was twenty-six, not eighteen. 'I've got work tomorrow. As do you,' she said, poking her finger into his belly. For a moment, it sank into the soft folds and she regretted her action. She snapped her hand back, but he didn't seem bothered.

'All work and no play . . .' he said, grinning.

Don't, Isla thought. Please don't say it. 'See you in the morning. In the glass dome. We can chat then,' she said quickly, before heading to the front door.

'I'll look forward to it,' he said.

Isla flinched. 'You don't know what's coming, yet,' she called over her shoulder. She wasn't sure if he'd heard her above the music, but a shiver tracked down her back as though his eyes were still on her.

Maybe he did know, after all.

Chapter Five

The doorbell rang just as Isla heard Zach's footsteps on the stairs. Good timing. She huffed out her breath, the sounds of voices at the door both comforting and alarming. It wasn't as though she were afraid of absolutely everyone – just *most* people. A healthy wariness, she concluded, given what had happened. Nicci had referred to Isla's reactions as similar to those of people who were suffering from post-traumatic stress disorder, but she disregarded her concerns. She would get over it. It was temporary. Two weeks was hardly any time at all, and she'd spent a few days in hospital, so there really hadn't been much time to recover yet.

Time was a good healer, didn't they say? She was doing okay – despite what Zach clearly believed. His over-reaction just now about her asking him to wait to shower had upset her. He seemed like he was becoming impatient, wanting her to make huge leaps of progress as fast as possible. She had an urge to tell him that if he was getting bored of being around her, then he should feel free to move back to his parents' place.

But she bit the inside of her cheek and smiled at Zach as he brought a tray in, placing it on her lap. No one else had jumped in to offer their help; Zach was all she had. And most of the time, she really was grateful he was there. Her mood swings were likely challenging for him to cope with and she was acutely aware she was unfair to him sometimes. Expecting him to know what to say, what to do. It wasn't as though he knew her inside and out, even before the attack. It must be really hard for him to adjust too.

'Thanks, babe. Smells delish.'

'Tuck in, then,' he said, sitting down beside her on the sofa. 'What's on?' He nodded towards the telly. 'Please, no more *Love Island*!'

'Hah! No, thought we'd watch *Gone Girl*.'

'Really? Haven't you seen it before?' Zach screwed his eyes up and inched his hand towards the TV remote. 'Not sure it's a good choice anyway.'

'Why?' Isla said. She put down the fork, then reached her good hand across her to grab the remote before Zach did.

'It's just, well – a bit violent in places . . . and God, I hate Ben Affleck.'

'Well, I don't. I think he's rather cute. For an older man. And anyway, it's all that's on. Apart from the usual reality stuff, which I do believe you hate even more than Ben?'

'Yeah, true. Well, if you're sure it's not too much.'

Isla stared at Zach for a moment before speaking, carefully planning out what she wanted to say in her head before engaging her mouth. 'It's okay, you know. You don't need to wrap me in cotton wool. I'm managing to do that very well myself – as you keep reminding me. Normal life *will* resume shortly. I have to start somewhere.'

Zach narrowed his wide-set eyes almost to the point of closing them, then nodded silently before refocusing on his food. Isla pressed play on the film.

She found her thoughts wandering, though – and hated to admit that some of the scenes did make her anxious, just as

22

Zach had prewarned. Her stomach knotted as snapshots of memories from that night flashed through her mind. A sharp pain in her head, cracking of bone, darkness enveloping her. Her limbs sprawled on the pavement, then the sensation of being dragged. A gasp escaped her lips and Zach turned sharply to face her.

'I told you this was a bad idea, Isla! I wish you'd listen to me more.' He moved the trays with the remnants of the take-away and sidled up to her, placing a protective arm around her shoulders. 'Come on, babe. Let's watch something else.' He took the remote and flicked through the channels. 'Here,' he said, 'this is more like it.' Isla stared blankly at the screen – at the face of Graham Norton – and cringed at his laugh.

'Sure,' she muttered.

'Laughter is the best medicine, so they say,' Zach said. He pulled her in tighter and she winced.

'Oh, shit. Sorry. Forgot,' he said as he relaxed his grip.

Zach faced the TV, leaving his arm loosely draped over her shoulders. Isla fought to focus on the show, but zoned out. A ping from the mobile phone brought her back to the moment. She slithered out from under Zach's arm and leaned forwards to take the phone from the table.

'Who's that?' Zach asked, not shifting his attention from the screen.

'I don't know yet; I haven't opened it. Stupid thing is so slow.' She was grateful Zach had given her a phone to use while she waited for a replacement, but going back to an older-style one was taking some getting used to. 'It's just a text from Alex,' she said when she'd finally opened it.

'Oh? What does he want?'

Isla sighed. 'I imagine he's wondering how I am? Like most of my colleagues.' She inhaled deeply. Her irritation was uncalled for – she knew that. She really needed to relax. The film had unsettled her and the fact Zach had known it would made her feel a bit stupid. As she read the message from Alex, though, her tension eased. He was always so light-hearted and funny, she couldn't help but smile.

Hurry up and get that lardy arse (because I know you'll be sitting down all day, snacking!) back to work, eh, chuck? Missing you. Well, missing your work ethic anyway – no one else here will do my paperwork or put up with my shit 😄 Or help me devour the midweek doughnuts. And you heard about the abysmal attempt in the escape rooms I assume? 😲 Jeez, love. We NEEDED you! Let me know if you require a compass to find your way back. Your favourite work colleague, Alex xx

Isla sniggered. No mention of the attack, no pussyfooting around her. She liked that. It was nice not to read a soppy message for a change. Although she really appreciated her mam's daily check-ins, they didn't exactly lift her spirits. Mostly, she just felt guilty after speaking with her or reading her texts.

'What's funny?' Zach craned his neck to get a better look at Isla's phone. 'What does he say?'

Isla tilted the phone screen away from him slightly. 'Says they could've done with my help at the escape rooms event. You didn't go then?'

'No. I didn't want to leave you, babe.'

'Oh. Sorry—'

'You don't have to be. That's why I'm here, remember? I want to look after you. And anyway, I hate those things. Is that all he said then?'

Isla frowned. 'Pretty much, yeah.' She placed the phone back on the table. 'Do you know who won?'

24

'The lock-in thing? Er . . . Maybe Graham's team. Didn't really take notice.'

'Oh, you don't know what you're missing out on, Zach. They're great fun. Don't you love trying to work out the clues?'

'Nope. I guess I don't think in the right way. All that cryptic nonsense – it's stressful, not fun!'

'That's a shame. It would be great to go as a couple. And I'd absolutely love to host a murder mystery night here when I'm feeling up to it. It would be a great way to finally make friends with the neighbours.'

'Oh, God, Isla. I can't think of anything worse. People dressing up and getting in character and everything. It's like bloody amateur dramatics – it's weird. I'd rather quiet, cosy nights in alone with you, not spending time with rowdy idiots all playing Miss Marple. Plus, you said yourself, the couple next door aren't even up for a coffee and chat, let alone a meal and daft game night.'

She was fighting a losing battle with this, she realised. 'Oh well, I'm sure we'll find something to occupy our time that we both enjoy.'

Zach grinned. 'I can certainly think of one thing, yes.' He slipped his hand under Isla's top, giving her breast a gentle squeeze as he lowered his lips to hers. She kissed him briefly, then pulled away.

There was something about the way the evening had played out that irritated Isla. As much as she believed Zach had her best interests at heart, and he seemed to be acting with care and compassion, the uncomfortable feeling that she wasn't in control of anything anymore forced its way to the surface. Before the night of the party, she'd been hopeful their relationship would progress to a more permanent status – she'd been starting to imagine him staying over at weekends, them lying in bed together on a Sunday morning eating breakfast and getting crumbs in the sheets. She'd even dared to think they had a future together. It struck her now, though, that everything was moving *too* fast.

If it hadn't been for the attack, he probably wouldn't be living in her house at this point. And maybe it would be better if Zach moved out again once she was deemed 'recovered'. Then things could return to how they'd been before life had catapulted them onto this path. Following the awful, complete head-fuck experience with Lance, she'd been adamant she would never rush into another relationship. She *had* allowed her feelings for Zach to flourish, and thought she'd found her soulmate, but now she'd lived with him for a couple of weeks, she found herself wishing they could move at a slower pace again.

The realisation she needed to take back some control was motivation to make some changes, if nothing else. Isla needed to pull her finger out and get with the programme. The quicker she could get back to her own life in her own space, seeing Zach when she chose to, the better.

Chapter Six

Christie's Crime Addicts – True Crime Podcast

Excerpt from Episode 161 – *The Couple on Maple Drive*

[GUEST] Yes, I knew them. Well. I knew *of* them, maybe I should say. Saw him coming and going mostly. Not her as much. But I *heard* them sometimes. You know – arguing one day, and . . . er, well . . . [coughs] . . . making up another.

[ED] And did you ever suspect anything untoward was going on?

[GUEST] It was none of my business, really. Live and let live is my motto in life. Only, in this case, I suppose that's the wrong phrase to use . . .

[ED] Where were you – that day when the police were called?

[GUEST] My sister's. Had the fright of my life coming back to find the road crammed with people, cameras everywhere, police vehicles . . . God, it was terrible – so much fuss. Poor thing. Bet they didn't think they'd get that much attention.

[ED] Murder tends to have that effect.

[GUEST] Yes, yes. I suppose. But still. No privacy these days, is there? Everyone is too keen to force their noses into situations they have no business in. All those onlookers . . .

nothing more than rubberneckers. Should be ashamed of themselves.

[ED] How has this affected you, personally?

[GUEST] It's made me ever so jumpy. I'm constantly looking out my window, checking the pavements for shadows. For strangers – or, at least for people I don't recognise as being from my road. I feel vulnerable. In case—

[ED] In case the story gets out and more people come to gawp at where it happened?

[GUEST] There's that, yes. But it's more about the issue of whether they took the right person away in cuffs, isn't it?

Chapter Seven

Zach sensed a shift – a pulling away. Not just physically, but mentally as well. Had he been too overprotective? Maybe Isla believed he was taking over – controlling aspects of her life: like enrolling her in the online therapy course, and saying what she should or shouldn't watch. Couldn't she see he was only being supportive? Someone had to take the reins because she certainly wasn't capable at the moment. It was more 'tough love' than being controlling. He had to be the stronger person. Ultimately, that's why she'd agreed for him to move in: to help, to take charge of things. At least until she was feeling stronger. Until she felt safe to live life normally again. Surely, she could see that's why he'd argued that the film choice was a poor one and why he'd switched channels to something light-hearted, funny.

He wanted to ensure Isla's mind wasn't returning to the horrors of the attack.

She couldn't remember everything about that night – the doctors said the head trauma in itself might be the reason. She'd taken a blow to the back of her skull, and although it wasn't fractured, she had been severely concussed. The team at Derriford Hospital had been fantastic, full of reassurances that all of her memories would return. Eventually. But not to rush it. And Zach got the impression that's precisely what Isla was trying to do. That's why she wanted to watch dark, crime films, in the hope it would shake a memory free. Personally, he believed that would be the worst thing for her recovery. Not remembering the awful details of an attack, moving on instead, *had* to be better. That was the key to her recovery – distraction. The therapy he'd suggested, after carefully researching the available online courses, advocated looking forwards, not back.

He had to make sure that's what Isla was trying to do. It was down to him to put her on the right path. Her moods were problematic; he had to admit that. They were all over the place and he couldn't predict what he was coming back to after work. He'd perhaps do some research himself, look into the after-effects of a traumatic event to ensure he was supporting her in the best way he could.

A small part of him wondered if he'd done the right thing suggesting he move in. After all, being the victim of a violent mugging threw so much more into the mix than a new relationship would usually have to cope with; it was inevitable it wouldn't be plain sailing. They would work out, though; he was confident of that. Once Isla had stopped trying to remember that awful night and was back at work, in a regular routine, her mind focused on her new role, she would come to realise that moving in together had been the best thing for them. And their lives could progress towards a bright future together.

All Zach had to do was remain in the house, offering his love and support to Isla.

Be patient.

And everything would be fine.

Chapter Eight

THEN – The night of

Isla hadn't wanted to make a fuss about leaving, not wishing to be guilted into staying at the party – she'd drunk too much and just wanted to go home and crash – but Graham had impeded her exit. Now, as she reached the front door, she turned around, curious to know if Graham's eyes were still on her as she sensed. They were. He was standing stock-still, a strange look on his face. He'd clearly heard her throwaway comment. She almost asked him what the matter was, but her gut was telling her the resulting conversation might not be the best one to have while intoxicated and at a party, so she bit her tongue. Still feeling a little unsettled, she left.

The cool air hit Isla as she stepped outside. She'd always found that alcohol seemed to ferment further in her stomach and once it mixed with the atmosphere, something happened – like a chemical reaction that made her instantaneously drunker than she'd been inside the warmth of a house. She tottered a little on the doorstep, one hand jutting out, reaching for the wall to steady herself.

'Whoa!' The voice was accompanied by a hand on Isla's arm. 'Steady on. Someone's had a little more than they should've.'

'I'm fine, thanks, Simon.' Isla sucked in a large breath, straightening. 'Just the cool air, that's all.' She shrugged him off and pulled her denim jacket on. It took several attempts to get her arms through and she caught Simon sniggering at her efforts. Isla glared at him, but he just laughed again, then drew heavily on his cigarette. He puffed out swirls of smoke, which curled around his long, thin face and thick, blond hair, before drifting upwards into the night. Every now and then, Isla wished she still smoked, and now, she inhaled the fumes greedily.

'You can *have* one,' Simon said, offering her the open packet.

'No!' The word came out as a yell. Being forceful was the only way she'd prevent herself reaching out and taking one. 'The nicotine would go straight to my head and I don't think I need an additional reason to stumble, eh?'

'Fair point.' He shrugged, slipping the packet into the inside of his black leather jacket. 'You still coming to the escape room next week? I need to be on your team after the last dismal performance put in by Graham's lot.' He snorted. 'For all the education he claims to have had, he hasn't got a bloody logical bone in his body.'

Isla frowned. Simon's words didn't make sense in her head; it was becoming fuzzier by the minute. 'Well, it's hard going up against the best. I *am* the office champion at locked room mysteries,' Isla said. It'd been her idea to have them as a monthly team-building event, but they were having to travel further afield now as they'd exhausted all the local venues.

'Anyway, I'm going.' She went to leave, but Simon continued. He was like this at work too – once you started him off talking, it was a real struggle to shut him up again.

'I thought Zach would be with you.' It was a simple statement, but one Isla was getting fed up with hearing from her colleagues.

'I'm allowed out without him you know,' she said, sharply. He must know Zach had to work late, too. Was he trying to wind her up?

'Ahh, having second thoughts about your choice of boyfriend? You and me are probably better suited,' Simon said, moving in closer. 'You just haven't given me the opportunity to show you yet.' He lurched forwards and made a clumsy attempt to kiss her.

'What the fuck, Simon!' Isla pressed both palms to his chest and shoved him. 'Go sober up, for Christ's sake, will you?'

'Wow, mate. Just joking.' He put his hands up, as if he were surrendering.

'If you think that's funny, you need to take a good hard look at yourself. I might be drunk, but that doesn't give you the right to make a bloody move.'

'So-rr-ee.' Simon lifted his shoulders. 'You know me – it was harmless. God, Isla. You're in a good mood for someone who just got a promotion.'

'Well, maybe it's just *some* people's ill-conceived jokes that have ruined it.' Isla shook her head and started to walk. Away from the party, away from Simon. She had to concede he was right about her mood though. It didn't match her achievement. And deep down, she knew why. She just couldn't tell anyone else yet.

'Shouldn't you get a taxi?' Simon called after her.

'Nope. I need the fresh air – it'll clear my head.' Plus, she'd use the fifteen-minute walk to call her mam. She'd be pleased to hear the news, finally. Rowan McKenzie had been keen for Isla to do well, to accomplish things she hadn't. Isla's mother's greatest achievement had been having her and her brother, Fraser. That's what she'd always told everyone. But underneath the words, Isla had heard the longing. The hoped-for, *wished-for* successes that had failed to materialise, mostly because Rowan had been the stay-at-home mam, putting any hopes of a career on hold to bring them up. And support her husband. Which made the fact he betrayed her again and again even more hurtful.

'It's never too late, you know, Mam,' Isla had said the first Christmas they'd been together following her father's death. They were all sitting around the open fire – her, Rowan and Fraser – crystal glasses topped with Famous Grouse whisky in their hands, the crackling logs sending orange sparks up the chimney.

'Oh, I think it is for me. Some things have to be grasped with open arms when the opportunity arises. Not everything, or everyone, will wait until *you're* ready. Don't you ever give up, Isla – promise me? You must fight for what you want.' Isla hadn't pushed her mother on exactly what it was she'd failed to do, or who hadn't waited. In that moment, looking into Rowan's glistening eyes, it hadn't seemed an appropriate time to seek answers. But, she'd internally blamed her father for whatever it was. He was also the reason Isla left Scotland in the first place. Once her brother had moved out, Isla couldn't bear to be the one left living with her parents in such a tense, unhappy place. So, getting as much distance between herself and the toxic atmosphere her father had created in the home had been the number-one factor when looking at universities. She chose Exeter because it meant she wouldn't have to visit home much. It'd been the one, and possibly only, bold and risky move Isla had ever made.

She had spent the first year with incredible guilt issues; every time she spoke to Rowan on the phone, they'd both end up crying. But it was her mam's choice to stay put; to stay with the man who continually let her down. Isla couldn't be responsible for that. She had to make her own way.

Isla turned the corner now, heading into Copelands Way.

She passed Cedars Bar, where she first met up with Lance, the man who she could thank for her reluctance to get into another relationship. She'd taken a leap of faith going on the dating app. She was usually so risk averse and jumping headlong into an online site was beyond the parameters she'd set herself. She should've known better – been prepared for the inevitable blow. It had come sooner than she'd imagined. Lance dropped her after a month – and just as she'd begun to believe they were a great match and the relationship was going somewhere.

Being ghosted was a first, and an experience she'd rather never have again. It'd been cruel. Knocked her confidence in men. In herself. What had she done that would make someone walk away from her in such a way? The experience made her reluctant to bother again. But life had a habit of throwing curve balls. So far, Zach was proving to be nothing but good. Not as if *he* could ghost her: she knew exactly where he lived, and she'd always see him at work. Although that would obviously make for a difficult situation if they separated. They wouldn't, though – she had a good feeling this time.

Zach was more intense than Lance, and more open about his feelings. Which made it easier for Isla to reciprocate, and bit by bit, he was dismantling the brick wall she'd constructed to keep herself safe. Despite being upset with him for working tonight, Isla knew he'd make it up to her, as promised. She smiled as she thought about him, warmth radiating through her insides. Or maybe that was due to the wine consumption, which Isla now cursed herself for; she'd been weak allowing Nicci to goad her.

She hadn't told her mam about Zach. She'd somehow kept her life in Devon fairly private from her, only really sharing work stories. Neither Rowan nor Fraser had been down for a visit – it'd been Isla who'd made the journey back home on the few occasions they'd got together since she left. Now she'd got the promotion and there was a reason to celebrate, perhaps they'd accept an invitation to *her* home. She could show them the local sites, introduce them to Zach. Although she would have to be careful there as her mam would no doubt mention marriage and kids within minutes of meeting him, keen for her daughter to settle. Reiterating that it was very early days and she wasn't thinking too far into the future would keep her mam's feet on the ground. But, secretly, although Isla had been taking the relationship relatively slowly, she'd started to think longer-term. Things like holidays together and even engagement had crossed her mind.

As thoughts of home, and her mam, filled her head, Isla slowed up and grappled in her handbag for her mobile. She needed to put some kind of cord on it – it always migrated to the bottom of her maroon leather tote bag and was hard to locate among the rubbish she kept in it. She stopped and leaned against a wall, rummaging deeper, her fingers pushing aside receipts and tissues.

'For God's sake,' she huffed.

Finally finding it, Isla carried on walking, her head lowered to the phone screen. All those contacts. Why did she keep all their numbers listed? More than half were 'friends' from her almost redundant Facebook account – and who lived in and around Glasgow – and the rest were acquaintances she rarely saw or spoke to. There was probably only a handful of people she actually messaged or called. A thorough whittling down was on the cards.

Her attention strayed to her notifications – three new messages and a missed call. She moved her finger over the WhatsApp message, but remembered she was meant to be calling her mam before it got too late. Although, it *was* too late, really, and she'd likely wake Rowan. Isla looked up just in time – she'd been about to collide with a lamppost. She laughed at her near miss; she really should pay more attention. Glancing at where she was, Isla realised it would be quicker to cut through the park. As she crossed the road to enter the gate, an uneasy sensation stopped her in her tracks. Instead, she circumnavigated it.

Better to be safe than sorry.

The thought struck her from nowhere. She'd never worried about taking the shortcut through the park before. She'd always felt safe in the bay, even with the recent spate of drug-related issues. It was only just gone midnight – not as if it were three in the morning. Must be the effects of the wine making her paranoid. Maybe she should have got a taxi after all. But it was such a short distance; by the time she called for one, waited for it, she could be home, tucked up in bed.

Isla looked back at her phone screen, finding 'Mam' in the list. She *would* call her – even if she woke her, she'd be pleased to hear from her daughter, and even more thrilled to hear about the promotion. Isla walked as the ring tone trilled in her ear, her mind now focused on telling her mam the good news.

She didn't register the rushing footsteps behind her – the heavy thuds rhythmically pounding the pavement – until it was too late. Her body plummeted to the ground, the air in her lungs snatched away with the speed of the fall. Her eyes snapped closed with the motion.

And stayed closed.

Chapter Nine

Christie's Crime Addicts – True Crime Podcast

Excerpt from Episode 162 – *The Couple on Maple Drive*

[DOUG] It's been a few days of theorising, delving into the lives of the couple at the heart of this investigation, taking apart possible motives, hypothesising. What makes a killer? It's something Christie's Crime Addicts have chatted about at length over the years – numerous podcasts have covered this very question. We've studied past serial killers, crimes of passion, premeditated murders – and at first glance, this one might seem to fit the crime of passion category. But, the evidence we've gained doesn't quite fit as snugly as it could. We have a strong suspicion there's more to this crime than meets the eye. More than the police are letting on, at any rate.

Are they worried about causing a local panic? Because, it might be that the one suspect we know the police have in custody, is *not* the person responsible.

And – more worrying still – is the victim we know of the *only* one?

If they don't have the right person in the cell – it could be a matter of time before the real killer strikes again.

Chapter Ten

The morning light shone through the dusky-pink curtains and Isla pulled the duvet up over her head to shield her eyes from its unwanted glare. She'd been meaning to replace the flimsy curtains for months with blackout ones similar to those she had in the lounge, but hadn't got around to it. Today, she felt like the streaming sunbeams were a judgement: 'This is how bright and cheerful you *should* be, Isla.'

She huffed. 'Bog off,' she replied to the imaginary mocking voice. She turned her body away from the window and reached a hand across the mattress to the space Zach had occupied for the past two weeks, gently running her fingers over the ivory-coloured Egyptian cotton sheet. She hadn't felt Zach leave the bed, but she did have a vague recollection of him kissing her on her forehead and saying goodbye. She supposed that would have been at around eight o'clock. Now, at almost ten a.m. she couldn't decipher if it were a real memory or an assumed one. It might have even been yesterday's memory, or the day before that. Every morning was pretty much the same.

After lying there for ten minutes more, she pushed back the duvet, stretched and rolled out of bed. Isla slowly made her way down the stairs, went into the kitchen and flicked the kettle on. The house was silent. The neighbours were generally pretty quiet, but she was usually *aware* of them: sometimes she heard a hoover, or the rhythmic thrum of a washing machine; occasionally she could hear muffled music or muted conversation – and rarer still, raised voices. This morning, though, there was nothing.

Isla turned on the radio while making her coffee. Heart Torbay was playing The Weeknd. A sharp pain immediately shot through her head. She pressed her fingers into her temples, gently massaging the area to alleviate it. A dizzy sensation caused her to sit down, right on the cold, tiled floor of the kitchen, afraid she'd fall otherwise.

Breathe.

The song had been playing at the party the night of her attack – she remembered it now. She'd complained to Alex about his choice of music and fiddled with Nicci's playlist, bringing this up. Hearing it now had somehow catapulted her back to that evening – to the moment she'd left the party. And a forgotten memory now forced itself into her mind.

Simon had been the last person Isla saw that night.

He'd been outside – had suggested she get a taxi. But she'd ignored him and walked off. He'd watched her leave, so knew which direction she was walking.

Why, if he'd been that concerned, hadn't Simon offered to walk her home?

Chapter Eleven

'How's she doing, then? Must be about ready to come back by now?' Kenneth Biggins was sitting at his desk, a bone-china teacup and saucer to one side of his computer, a leather-bound diary open in front of him and various folders littering the surface.

'No, Dad. She's not,' Zach said, shifting his weight from one foot to the other. 'I mean, she's doing better. Physically, anyway. But . . .'

'Oh, nonsense. She should get right back in the saddle; it's the only way, lad. Sitting wallowing at home won't do her the slightest bit of good. Tell her we need her back. God, I'd only just promoted her!'

'Yes, she's aware of that, Dad. It's not as if she asked to be mugged, is it?'

'No, no. Of course, not. That's not what I'm saying.' Kenneth's jowls wobbled as he spoke. He wasn't hugely over-weight but did carry excess fat in his face. Zach hoped it was a trait he hadn't inherited; he'd managed to gain his brooding, striking good looks from his mother and prayed he aged as well as she had. 'But business is business.' Kenneth slapped a hand on the desk, the teacup tinkling in its saucer. 'And the longer she stays away, the more difficult it'll be for her to slot back in. What with new responsibilities and a different role to learn, she'll fall behind. Lose confidence.' He absently shuffled some papers on his desk, then with his eyes locking onto Zach's he added, 'Maybe I should look into keeping her downstairs a while longer. There are other people in line for promotion, you know.'

Zach pursed his lips tightly. He didn't immediately respond to his dad's line of thinking – he knew better than that. His father wasn't, as you might be fooled into believing, asking for his opinion. It wasn't a question. It didn't require any input from him. Kenneth Biggins was merely using his son as a sounding board. Zach's thoughts on the matter were largely irrelevant. So, he waited, standing on the opposite side of the desk, like an obedient puppy awaiting his owner's command.

'Speak to her,' Kenneth said finally. 'See what she thinks.'

That had been an indication he was now allowed to respond. 'I will,' Zach said, giving a curt nod. 'It might be more beneficial to give her time to recover before expecting her to step up.' This was a wise choice of reply because it served two purposes. One, it made it sound as though he were agreeing with his father's assessment of the situation, and two, it would buy more time. Isla would be able to recover at a sensible pace if she wasn't rushed into coming back and fulfilling her new, more demanding job role. Zach's eyes remained on Kenneth, watching for the sign he had indeed said the right thing.

Kenneth nodded and Zach's shoulders relaxed. 'It's disappointing, of course,' Kenneth mumbled. 'But the business will go on without her, and the needs of the company do have to come first. You know that don't you, Zach?' Kenneth's dark, hooded eyes bored into Zach's, making him squirm. 'And I'm sure she'll understand that, too.'

I'm sure she won't.

Kenneth lowered his gaze, snatched up a pen from the desk, then began scribbling into his diary. This meant Zach was no longer required in his office; he was dismissed. The way his father treated him really hurt. Sometimes Zach could brush it off; other times he took it to heart. It'd been the same for as long as he could remember. Memories from as early as four years old told the same story – Kenneth had always been abrupt and standoffish towards him. Had the man even given him a hug? Been warm and loving? Zach was determined that when he had children, he'd be sure to shower them with love and praise, not leave them feeling cold and irrelevant. Even now, no matter how hard he worked, how much time and effort he put into the business, it was never enough. Apparently it didn't even warrant so much as a 'you're doing a great job, son', or 'I'll be leaving this business in the best hands'. In fact, there'd been little mention at all lately of Zach taking over when Kenneth had deemed it time to take a back seat. Would he ever? He didn't want to dwell on his father's plans; it made his stomach cramp at the thought he might bypass him altogether and favour Graham instead.

But blood is thicker than water, surely?

As Zach turned to leave, he made the decision not to talk with Isla about any of what had been discussed. There was no way he was going to take the inevitable flak. She'd shoot the messenger without fail.

Not that he was a coward, he told himself. He could just do without the confrontation.

He had enough to worry about.

Chapter Twelve

THEN – *The day after*

Isla was greeted with concerned eyes when she finally opened hers. She tried to sit up, but sharp pain – first in her wrist, then in her head – prevented it. She winced as she touched the fingertips of her non-injured hand to the base of her skull, finding a large lump.

'Don't try and move, Isla, love,' a female voice with a strong Plymothian accent said.

She must be in Derriford Hospital. Isla blinked, clearing the blurriness. The shapeless blue form came into focus and Isla saw a kind-faced nurse, dressed in scrubs.

'What happened?' Her tongue stuck to the roof of her mouth as she spoke. She turned, searching for a glass of water.

'Here. Sip this.' The nurse tilted a glass with a straw towards her lips. Isla sucked greedily.

'Whoa, take it easy. Don't wanna be sick.'

Why would she be sick sipping water?

As if reading this thought the nurse, Heather, explained how Isla had been unconscious when first brought in, then had been treated for a fractured wrist and severe concussion. Heather informed Isla she'd been found in a park close to her home at two that morning and an ambulance called.

'Do you remember any of that?'

A wave of nausea swept through her as she shook her head – forgetting Heather's warning not to move. 'No. Did I fall? And why aren't I at Torbay Hospital?'

She'd been at the party at Nicci's – she knew that. And she'd drunk too much wine. This was precisely why she usually avoided wine and stuck to weak, pre-made G&Ts. Alcohol and her just didn't mix well.

'Brought you here because of the suspected head injury, love. And it's probably owing to the concussion why you can't remember,' Heather said, offering a sympathetic smile. 'Can play havoc with the memory. It'll come back to you in time. But rest now, love. We'll talk again later.'

Isla noted Heather's avoidance of the question. So, she hadn't fallen? And why wasn't anyone else here with her? Maybe it was still early in the morning.

She let her eyelids flutter closed.

Heather was right. She should rest – she felt so tired. Her questions could wait.

Chapter Thirteen

When her bottom became numb, Isla picked herself up from the kitchen floor and went into the lounge, immediately slumping onto the sofa. It was no use thinking about what might've happened had Simon asked to walk her home. She knew she would've declined his offer anyway, so the outcome would've been the same: she'd have been mugged. But still, for some reason, the knowledge he was watching her walk away, aware of the direction she was taking, niggled in the recesses of her mind.

The police had informed Isla they had nothing much to go on, bar her bloodied clothes that may, or may not, be helpful in terms of DNA and possible fibres. But, even if there were any, they'd need something to match the samples and fibres *with*. As Isla was unable to give any form of description of her attacker, they had no images they could circulate – no starting point. None of the stolen items had been recovered and her mobile phone hadn't been used. The last area it pinged in was where the attack had occurred. And, adding to the lack of evidence from her was the fact that apparently the CCTV in the area had been vandalised the night before – by hooligans. Druggies. Wannabe gangsters. Who knew. The officers were extremely apologetic, citing lack of staff and resources both from them and the local authority, in getting it back online sooner. It was in working order *now*, though. They made sure to lock the stable door after the horse had bolted.

It was down to Isla to piece the events of the night together. She held the key to what happened. Somewhere, locked in her memory was the identity of the man who attacked her. For a few moments, she considered going for a shower – she could manage if she tied a bag over her plastered arm – but decided she'd rather stay in her pyjamas and catch up with her crime shows instead. Grabbing the TV remote, tucking her legs up beside her on the sofa, and arranging the cushions comfortably, Isla settled down to watch Netflix.

Hours passed before she moved, and then it was only to visit the bathroom or to snatch a packet of crisps and biscuits from the kitchen cupboard. Once she'd gathered supplies, she repositioned herself on the sofa and switched on the laptop, scrolling to the podcast shows in her favourites list. *Christie's Crime Addicts* was top. They were one of Isla's first choices to listen to, largely due to the fact they covered local crime stories and they added an element of live shows to the mix, which intrigued her. It was like listening to real-time investigators reporting from the scene rather than just relaying past crimes and how they'd been investigated and solved. Since she was convinced that her attacker would strike again, she needed to keep on top of issues concerning the Torbay area and the live aspect definitely helped with that.

From what Isla had learned over the last few weeks about criminal behaviour, she was certain she'd hear of another mugging or violent attack. Or, maybe it was a death similar to the local one recently reported that she should be listening for. He may have become braver, or merely more successful, since his failed attempt with her.

Her scalp tingled, the sensation tracking all the way down her spine as from nowhere she suddenly recalled the overheard conversation between two nurses while she was laid up in hospital: 'She was lucky – I'm not so sure they meant to leave her alive.' It'd possibly been a passing remark, not based on anything factual. All the same, it made her go cold thinking about it. Isla shook off the feeling, quickly clicking on one of the recorded podcasts.

It was Jase leading the discussion. The topic – his smooth, clear voice stated – was the increase in drug-related crime in Devon, with the focus of the episode being on the recent stabbing incident in Newton Abbot. Two men had been seriously hurt following an altercation in a flat belonging to alleged drug dealer, twenty-four-year-old Matthew Durnsley, who was left beaten and with a serious head injury. The other victim had managed to leave the property with a stab wound to his stomach. Witnesses claim he stumbled towards the train station where he collapsed on the platform. Police attended shortly afterwards and reported that both men were taken to hospital. Jase relayed the timeline and ongoing investigations but ended by saying the men were each blaming the other. A large quantity of drugs and cash were subsequently found at Mr Durnsley's rented flat.

Isla considered this story carefully. One of the theories about her attack was that it was drug-related – that the culprit needed cash for a deal and Isla had been in the wrong place at the wrong time. She was less inclined to go along with that, though. It didn't feel right. A simple mugging would've sufficed in that situation. There'd been no need to hurt her so badly, surely? She clicked off that podcast, moving on to the next.

The next one was about the tragic death of an unknown man who'd been found washed up on Meadfoot Beach. It was so sad to think no one had even reported him as missing, that no one came forward to say they knew him – although there was only a description to go on because police hadn't released photos. She supposed, given that he'd been in the sea a while, his physical appearance had been grim. The consensus had been he was a homeless man, but with no identification, his name remained unknown. The death, investigating police said, wasn't being treated as suspicious at that time. Now, Jase was talking to his co-hosts about the circumstances surrounding the case.

Isla's forearm beneath the cast itched. Her mother would say that was a sign of it healing. She smiled – if only her mam lived close by. Although she knew Rowan would be overprotective, running around after Isla as though she were ten again, having her mam to look after her would make her feel safe. There was nothing comparable to your mam to comfort you through a dark, scary time. Phone calls were all very good, but not the same as physical contact. She missed her mam's hugs. Tears pricked her eyes. Quickly blinking them away, Isla reached down the side of the sofa and took the knitting needle, sticking it inside the cast. It was one of her mother's tips and she'd sent her the needle because Isla hadn't knitted in her life. Thankfully, the swelling had subsided, leaving a gap between her skin and the cast, so reaching the itch was relatively easy. Despite being instructed *not* to stick anything inside the cast by the orthopaedic team, Isla couldn't bear the irritation any longer and it was such a satisfying feeling when the itch was scratched, she felt zero guilt going against their advice. It was a relief to know she only had to put up with the discomfort for another two weeks, then she'd be free of the cast. She was lucky, she'd expected to suffer a full six weeks with it on, but was told four should be ample for the simple fracture she'd sustained. If she did what she was told.

Isla tucked the knitting needle back down beside the sofa,

then leaned forward to skip the podcast to another episode. Again, this one wasn't quite what she was searching for; she was keen to find crimes that fitted with the one she'd been a victim of. There were over fifty to work her way through – although some she could more easily prioritise over others as the titles of the show made it obvious the victims had been male. Not that she'd rule these out entirely, but the focus for now was on females. She also decided to skim-listen to a few, hitting fast forward to see if it was a relevant case, but there were some, like the most recent one, that were ambiguous, so she'd have to listen to the full hour, focusing intently.

That wouldn't be a problem, though. It wasn't as though she had anything better to do.

Chapter Fourteen

Isla's only interruption to her afternoon's planned activities of podcasts and crime documentaries came from a phone call. The refurbished phone Zach had given her as a temporary replacement only had a handful of contacts saved in it. Zach, Nicci and her mam being the main ones, along with Alex. She'd had a couple of texts from other work colleagues: vague 'how are you doing?' ones, which she'd responded to with a standard, 'getting there, won't be long before I'm back to my usual self,' and 'Zach's doing a great job looking after me'. She hadn't gone too deep, keeping her actual feelings to herself. So far, Rowan had called every day to check up on her, but Nicci had mainly just messaged – so seeing it was her calling now surprised her.

'Nicci, hi. You not at work?'

'Of course I'm at work – no days off lounging around watching TV for *me*,' she said, her upbeat tone loud in Isla's ear. 'Had five minutes spare and thought I'd check in with you, see how you're doing.'

'Oh, well. You know . . . as you say, just watching TV. I've done my therapy for the day,' she said, heat rushing to her face at the lie. Good job it wasn't a video call.

'That's great, Isla. And is it helping?'

How could, or should, she answer that? The easy option would be to say yes. The honest answer would be to admit she'd given up on it, and mostly let the session videos play out to themselves so that it would appear, if anyone could access it and check what she'd watched, that she had indeed viewed them in their entirety. Isla wasn't proud of this deceit – it hadn't ever been one of her traits prior to the attack. Somehow, now, being guarded, secretive even, was becoming second nature.

'Not sure if *helping* is the right word,' she said. 'I don't feel hugely different to two weeks ago. But it's early days – everyone is saying not to rush things, so I'm taking that on board. Each day as it comes, and all that.'

'That seems wise. Well done, Isla.'

'Do I get a gold star?'

'Sorry, I didn't mean to come across as condescending. It's hard trying to say the right things.'

'Don't be sorry, Nicci. I'm grateful, really. I don't think there *is* a right thing to say – no one prepares you for these kinds of situations. It's not easy trying to navigate a path through, whether you're the one experiencing it, or the one offering support, is it?'

'No, but I should be doing *more*. Zach rushed to your side quickly enough, and I'm flapping about on the sidelines – I feel useless.'

'Don't! Trust me, I'm feeling useless enough for the both of us. You're on the end of the phone – I know that. I can call you whenever I need to – that's huge, Nicci. Knowing you're there is what matters to me at the moment. Zach's taking care of my physical needs—'

'I bet he is!'

'Oh, you! You know what I mean. Although, admittedly, *that* takes my mind off things, too.' Isla laughed.

'Good to know someone's getting it. At this rate, I'll become a virgin again.'

'No luck on the dating front then?'

'Nope. And now you've taken the only eligible male under thirty who's even remotely intelligent and attractive, there's nothing for me at this place, either.'

'Oh dear. Graham not up your street, then?'

'Is Graham up anybody's street?'

'Well, everyone has a match somewhere, don't they? Even Graham. Especially if you like balding, overweight, opinionated, sexist . . .' Isla was about to add more, but her train of thought was momentarily derailed, the words she was going to say completely slipping her mind. She stuttered, attempting to regain her thoughts, but fell silent when nothing came.

'You okay, Isla?'

'Sorry. Completely lost focus . . . mind went blank.'

'I got the drift, anyway. Maybe you need to rest.'

'It's awful, Nic. I'm not usually so . . . well, *woolly*. Can concussion last forever?'

She said it jokingly, but Isla's insides wrenched. The doctor had said the symptoms of the concussion could last two weeks, but mentioned that in some cases it could go on for several months, so maybe she shouldn't worry just yet. The thought of it going on for a longer time, though, was depressing. She needed to be back on her feet, fully functioning within the next few *weeks*, not the next few months.

Following some reassuring words from Nicci, a short precis of what was going on at work – which wasn't a lot according to her – Isla hung up, then lay down on the sofa. Her body ached; her neck was tight. Talking to Nicci for half an hour had really taken it out of her.

In the depths of her mind, what she was going to say about Graham floated around, just out of conscious grasp. What was it about him that made her lose her train of thought? It was something to do with work, her new job role – something she had to talk to him about?

Maybe if she relaxed, it would come back to her.

Her eyes closed, and she drifted.

Chapter Fifteen

When she opened her eyes, Zach was standing over her.

'Jesus Christ! What are you doing sneaking up on me like that?' Isla bolted upright, her blood pressure plummeting, making her dizzy.

'Sorry, was going to wake you with a kiss,' he said, backing off.

The shock of seeing a man's face looming over hers had jolted a memory free. Not a fully formed one, more of a blurry, soft-around-the-edges one. But, it was from that night, she felt sure.

'I must've dozed properly. I only meant to rest my eyes. I think I was dreaming about . . .'

'Oh, Isla.' Zach squashed up beside her on the sofa, laying an arm over her shoulders. 'Can I get you something? A water, or a cup of camomile tea?'

'What?' Isla frowned. 'When have I ever drunk that? No, I'm fine, Zach. Thank you.' She felt irritated, for no real reason. It must be the aftershock of the dream – the remnants of fear still remained in her bloodstream, pumping adrenaline around her tired body. 'Just please don't do that again, okay?'

'Sorry. I did call you – not my fault you didn't answer.' Zach got up abruptly and strode back out of the lounge. Isla heard him mutter, 'I can't do anything right,' as he disappeared into the kitchen. She reached and grabbed her phone. Dead. Some refurbishment. Damned battery forever needed recharging. After plugging it in, Isla sank back into the sofa cushions. She hadn't meant to be so snappy towards Zach, but he'd given her a start. She'd attempt to make it up to him later – snuggle up together, watch a film – maybe even instigate sex. Contrary to what she led Nicci to believe, they hadn't been intimate since the mugging. It hadn't been at the forefront of her mind, but now, thinking about it, it would be nice to feel wanted. Loved. And she supposed it would be good for Zach, too. He'd done so much for her, she wanted him to know she appreciated that. And even when she was better, and the time came for him to move back to his parents', she did want their relationship to continue. She needed to nurture it more than she'd been doing.

Before the nightmare that started two weeks ago, Isla had been on the verge of declaring to all that she'd found 'the one'. Her feelings for Zach had initially been a slow burn, quietly growing in a way that had snuck up on her. Maybe because she hadn't been looking for it – determined to stay clear of relationships for a while. Once she acknowledged she did in fact fancy him, though, everything sped up. She no longer avoided him at work, stopping to chat instead. She openly flirted. And contrary to the voice in her head that wanted to put the brakes on because of her insecurities and the fact he was the boss's son, Isla silenced the doubting voice, deciding she couldn't possibly be burned the way she'd been with Lance. Lightning didn't strike twice in the same place.

She had to remember how he'd made her feel prior to the attack. She'd been happy because things were falling into place. She was in a 'proper' relationship, work was going well – the promotion in sight – she'd finally reached the place she'd expected to be at twenty-six. Now, she was sabotaging it all due to what a mindless, violent individual had decided to do. If she allowed him to steal any more of her, then he'd won. Her mind made up, Isla went into the kitchen. Zach was sitting at the breakfast bar, his head in his hands.

'I'm sorry,' Isla said, giving him a kiss on his cheek. 'I'm glad you're here.' Then, she grabbed a plastic carrier bag from the larder, and went upstairs for a shower.

Chapter Sixteen

Zach's lovemaking had seemed almost apologetic. He was slow, gentle – but instead of feeling sensual, erotic, his feather-light touches and unhurried thrusts felt more remorseful – as though what he was doing was wrong, or unwanted. Was he under the impression she wasn't ready? That she was only doing it to appease him, or keep him happy?

That *was* what she was doing though. Maybe he could sense it.

Afterwards, as they lay in each other's arms, it was the smell that caught Isla off guard. With her face nuzzled into his neck, she breathed him in. And the fragrance of day-old aftershave hit her. It was the same aftershave he always wore, but somehow it seemed different. Possibly because before he moved in with her, she'd only ever smelt it when it was fresh. And now, this being the first time they'd had sex since he'd lived with her, she was experiencing it in a different context.

And the smell immediately took her back to the night of the attack. Isla knew smells could trigger memories – there'd been countless times when a waft of a scotch egg transported her back to her childhood and flashbacks of family days out, picnicking with her mam and Fraser, always came to her.

Specifically, the time Fraser had pushed her over and she'd sat on her plastic food-filled plate and he laughed so hard he'd thrown up. But of course, common smells would have links to numerous memories. The smell could very well have been a recollection of an aftershave worn by someone at the party. And many men used the same aftershave, or ones that had similar fragrances. It might not have even been aftershave, just the attacker's natural scent. Or deodorant. Or his clothes.

Isla unwrapped herself from Zach's arms.

'You okay?' he said. 'Was . . . that . . . you know? All right? I didn't hurt you?'

'No, of course not. Why would you think that?'

'Well, after . . .'

'I wasn't raped, Zach. I was mugged.'

'I know that! But you *were* hurt. I was being sensitive. I thought, anyway,' he said, his tone defensive. She'd clearly hurt his feelings.

'But that's not how it sounded. And you were overly gentle – it felt a little like you didn't even want to touch me. Why?' The thought he may not have really wanted to have sex with her was suddenly mortifying.

'Seriously, Isla? Come on, babe.' Imploring eyes searched hers.

'That's not an answer, Zach.' She looked away.

'I'm really not sure how to be around you at the moment. I'm sorry if I'm doing it all wrong – it's not like I've dealt with this sort of stuff before in relationships. I'm trying my best.'

'Hmmm.' Isla sat on the edge of the bed, contemplating what to say next. The awful, creeping feeling inside her made her question how Zach was being with her. At the same time, she wanted to give herself a good shake. He was doing nothing wrong. Was she experiencing some kind of behavioural reaction as a way to protect herself? It was as if she was pushing the person closest to her away and purposely causing a rift. Why then, when she knew that was exactly what she was doing, was she compelled to keep pushing? The fact his smell catapulted her back to that night was a coincidence, but all the same it did put her on edge and terrible questions flooded her mind.

'You know the night I was attacked?'

'Of course,' Zach said, getting up and dragging on his dressing gown. 'What about it?'

'You didn't come to my party and I can't remember why now.'

Zach's mouth twitched and he didn't respond immediately, slowly tying the material belt of the gown, his eyes downcast. He breathed out a long sigh before answering.

'We did talk about this when you were in hospital. I felt so terrible – so *guilty* – for not being with you that night. It's my biggest regret, Isla. Believe me, I've been over and over it, torturing myself with what-ifs and alternative outcomes had I gone with you to the party.'

'Yes, I remember you saying you felt guilty. But why hadn't you been with me? Were you working?'

'I'd stayed late at the office, yes. Do you remember the big fuss my dad was making over the new investment account he'd secured?'

Isla took a moment to cast her mind back. Yes, she did remember Zach being stressed about a contract with a large company, but as he'd just said, his dad had secured it, so why was *he* working late?

'Sort of,' she said.

'Well, Dad being Dad, he tasked me with going over the contracts again with a fine-toothed comb to make sure there was nothing amiss.'

'Surely that would've been done prior to the signing, Zach? That's what the company lawyers are for.'

'As I said, it was Dad being uber-careful. It was a huge account, and I think he was concerned – but of course, he'd never admit to that.'

'And it couldn't have waited until the following morning? And why on earth didn't he get his second in command Graham to do it? I thought he was the trusty sidekick.'

'What is this? Twenty questions? Should I get my lawyer?' Zach laughed, but his face remained stony.

'Do you think you *need* your lawyer, Mr Price?' Isla said, remembering how she'd been thrown by his surname when Zach had first introduced himself, assuming it to be Biggins, like his father. She smiled now, attempting to lighten what had become a very tense moment. One she'd created and was fuelling. Maybe it was the concussion causing some odd misfiring in her brain. She needed to rein in her reaction to it. If she pushed Zach away, she knew she'd forever regret it. Isla reached out to him, pulling at the tie to his robe.

His posture relaxed and he bent down towards her, placing his hands either side of her and lowering his face to hers. 'You can interrogate me anytime, Miss McKenzie.' He kissed her more urgently now, pressing himself into her and pushing her back down on the mattress. This time when he made love to her, he went in hard and passionately.

There was nothing apologetic about it.

Chapter Seventeen

Zach bundled some fresh clothes into his holdall, trying to be as quiet as he could so as not to alert his parents to his presence. He didn't want to get into a conversation, be asked questions about Isla. Or work. Seeing his dad at the office was enough. He certainly wasn't missing being within metres of him at home too. Staying at Isla's was liberating in some ways – he at least felt more normal, like a thirty-year-old should. His father had managed to make him feel like a child – dependent on them for survival. Zach knew he'd only been employed by him to ensure Biggins & Co had an heir. Kenneth had worked hard building it up from scratch and was adamant the business should be kept in the family. This had meant, in reality, that Zach had little choice of which career path to take. It was a given he'd step up to the mark once he'd hit eighteen.

Had Kenneth and Viola Biggins had more children, he imagined the pressure on him would've been less. He would never have been first choice to succeed Kenneth. But, as it was, his mum had been unable to sustain further pregnancies, each attempt resulting in miscarriage and a great deal of grief and resentment.

Zach never made up for their lack of other children. He

was, as he'd come to realise, a complete disappointment to them. Of course, his mum did her best to hide it, and when he was younger, he hadn't felt it quite as much as now – she'd played her part well and managed to make up for his father's shortcomings. But, Kenneth hadn't quite pulled it off – then or now. He wasn't able to cover his emotions as easily and, from time to time, they would slip through the barrier – his little digs, sarcastic criticism, belittling or condescending remarks, all pointed to the truth of the matter: Kenneth Biggins didn't really *like* his son.

But Zach was all he had. Therefore, he had no other choice.

There was a time when Zach believed his father would hand it all over to Graham – they'd been thick as thieves for as long as Zach could remember. But Graham was only six years Kenneth's junior, so hopefully, this took Graham out of the running. There were occasions when Zach found himself fantasising about the day his father died. Then he'd be able to get on with it; take on the business, possibly even sell it. But, as it turned out, his father had thought of that and had recently informed him that it would be a condition of his will he wasn't to sell up. No doubt Kenneth would also have it written in that Zach would have to change his name back to Biggins. He'd used his mother's maiden name on all but official documents since he turned sixteen. Changing it by deed poll a few years later had been a clear way to distance himself from his father's shadow as he prepared to work for him at Biggins & Co. He didn't want everyone thinking he'd only been employed because he was the boss's son. His reasoning had run far deeper than that, though. A part of him wanted it to feel like a kick in the gut for Kenneth; his only child not wanting to share his surname would undoubtedly hurt no matter how disappointing that child was to him. A small 'win' for Zach among the innumerable 'losses'.

Zach zipped up his bag and took a look around his studio.

The main house was substantial and the annexe, or studio as he preferred to call it because it sounded fancier, was adequate for him. The property was situated in the sought-after Ilsham Marine Drive, overlooking the little island, Thatcher Rock, which was near Meadfoot Beach: a place Zach had spent much of his time growing up.

Although many of his mates and work colleagues, and probably even Isla, thought of him as 'still living with Mummy and Daddy', he had, in fact, been self-contained in the grounds of their gated mansion since he was eighteen. It had been something Viola had convinced Kenneth should happen given he'd begun working full-time for the company. He needed some independence, she'd said. And Zach had mostly fended for himself and didn't go running to his parents at every opportunity, as he suspected others believed. But still, being out of their grasp now, out of their sight and living completely independently from them, did have its advantages.

Having checked all was in its place, he locked up and slowly slid the glass doors open.

'Thought I heard you sneaking around.' The voice – deep, strong – came from outside, to the side of the studio.

'Bloody hell!' Zach took a few deep breaths, his heart racing. 'I wasn't *sneaking*.' He turned away, hiding his guilty face. Typical, his dad had caught him doing just that. Zach closed and locked the door, pocketing the key.

'Looked like it to me – here under the cover of darkness,' Kenneth said. He had his long, velvet, burgundy smoking jacket on, and Russell & Bromley slip-on loafers, so Zach knew he'd been in his study. His mum would've been in bed at nine, as usual. How had he even heard him from his study?

'Well, I wasn't. It's late because I waited for Isla to fall asleep before leaving her. I was just getting some fresh clothes, that's all.'

'Still insisting on keeping an eye on her, then? Thought she might've thrown you out by now.' He gave a short, sharp laugh. Zach wasn't in the mood for his below-the-belt digs.

'Yep, she needs me. There are *some* people who think I'm worthy, Dad. Believe it or not.'

'Hmmm . . . well. Yes,' he muttered, turning now to make his way back to the main house. 'Make sure to be in early in the morning. I've got something I need to discuss with you before everyone else piles into the office.'

'Oh? Like what?'

'Seven-thirty sharp, Zach. My office. We'll discuss it then,' Kenneth said, with a dismissive wave of his arm as he disappeared up the path and into the house.

Chapter Eighteen

Christie's Crime Addicts – True Crime Podcast

Live stream:

[CHRISTIE] Christie here, live and ready to take any questions relating to the recent murder in the bay. Have you got any information about the case? Do you know the couple on Maple Drive? Maybe you worked with one of them, or were friends. Do you have any theories as to what happened that night? Don't be shy – no theory is too mad, no question too bad. You can type your comments and questions here, on Facebook, or contact us via the usual means. Myself, Ed, Doug and Jase are all here awaiting your input.

Don't forget to listen to our most recent episode. It details the case of the brutal attack and murder of twenty-year-old Magdalena Kaminski, a Polish exchange student attending Torquay's language school, who was found in the early hours of the morning in Cary Park. I'll be giving the basic details and Doug will take you through the witness statements and timeline of how the police pieced together Magdalena's last known movements. Ed will then bring us up to date on the case as it stands today – because, you guessed it, sadly this is an unsolved crime. I'll be back live this evening. In the meantime, Christie's Crime Addicts wish you a safe day in the bay.

Chapter Nineteen

Zach hadn't been in the house when Isla awoke at six-thirty. He must've left early for a meeting, although he hadn't mentioned it last night. Thinking about it now, she couldn't recall him even coming to bed. Had he? After they'd had sex, they'd both gone back downstairs, eaten a stir-fry, then watched some banal film she couldn't even remember the name of. She'd gone to bed first, leaving him flicking through the news channels. She'd give him a call later, see how his day was going.

After her usual routine of rolling out of bed, grabbing a bowl of cereal and planting herself on the sofa, laptop open on the coffee table in front of her, Isla switched on the news and simultaneously started up a new episode of the Christie's Crime Addicts podcast.

As yet another political rant played out between guests on *Good Morning Britain*, something from the podcast grabbed her attention. She quickly muted the TV and lurched forward to hit the volume button on the laptop. Finally, one of the topics on the podcast sounded relevant to her own case. The episode was detailing a local murder, and the similarities with her attack were marked.

The case was still open because there'd been few leads, Ed,

one of Christie's co-hosts, was saying. What they knew was that the attacker had approached the victim from behind and she'd been struck on the head with a blunt object to incapacitate her. This had not been the cause of death – she was dragged into the park where she was sexually assaulted, then strangled.

Isla considered the facts. She'd been attacked from behind, but according to police, they believed her head injury was sustained from the fall, not from being hit. She had been dragged into a park, though. But there had been no evidence of sexual assault, and he hadn't strangled her. So, on balance this case didn't at first glance seem to be like her own. However, she remembered overhearing the nurses speaking to each other saying they didn't think the perpetrator meant to leave her alive. So, had he been interrupted? Maybe he would've sexually assaulted her and then strangled her if he'd had the chance.

The memory of the smell came back to her again – and how last night Zach's aftershave had transported her to the night of the attack. *Had* he still been working late at the office? Her sudden mistrust of him made no sense. Why the hell would her own boyfriend lie about working, let alone try and hurt her? And he most definitely wouldn't want her dead. Zach had been ultra-keen to go out with her, and when she'd finally agreed, he was off-the-scale happy – doing all he could to make her happy too. Even now, in the face of all the challenges, he was with her, by her side, supporting her. As he had been right from the night she was attacked when he rushed to be with her at the hospital.

'Of course,' Isla said aloud, the obvious conclusion now hitting her. She'd been out of it that night; concussed. She had no recollection of it, was only able to remember what the nurses and doctors had informed her afterwards, and even that was sketchy. But now she thought about it, it made perfect sense that she would link Zach's aftershave smell with the attack. It was because he was by her bedside the entire night. Relief, mixed with guilt, washed over her. This whole thing was making her crazy. It was the knowledge it was likely someone who knew her that wouldn't leave her mind. It was a constant nagging voice, making her question everyone. And now she'd ruled Zach out, maybe she should look more closely at Simon and Graham.

'No, no, no!' Isla ran the fingers of one hand through her hair, catching them in the knots. She wished she could stop torturing herself. Why couldn't she let it go? It was as if a rat were gnawing away, bit by bit, at her mind, slowly burrowing its way in, trying to reach a buried prize. A memory, in Isla's case. Something held deep inside, waiting to be unearthed. Someone wanted to hurt her, *kill her*, even, and their reason for that was in her subconscious. Who it was, was there, too.

Whoever it was, something – or someone – had disturbed his act, and he'd made a quick getaway before he was able to finish her off.

Would he now be worried that Isla could potentially identify him?

Because if he was, he might want to return and finish the job.

Chapter Twenty

THEN – The week before

Isla popped her AirPods in and fluffed her hair up with her fingertips, bringing it forwards to cover her ears so her colleagues wouldn't spot them. Not that any of them would call her out on it – it wasn't as though they were at school and it was against the rules to have your phone out – and being in the upstairs glass dome, alone in the filing room, she doubted she'd be sprung anyway. But Kenneth Biggins had eyes everywhere and wouldn't be best pleased if he realised, because he liked them to have one hundred per cent attention on their work-related tasks. The fact she could listen to podcasts and it actually increased the likelihood she'd get more work done, would be neither here nor there to him. Although, if she bothered to look, she expected it would be 'company policy' not to have distractions such as earphones during working hours. Currently, while sifting through hundreds of files, both physical and digital, it was the only way Isla could see her way through to completing the task without falling asleep.

'What are you up to?' Zach's voice made her jump, and she spun around to face him.

'I'm having a tidy-up. Some of these go way back and need archiving and the data on the computer is all over the place.

It's not an efficient way of filing – how has this not been addressed before?'

'Because we didn't have anyone as super-efficient as you? Some of Dad's practices are a little . . . archaic, I guess.'

'I'll say. I assumed all this was covered by the secretary?'

Zach shook his head. 'Nope. Dad likes to keep this stuff up here, away from prying eyes. Doesn't trust many with the ins and outs of each and every one of his business dealings. I'm surprised he's let you loose in here if I'm honest.'

'Well, that sounds decidedly dodgy, Zach.' Isla raised her eyebrows. 'Who else has access to this?'

'Why do you ask?'

'No reason, just curious.'

'Dad, Graham, me and now you, it seems.' He gave a tight smile.

'Right. I feel so privileged,' she said, the sarcasm obvious.

'Dad didn't mention you'd be doing this. Haven't you got anything more important to do?'

'This is important, Zach. Not that he specifically tasked me with doing it.'

'Then why the hell are you?'

'I'm in line for the promotion. I want to gain all the knowledge I can, as well as ensure everything is shipshape for when I'm up here in the glass dome full-time.'

'Well, I think you're wasting your time, Isla. Half this stuff isn't worth worrying over. It's new accounts you need to focus on, not old ones.'

'Maybe.'

'Why don't you give it up? Come on, I can show you far more interesting things – just step into my office.' Zach gave her a wink.

'Hah! And get fired for professional misconduct before I'm even officially promoted?'

'Spoilsport.'

Isla checked her watch. 'An hour to lunchtime – we could sneak off for half an hour. A lot can happen in thirty minutes,' she said, pushing her body up against Zach's and tilting her face up to his. They kissed, but Isla pulled back before they got carried away.

'Oh, God, I want you right here, right now,' Zach said, his breathing heavy.

'Go on, away with you. Go do some work. Don't want to be told off by Daddy.'

'You drive me nuts, Isla. I'm keeping you to your word you know. In an hour, you're mine,' Zach said. He turned and left.

Isla felt off kilter, her desire for him momentarily taking control. She needed to be careful at work; she really couldn't afford Kenneth Biggins to catch her having a sneaky snog with his son. And from the way Zach had responded to where she was, she wondered if Kenneth would also be upset about her digging around in his filing room. Zach had seemed like he was actively trying to stop her from looking further into the files. Did he know that some of his father's past deals might not have been altogether 'above board'? Because some of the data was a little off. And so far, Isla had come across at least two discrepancies between the physical and digital files. They could have been incorrectly transferred to the database, but she got the feeling there was more to it. A few of the accounts that had jumped out for Isla had been signed off by Graham Vaughan. But, as she looked closer, she realised they weren't deals actually done by him.

And the money that passed between the company and the account holder didn't add up.

'This is where you've been hiding yourself.'

'Blimey! What's with people creeping up on me today?' Why had her movements suddenly become so important to her colleagues? No one usually bothered where she was at any given moment. But now, as she was trying to stay under the radar, it appeared everyone and his dog wanted to know what she was doing. 'I'm filing, Simon. I mean, I realise you have no idea what it is to file something away, given the state of your desk . . .'

'No need for that, is there?' He walked in, closing the door behind him.

She wasn't in the mood for chitchat; she wanted to finish what she'd started. 'Why are you bothering me? No work of your own to do?'

'Just wanted a private chat, that's all,' Simon said.

Isla frowned. 'Oh? About what?' She placed some files back on the table, and crossed her arms. It was uncomfortably snug in the filing room, no windows to let in light, and the rows of metal cabinets lent a cluttered feel to the space. As Simon took a step towards her, she took one back.

'It's a bit, well, awkward, really.' His eyes flitted around, not making contact with hers. She'd worked with Simon for five years, but this was the first time she'd felt cornered by him. He'd been slightly offhand with her since the mention of her upcoming promotion and she couldn't help but assume it was jealousy. He'd been at the company for the same amount of time as her, but she'd excelled, and he had merely coasted. It was down to him, his lack of drive, nothing to do with Isla getting promoted before him of course, but he'd come across as bitter. She hoped it wouldn't affect their working relationship, but this forced encounter was looking rather like it might go that way. She stared at Simon, waiting for him to continue. He chewed at the side of his thumbnail.

'Well?' Isla said, her patience taking a dive.

'You're *with* Zach, aren't you? Like, a couple . . .'

'Yeees. You know that. As does the entire office, I believe. Why?'

He shrugged and screwed up his face. 'It's just, you were keen on that other bloke not long ago, and I just . . . am worried, I guess . . . that you're maybe rushing in.' His cheeks flushed as he finally made eye contact with her.

His sudden interest in her relationships struck her as odd. But, not wanting to extend this conversation for any longer than necessary, Isla just nodded, then thanked him for his concern but reassured him she knew what she was doing. 'Hadn't you best be getting back to your desk?' she asked.

'I don't want you to think I'm being nosy. I genuinely just want to be a good friend, that's all. And I've wanted to talk to you about it for a while, but kept putting it off, thinking it was none of my business. But as Zach works here and I've known him as long as I've known you, there were certain things—'

'Simon,' Isla said, putting her hands up towards him. 'Thanks. But you're right – it really isn't any of your business.' Isla glanced at her watch. Christ, she'd been waylaid for thirty minutes by Zach and now Simon. She'd never finish going through the files today at this rate. She carefully walked around Simon and opened the door. 'I'll catch you later,' she said as she held it for him. He got the message and left. She hammered out a text to Zach:

I'm not going to make our lunch date, sorry. I need to work through break. I'll owe you the thirty minutes 😉 🖤

She wasn't going anywhere just yet.
She'd started something now – she had to see it through.

Chapter Twenty-One

Her adrenaline was pumping for the first time in weeks; it was the most energetic she'd felt. Isla paced the lounge, her mind filled with questions and theories. Her gut was telling her she'd been attacked by someone she knew. That it was planned, not random or opportunistic. But, if that had been the case and she'd been personally targeted, what could possibly have been the motive?

Her thoughts kept returning to Biggins & Co. Her colleagues were the only people who knew exactly where she'd be that night. It went against everything she knew to even consider that one of them would wish to attack her. Let alone kill her. However mad it seemed, though, they were currently the only people who fitted her theory.

The business accounts.

The memory flashed through her mind. Maybe the doctors were right – it was only a matter of time before she would recall everything. Isla focused her thoughts: a week or so prior to her official promotion, she'd been working on archiving paper files, and updating the computer database. And she'd found financial discrepancies. Something to do with a group of investments.

Why couldn't she remember which ones – or what, exactly, the issue had been, though?

'Think, Isla, think.' She continued pacing, her head aching. The memories were on the periphery; they were hazy. She knew she'd uncovered something that appeared 'off' but couldn't bring the detail to the forefront of her mind. At least memories were beginning to return. She shouldn't force them. Bit by bit, everything would come into focus.

A loud series of bangs interrupted her train of thought and Isla stopped walking mid-pace, her senses on high alert. The deep-sounding thuds came from the direction of the hallway. Silence followed and Isla let out her held breath. When she felt certain the noises had come from next door, not outside – or more importantly, not from inside her own house – she tiptoed towards the stairs. She cursed herself for being so ridiculous – why was she tiptoeing?

Get a grip.

Putting her ear to the wall, she listened intently for further bangs.

Nothing.

Earlier, she'd assumed no one was in next door, and she couldn't remember hearing any movement since concluding they must both be out. So, what had the noises been?

The rhythm of the bangs made her think of someone falling down the stairs, bumping and crashing on each stair as they went. Maybe she should pop around, knock on the door to check all was okay.

Her heart jittered, and for what was probably five minutes, she sat on the bottom stair while contemplating whether she was over-reacting. A few bumps didn't mean anyone had come to harm. But if she didn't at least attempt to be a good neighbour and go and check, and then she found one of them had fallen, she'd have extreme guilt.

Her mind flitted to the Netflix true crime series *The Staircase*. In that, a woman had fallen down the stairs and died, with the resulting death being put under the microscope as it had appeared her injuries were more serious than a mere fall. Police determined they were more consistent with a beating *prior* to being pushed. Blame was attributed to her husband. However, her husband was resolute in his innocence. Isla, on the other hand, had been convinced he was as guilty as sin.

She barely knew the couple next door – could something like that have just happened? Isla had lived in her rented semi for five years, having found it as soon as she'd graduated and left the student accommodation in Exeter. The owner, Mike, had inherited his parents' house and moved in, but wanted to keep his as well. The timing had been perfect, and he told Isla he was keen for it to be a long-term let, 'none of that fussing about with a short-hold, six-month tenancy rubbish'. His preference for no fuss also meant he hadn't bothered her much during her time there. Just the odd visit to check up on appliances, and general upkeep of the building, and a phone call here and there to arrange for the boiler service and landlord safety checks.

The current neighbours had only moved in last year, and they were renting too. She'd noticed the 'To Let' sign go up and been hopeful for some young, friendly neighbours. Unfortunately, the letting company didn't get that memo, and let it to a middle-aged couple who mainly kept to themselves and who hadn't even bothered with introductions. An odd pair by anyone's standards. She knew they lived in a town, not a cosy village, but *some* neighbourly interaction would've been nice.

But still, it was unlikely the banging noises she'd heard were anything sinister. She'd been watching far too many true crime shows and was becoming fixated on attributing criminal explanations to everything. Now the question was firmly lodged in her mind, though, there was no way she could ignore it. She'd have to leave the house and go next door to check everything was all right.

Chapter Twenty-Two

It should be easy. She was only popping to the next house, but as Isla put her hand on the front door handle, she paused. This would be the first time she'd left the safety of her home since the attack.

'For God's sake. It's broad daylight and you're only walking down your path and up the one next door!' Her positive self-talk was immediately countered by her negative mind.

You've seen enough true crime now to know attacks happen in the daytime, too.

She hadn't heard further unusual noises from the neighbours – she'd probably be wasting her time anyway. As Isla began to withdraw her hand, the doorbell rang, causing her to reel backwards. She wasn't expecting anyone. Would her attacker be so brazen as to seek her out? Come to her *house*? The thought was horrifying. She backed out of the hallway, retreating to the lounge, then cautiously pulled back the lounge curtain an inch or so.

Nicci was standing on the top step.

With a sigh of relief, Isla went back to let her in.

'Well, you took your time. Thought you were hiding from me,' Nicci said. She stepped inside, appraising Isla's appearance with one up-and-down glance. 'You look like shit. When did you last take a shower?'

'Cheers. Lovely to see you, too.' Isla's shoulders slumped as she watched Nicci disappear into the lounge, noting that, as usual, she looked like she'd walked straight out of the pages of a fashion magazine – her boho-chic style seemingly effortless. Isla was well aware she looked the worse for wear, of course, but hearing it from her friend was like a smack in the face. She slammed the front door and sloped after Nicci; her concern over the banging from next door would have to wait.

'No wonder you were avoiding seeing people,' Nicci said. She averted her eyes and began rummaging in her black leather tote bag.

'New bag?' Isla asked, ignoring Nicci's comment. She squinted, moving closer. 'Wow, a Mulberry. Nice. Did you get a pay rise?' She laughed, but Nicci's expression remained neutral.

'Oh, got it from eBay,' she said dismissively, as she pulled a small, box-shaped item wrapped in purple floral-print paper from it. She smiled, handing the gift to Isla.

'What's this?'

'A little something to cheer you up. Zach said you were struggling,' she said matter-of-factly.

Isla forced a smile, at once feeling both cherished *and* annoyed. Why was Zach talking about her like that to her colleagues?

'Oh? He said that did he?'

'He's worried about you, that's all, Isla. And I feel so terrible not coming around to see you before now.' Finally, Isla heard a softness in her friend's voice. Nicci was often abrupt and up-front when speaking; it was her way – and it hadn't really bothered her before now – but today, Isla was feeling a bit sensitive, and hoped she'd be more sympathetic and less judgey.

'I suppose I did ask you not to.' Isla shrugged. It was true – she had tried to put off visitors since the attack, preferring to stay tucked away, hermit-like, until she was ready to face the world again. But if she were being honest with herself, she had been a little upset that Nicci had only texted and called instead of being her usual bolshie self and just turning up.

'I should've ignored you,' she said, as if reading Isla's mind. Nicci smiled, a genuine concern in her expression. Isla stared into her eyes to see if the smile had reached those, too. Despite her heavily made-up, smoky-grey lids, Isla saw that it had. She felt the threat of tears, and when she tried to speak, her voice wobbled.

'Okay if I make myself comfy?' Nicci asked, moving to sit on the sofa. It was as though she'd sensed an onslaught of emotion and was trying to avoid it now.

'Sure. I'll make us a coffee,' Isla said, overly brightly to compensate.

'Lovely, thanks. I can't stay long, obviously – I've told work I've got a dentist appointment.'

'Hah! And they haven't queried the fact it's your third appointment this month?'

'Nah! I swear they don't even listen when I speak, Isla. I think all they hear is *blah, blah . . . blah, blah, blah.*' She snapped her thumb and fingers together in a mocking hand-puppet motion.

Isla laughed and thanked Nicci for the gift, placing it, unopened, on the large, gloss-white shelving unit. 'I'll save it for later if you don't mind. My days drag somewhat; it'll be nice to look forward to something.'

Nicci shrugged. 'Whatever floats your boat.'

Isla fumbled around in the kitchen, her mind contemplating the reason Nicci had turned up the day after calling her. Had she said something to worry her friend? She made two coffees and grabbed a packet of custard creams, putting them on the bamboo tray. 'Nicci?' she called. 'Can you help me in with these, please?'

Nicci carried the tray in, setting it on the coffee table, then they sat one at each end of the sofa.

'How are you doing, then? Tell me honestly because I think you were telling me what you thought I wanted to hear on the phone,' Nicci said, her mouth stuffed with a biscuit.

So, she'd been right, then. The reason Nicci had come over was because she didn't believe Isla's assertions she was doing okay. Isla quickly weighed up the options of offering Nicci the truth, versus lies and decided on a mix of the two. 'Like I told you, I'm slowly recovering,' she said. *Truth*. 'The online therapy is helping.' *Lie*. Nicci might relay this conversation to Zach, she thought, so she should play it safe. 'But I can't stop thinking about the attack. Zach's right, really – I am struggling. Finding it hard to move on from it. And I'm thinking the person who did it is someone I know.' *Truth*.

Isla paused; she'd said enough for now. She didn't want to tell Nicci all her inner worries. Like the fact she thought Simon was the last person to see her after she left the party and had known which way she'd walked. Or that when she'd had sex with Zach, the smell of his aftershave had taken her back to that night. She'd refrain from mentioning that a memory had returned of her uncovering some financial discrepancies in the files she'd been sorting a week prior to the attack.

Quite why she was afraid of sharing this information, Isla wasn't sure. Nicci wasn't just a colleague, she was also her friend – her only real friend in Devon, in fact. Not only was she someone she regularly socialised with, they also had a laugh together. She was Isla's 'go-to' when she was feeling despondent about work, or lack of a man in her life. While she loved Alex, they rarely spoke outside of work, only at the odd social gathering or team-building event. But even taking all this into account, as had been the case before any of this, Isla still didn't *completely* trust Nicci. Those eyes. There'd always been something behind her eyes that meant Isla held back from opening up to her entirely.

'Christ, Isla. Really? What makes you think it could've possibly been someone you know?' Nicci's face paled as she slammed back hard against the sofa.

Again, Isla sensed she needed to be careful. She didn't want Nicci to know she'd become obsessed with true crime, spending her days watching documentaries and listening to podcasts; that would only make her think she was out of her mind. Would make what she was saying less believable, verging on being hysterical.

'Because the attack wasn't random, Nicci. I wasn't a victim of an opportunistic crime, I'm certain of it. Yes, my bag and phone were stolen, but I think that was to make it *look* like a mugging. In all likelihood, the attacker meant to kill me that night.'

'Whoa!' Nicci sat forward, a stunned look on her face. 'Okay, if that's true – why . . . the . . . *hell* . . . would anyone want to kill you?' she said slowly. 'It doesn't make the slightest bit of sense, Isla. You're overanalysing, overthinking it. It was a mugging. Some nasty lowlife, who probably wanted your stuff so they could sell it to fund their drug habit, saw you walking alone – appearing drunk and vulnerable – so took the opportunity there and then. That's it. All there was to it. No one wants you dead. That's ridiculous.'

Without divulging the rest of the information, Isla could understand Nicci's reaction. In fact, she was probably right and Isla had completely over-reacted, making the attack something it wasn't. There was a strong possibility what she was thinking, believing it to be a personal attack against her, could be a normal reaction for people who'd had this experience.

'It does sound ridiculous now I've vocalised it,' Isla agreed. She decided she'd say no more about it to Nicci. 'Ignore me. It's just some process or other I have to go through. Apparently it's normal – so says my online therapist.' *Lie.*

Nicci looked thoughtful for a moment. 'I don't want you to think I'm dismissing your concerns out of hand. I'm only worried that you're never going to get back to normal if you insist on obsessing over it. You need to focus on returning to full health and getting back out there again – back into society.' Nicci waved an arm towards the window, then stood abruptly, pulling the curtains fully back. 'You're like a hermit in here, tucked away from reality. It wouldn't have hurt you to come to the locked room mystery thing the other night, but Zach said you refused the opportunity. They are your favourite things to do, Isla. And God, you were missed.'

'Sorry. I'm kinda in the middle of my very own locked room mystery at the moment.'

'No excuse, missus.' Nicci wagged her index finger, but was smiling. 'And more importantly, you need to come to work!'

'Ah, you're missing me?'

'Of course. Although you won't be working with me when you get back anyway – I know that. But having you around, seeing you at breaks – that would be great. I'm so bored not having you to share my lunchtime gossip with. No one can replace you, you know?'

'That's great to hear. Thanks, Nicci. But as I've had this time off, and don't actually know a date of return, I'm surprised old Scrooge hasn't replaced me.'

'Well . . .' Nicci's eyes widened. At first, Isla attributed this fleeting look of shock to her statement, but then her pulse jolted. Was Nicci about to tell her that he *had*, or was thinking

92

about replacing her? Her jaw slackened as fear of how Nicci was going to finish that sentence stalled her. All she could do was give her an encouraging nod, so she'd continue. Nicci sighed. 'It *is* all a bit chaotic at the moment,' she said.

'Just because you're one down?' Isla said.

Nicci shook her head. 'No, what with Simon off, and Graham appearing to buckle under the strain – seriously, the whole place seems to be falling apart. Your mugging started off some weird chain reaction.'

Isla frowned. 'Oh God. Sounds a nightmare. I bet that's why Zach's been going in early then. He didn't even tell me Simon was off. Two people down – no wonder Graham's feeling the strain. What's wrong with Simon?'

'No one knows – well, no one on *our* floor. He went off the same time as you.'

'That's interesting,' Isla said. She was distracted now she'd learned this. Simon being off since her attack seemed like more than a coincidence.

'Yes, and bloody Graham – him and Scrooge are thick as thieves and disappearing for private meetings all the time. Makes you wonder if the business is in trouble.'

'No, surely not.' Isla considered it for a second, and realised it wasn't necessarily a far-fetched theory. She closed her eyes, taking a long, deep breath in, releasing it slowly. 'Bloody hell,' she added.

'Oh, I'm sorry, Isla. Adding to your worries here, aren't I? I'm positive it'll all work out once the team are at full capacity again.'

'Maybe there is something going on, though – and only the men at the top know.' Isla was only half-speaking to Nicci, her words more for her mind's benefit. 'Them in their fucking ivory tower. When I think back to the party, from what I remember of it, Graham was a little odd, wasn't he? I mean, odder than usual? Flustered.'

'I can't say I noticed a difference, no.'

'A memory of the night came back to me,' Isla said, choosing her words carefully so she didn't reveal everything she'd remembered. 'When I left, I said something to him – I can't recall what, exactly – but he gave me this really weird look. Worry, mixed with anger, if you can imagine that.'

'Sort of. Maybe that's why he left right after you did. He didn't even bother to come and say goodbye.'

'What? I left and he stayed, didn't he?'

'Nope. I saw him walk past the window a minute or so after you.'

'He was walking?'

'Yeah, I assumed he was walking up the road a bit so it was easier to get a taxi. He said he'd come straight from work and hadn't driven.'

Which meant Graham had walked the same way she had, only moments behind her.

Chapter Twenty-Three

'Hey, you.' Zach walked into the lounge and kissed the top of Isla's head. 'Sorry I'm late back.'

'I was beginning to get worried. What kept you?'

'Trying to catch up on stuff, nothing major,' he said. 'But I still haven't finished, I'm afraid. Maybe an hour or so in the spare room, then I'll join you.'

'Oh, right. Okay.' Isla's brow creased. 'Have you eaten?'

'Yeah – Graham ordered in some pizzas.'

Isla refrained from commenting, but her senses pricked. She wanted to grill Zach about Graham, ask if he'd been acting strangely at work, or if he'd been asking after her. She was put out that he was going to go straight upstairs. Zach hadn't once been late back from the office during the two weeks he'd been staying. And he hadn't used the spare room at all even though she'd set it up for him to use as his home office when he moved in. Why tonight?

'I'll grab a drink and go on up. Can I get you anything first?'

'No. Thanks. I'm good.' She wasn't, though. She was on high alert – her thoughts running wild.

*

She waited until the end credits of *Making A Murderer* rolled, then crept upstairs to check on Zach. As she was about to push the door, it flung open and Zach came through and closed it behind him in a swift movement.

'You made me jump,' he said.

'Sorry, just wanted to know if you were almost done,' she said, adding, 'I'm missing you.'

They were standing close, facing each other, and Isla was suddenly unsettled, feeling as though she'd caught him out doing something he shouldn't. He appeared guarded. Secretive. Isla noticed Zach slip something into his trouser pocket. It looked like a phone – but not his usual one; it was smaller, but chunkier, than his sleek Samsung Galaxy.

He has a second phone.

That could only mean one thing. What, or who, was he hiding from her?

After a few awkward moments, where both of them silently faced each other, Zach said he was finished for the night. They went downstairs and sat together on the sofa. Despite the fact they were side by side, bodies touching, Zach was distant.

Isla took a breath and twisted to face him. 'Is everything okay? Or is there something wrong at work?'

Zach's gaze didn't meet hers. 'Nothing I can't handle,' he said, his focus remaining on the TV.

'If you want to talk about it, you can. Don't think because I'm off sick I'm not capable of supporting you. Tell me.'

'Nothing to tell, Isla. Really. I'm fine.' He turned then and took her hands in his, finally looking her in the eye. 'It's you who's important. How are the therapy sessions going?'

Isla's cheeks burned. 'Yeah, good. I'm definitely giving less space in my head to the negative thoughts . . . you know . . . and focusing on the future.' God, she hoped he didn't delve any deeper, question her on any specific methods she'd learned from the therapist.

'Are you sure about that? Not just telling me what you think I want to hear?'

A knot formed in Isla's stomach. They were almost the exact same words Nicci had used earlier. 'No. Why would you say that?'

Zach shrugged. 'Oh, I don't know. A gut feeling. Call it a hunch.'

Isla didn't believe it was any such thing; Nicci had obviously gone straight back to him to report what she'd said earlier. She tried to keep the disappointment from her voice when she asked: 'Did you send Nicci to check up on me, Zach?'

'No, of course not,' he said a little too quickly, straightening his back and pulling a face. His indignation was exaggerated, and he seemed to realise it, too, as he conceded and added: 'I did happen to say I was concerned about you, though. And thought some company would do you good. I assume she took that opportunity, then.'

'Yes. She came over earlier.' She narrowed her eyes as she told him, getting the feeling he knew full well already. What else had he and Nicci cosied up about? She tried not to read too much into it, but the image of his second mobile lay stubbornly in her mind. She bit her lower lip to stop herself asking about it. Instead, she decided to take this opportunity to dig a little more about Simon. 'She said Simon was off sick. What's the matter with him?'

'Oh, some virus or other knocked him for six apparently. Graham went and saw him over the weekend, says he's very low.'

'Hmmm.'

'What?'

'Nothing. And Graham – he's the same as ever?'

'Yes, I guess. What's with the interrogation? I said everything at work was fine.'

'I know you did. Sorry, I'm only interested in what's going on in the company while I'm off.'

'You've enough to be worried about. I don't want you to be focused on work issues when you should be concentrating on yourself – on getting better.'

'I am getting better.'

'I know, babe. I know.' The atmosphere had become tense and she got the impression Zach was trying to placate her with his 'babe' talk. He smiled. 'Now, can we change the channel? Or shall we just head to bed now. It's late and I'm knackered.'

Chapter Twenty-Four

'How are you doing today, sweetheart?'

Isla sighed deeply. 'Okay, mostly.' She sat on the sofa and leaned on the arm, the mobile tucked in between her shoulder and chin. Then she switched her laptop on, balancing it on her thighs.

'Well, that doesn't sound convincing, now does it?' Rowan's Glaswegian accent made Isla ever so slightly homesick, but the words came across sharply, sounding more like she was receiving a telling-off, and Isla immediately went into defensive mode.

'Some days are better than others, Mam. You of all people know that.' She clenched her teeth, aware she'd just punched below the belt. Rowan had done her best to shield Isla and Fraser from the intensity of her arguments with their dad, avoiding showing her true emotions until they were safely tucked up in bed. But Isla had heard her mam's muffled tears on more than one occasion. She'd been afraid her parents would split up at first, then later, wished they just would.

'I know, love. And aye, you're right about that. You know I have my regrets. I thought I was doing the right thing, but he wore me down to the point I spent most of my time completely scunnered.'

Even though hearing her mam say this was sad, her mention about being scunnered raised a smile. 'I can certainly relate to that, Mam. I'm a little fed up myself at the moment.'

'You heard from the police yet? Any update whether they've made an arrest?'

'No, Mam. Maybe they won't.'

'I don't like the thought he's still out there, doing Lord knows what. The bastard should be behind bars. What if he comes at you again? You have to be careful – no more walking alone, all right?'

Isla knew Rowan was only vocalising the same fears she herself had, but they weren't particularly helpful to hear. 'It's okay, Mam. Look, it was some druggie needing money for his next hit I expect. Totally random, as the police suggested, and I'm sure it won't happen again. I'll be fine.'

As the words left her mouth, Isla realised she didn't believe it at all.

She changed the subject and soon they were chatting about Fraser and his girlfriend. She was surprised to hear that they'd announced their engagement the previous evening. Shame he hadn't bothered to let her know personally. Did he think offering her good news was inappropriate given her attack? Fraser could be quite sensitive when he wanted to be, but he hadn't been in contact much lately. Obviously wrapped up in his own life. He had sent the odd text here and there, but mainly it was Rowan who passed on messages from him.

Tired from talking now, Isla thanked her mam for calling in an attempt to bring the conversation to a close. She was desperate to get onto her laptop and scroll through some crime podcasts. 'I'll ring you tomorrow, Mam.'

'Och, awayyego!'

She was right – it was highly unlikely. 'Okay, then. You call me,' she conceded.

The phone's battery bar was low after talking to her mam. Isla reached down to the socket beside the sofa and plugged it in to charge, then clicked onto her list of real-life crime podcasts. After the chat with her mam, she was even more certain her attack wasn't an isolated one.

Each podcast episode she listened to confirmed what she'd already been thinking – that she'd been attacked by someone known to her. That wasn't to say it was a close contact, but maybe someone who knew her movements, where she worked, lived. Her mind whirled as she considered those working at the local grocery shop, the butcher's, the supermarket, the bus drivers, taxi drivers. People she saw or came into contact with week in, week out, who she rarely paid attention to. But what if one of them had been paying close attention to her?

It was the same for many people these days – they lived in their own bubble, going about their daily routine without really *seeing* others. Lost in thought about the stresses of their lives, worrying about where they were meant to be, what appointments they had. And Isla was guilty of being the person who didn't look up, didn't observe those around her; the person who was often rushing around, too self-absorbed and pre-occupied to be aware of who might be watching her. From what she remembered, it'd been the case the night of the attack, too. Oblivious to her surroundings, unaware of the danger until it was too late.

Hours had passed, and Isla realised she hadn't moved off the sofa – not even to get snacks. Her obsession was really taking over. Stiff from inactivity, she did some stretches, then made her way to the kitchen, rummaging through the cupboards for something resembling a meal. She settled for a crisp sandwich, which took an age to make with one hand. The cast was beginning to get on her nerves now – maybe she should see if she could bring the hospital appointment forward, get the thing cut off early.

Once she'd eaten, Isla went upstairs to retrieve her journal from the top shelf of the wardrobe. She sat on the bed, scribbling a few notes about her current theories, adding shop workers, regular customers, bus and taxi drivers to the list of suspects. How she was meant to investigate this theory was beyond her, though. She could call the police and share her list, but she got the feeling she'd be fobbed off. They'd categorised her attack as a robbery – crime against the person – not even an aggravated assault despite her head injury. Without solid evidence, she didn't think that would change.

She was on her own.

Chapter Twenty-Five

Catching sight of herself in the hallway mirror as she reached the bottom of the stairs, Isla paused. She'd done her best to avoid her reflection of late, not wanting to face reality; not wishing to know just what Zach saw when he came back from work each evening. Her skin was pallid – it hadn't had an iota of make-up on it for weeks, and no doubt lack of sunlight didn't help. She was reminded of the undead as she stared at herself – but at least she *had* a reflection, so that was a plus. Her pyjamas hung off her diminishing frame, a stark reminder she wasn't eating healthily, and her hair fell to her shoulders in greasy clumps.

'Dear God, woman. You do look like shit. Nicci was spot-on about that.' She turned and headed back up the stairs to the bathroom.

Feeling better from the shower, she blow-dried her hair. Once she'd done that, it resembled a wig that'd gone through the tumble dryer. She'd have to straighten it now. Ducking beneath her bed to get the straighteners, she caught sight of her new curling wand. Curls would be good; Zach would definitely notice if she'd taken the time to tame her hair. She plugged it in and while it heated to the ridiculously hot temperature, got dressed – into day clothes for a change. Only jogging bottoms and a T-shirt, but an improvement on PJs.

As she knelt in front of the large, oval mirror and took the curling wand in her good hand, she realised it was going to be a challenge. 'Damn.' She had limited range of movement in her fingers due to the cast, but made a clumsy attempt to hold a chunk of hair while she wrapped it around the barrel. Her mind wandered until she smelt burning-hot hair and quickly removed the wand. She'd kept it in the same position for too long; the smell reminded her that she'd done the same thing the last time she'd curled her hair.

On the night of the party.

Maybe he did know.

The words came into her mind from nowhere. A memory. Had she spoken them? Or had someone else? She repeated them in her head until she was able to latch them on to something that made sense. She'd *thought* them, that was it. She'd been about to leave the party – she could envisage Nicci's hallway, hear the music playing, could see Graham. Then it was gone. Isla shook her head. It was so frustrating getting these fragmented memories bit by bit. It seemed smell was a big trigger in the recollection of some of them. She'd have to try that more. If she were lucky, everything from that night would return to her.

She went downstairs and sat back down on the sofa, reaching down the side to unplug her phone. Seven new texts had arrived since she last checked. She scrolled through the messages – all of which asked her the same thing in different ways – enjoying guessing who they were from just by their tone and language use, because all of them were from unknown numbers. She'd concluded there was little point in programming them in because some were from colleagues she barely spoke to at work anyway and the others from old friends in Scotland she engaged with via DMs from her social media accounts from time to time; the important names were in there and that's all she was bothered with. Besides, her new phone must be on its way and her contacts should be transferred across to that one. Although, the company were really dragging their heels; it'd been ages since they said a replacement was being sent out.

Zach had made several calls to them demanding a quicker service, but told Isla they'd been trying to wriggle out of the insurance claim. Isla didn't understand why – she paid enough for the privilege and it was a simple enough claim. In fact, she should take control and call them about it herself; threaten them with Ofcom or something if they didn't hold up their end of the contract. Suddenly motivated, she found their number and used the landline to make the call.

Twenty-nine minutes later, Isla was exhausted from the hold music and was ready to give up when finally, the music stopped. *Please don't be on a loop.*

'What can I do for you today?' an equally exhausted voice said.

'At last! Right, I'm getting fed up with waiting for my replacement iPhone, which was stolen over two weeks ago.'

After going through the usual security questions and repeating her insurance claim number a dozen times, Isla was left more frustrated than ever.

'I'm sorry, there doesn't appear to be a claim under that number.'

'There has to be!'

'When was the claim made?'

Isla couldn't remember. A sharp pain above her eyes caught her off guard and she dropped the phone to grab her forehead, scrunching her eyes up until it passed. There'd been a few episodes of short, sharp headaches since her injury, which she'd been told not to worry about. Unless they became worse, which she hoped wouldn't be the case. Taking a breath, she composed herself and slowly reached down to pick up the receiver. The line was dead.

'You've got to be shitting me? After all that?' There was no way she was starting from the beginning again. And without all the details, she was probably wasting her time anyway. She'd be sure to get Zach on the case later. Glancing at the time, she realised she wouldn't have long to wait until he walked through the door. Hopefully, he'd be impressed to find her clean and dressed; she needed to show him she was making an effort.

The slamming door woke her. Disorientated, Isla shot up from the sofa, her blood pressure plummeting. She immediately sat back down.

'I didn't think you'd still be up,' Zach said, coming into the lounge, his briefcase still in his hand.

'What time is it?' Isla rubbed a hand over her face.

'Ten-thirty. Sorry, babe. Didn't intend to be this late back.' He bent to kiss her. 'Oh!' he took a step back, appraising her. 'You look nice.'

Isla managed a sleepy smile. 'Thanks. Though getting dressed is over-rated.'

'Maybe, but sadly a social requirement.' He laughed, but his faced appeared taut, tiredness – or stress – pulling at his features. He turned to leave. Isla realised he hadn't placed his briefcase in the usual position by the hall table. Which meant he was going up to the second bedroom. She got up, following him out.

'Late back yet *still* not finished work?' she said, her tone a little too accusatory.

'Yeah, I know.' He paused at the bottom stair. 'But I assumed you'd be in bed anyway, so wouldn't mind? Besides, I'm literally going to be half an hour – that's all. Then I'll join you in bed.' In contrast, his own tone was calm. Isla leaned against the doorframe and sucked in a breath instead of responding. She wasn't sure why she was even annoyed with him. Maybe because she'd made an effort and hoped for positive reinforcement – more compliments, praise for making progress. But really, what was she expecting – a sticker for her reward chart? Maybe he was no longer bothered about her appearance because he was getting attention from elsewhere.

The second phone. She had the urge to ask him about it now. Her mind flitted between thoughts – all bad ones – as to why he had it; why he was hiding it from her. Why he was late for the second night in a row. One thought dominated. Nicci's visit yesterday had been the first since her attack, whereas before they'd regularly spend time at each other's places. She was well aware that Isla couldn't face leaving at the moment, so why hadn't she popped in more? She thought about the fact she herself had put off visitors, but really, that wouldn't stop a true friend from at least trying. It was almost like Nicci was avoiding coming over because Zach was there. The memory of Nicci's words came hurtling back to her:

'You've taken the only eligible male under thirty who's even remotely intelligent and attractive.'

Was she jealous? Did she want Zach for herself?

From the lounge doorway, Isla watched her boyfriend ascend the stairs and couldn't help but ask herself the question.

Was something going on between Zach and Nicci?

But surely her friend wouldn't betray her in that way.

Chapter Twenty-Six

Zach had joined her in bed after about half an hour, as he said he would. Isla had to accept she was maybe overthinking, over-reacting. Being on her own, shut away from the world was probably doing her no good and it merely added to her anxiety. That, and listening to real-life crime podcasts and watching crime documentaries. But she hadn't imagined Zach's second phone, or the fact he seemed secretive. As much as he'd denied issues at work, there had to be something going on to account for his extended working hours. If it was just a new deal, he'd have said. Blaming problems at work was at least preferable to her considering the other, more hurtful one of him having an affair with her best friend.

Isla snuggled up to his warm body, eventually drifting into a fitful sleep.

The mattress shifted, bringing Isla out of her dream. Her eyes felt puffy and sore; she hadn't been asleep that long. She was about to ask where Zach was going, but instead, stayed still, and silent. Shadows skittered across the ceiling as he crept from his side of the bed and moved towards the door. When he'd disappeared from view, Isla checked the clock. Two a.m. Was he going to the bathroom? She heard the muffled creaking of the office chair as his weight lowered onto it, ruling that out. She waited for ten minutes, assuming he'd come back to bed. When he didn't, she swung her legs out, sitting on the edge of the mattress, her ears straining for any sounds.

Nothing. She'd have to get closer. Slowly and deliberately, she placed one bare foot in front of the other until she was standing directly outside the spare room. First, she put her ear to the door, then, hearing only a few clicking noises, edged her face closer to the crack he'd left. The upstairs bedrooms had locks, but she had never used the keys; they were tucked away in the downstairs utility cupboard, the doors always remaining unlocked. Zach hadn't asked for the key to the room, maybe because he didn't want to alert her to there being anything to hide. Now, gazing in, she could see the small table lamp illuminating him. He was sitting with his back towards her, hunched over something on the desk. He looked different in the soft, yellow light. Older, somehow, than his thirty years. Not recognisable as the Zach she knew.

He *must* be worried about work for it to have woken him – or prevented him from sleeping in the first place. Isla put her hand on the door, about to push it open when he scooted back from the desk. She withdrew her hand; held her breath. She wasn't sure why, but her nerves were on edge: jumping, making her skin tingle. She carried on watching him as he put some files – and another item she couldn't decipher from her position – into his briefcase, locking it. He dragged his fingers through his hair, pausing, keeping a grip on the clumps in either hand before pulling at them while muttering to himself.

Was he up to no good? Her gut was twisting in a way that made her suspect that was the case. He'd been leaving early and returning late, hiding a second phone, becoming annoyed when she dared to ask questions, and at times he was acting strangely towards her. All of which could be attributed to him engaging in some form of illicit activity. She thought about the recalled memory about the dodgy deals; the accounts not quite adding up. Maybe Zach was involved in them. Or was covering for the person who was. *Kenneth*?

Isla almost gasped. He could be covering for his father. And a week before her attack, she'd been delving into the company's financial files. She might not recall everything, but she knew Zach had come into the room that day and asked what she was doing.

Was Zach staying with her so that he could be the first to know what she remembered?

Keep your friends close, but your enemies closer.

Was it really possible that Zach was involved with illegal deals at work? If so, what lengths would he go to stop people finding out? Her mind jumped from one outrageous thought to the next. What if he'd been the one who'd attacked her? Or, he'd got someone else to do it in order to get her out of the picture?

Tears stung her eyes – even thinking Zach could be capable of such a hideous thing was awful. While Zach may or may not be capable of some underhand deals at work, that was a far cry from harming his own girlfriend. The time of the attack being while he was supposedly working late had been a coincidence and she should stop trying to make it otherwise. If she continued like this, she'd lose Zach, Nicci, her job; everything she'd worked hard for.

On the other hand, if Zach *had* played a part in her attack, then that spoke volumes about her ability to judge character. Lately, she'd made one poor choice after the other where men were concerned. Lance ghosting her had been gutting. Questions about why *still* haunted her. Was it something she'd said, done? Perhaps she'd come on too strong, although she thought he felt the same. She'd even spoken of him in a way that most would intimate meant they were in a serious relationship. Even now she blushed at the memory of her gushy outpouring at work, where she'd told anyone who'd listen just how perfect he was. That it was 'meant to be'.

She must've frightened Lance off – been more serious than he was about her. Perhaps after he'd had his bit of fun he'd gone back to his ex-girlfriend. Whatever his reasons, it had been the most painful experience of Isla's love life up until now. But maybe she'd hit a new low – at least Lance merely disappeared from her life; he hadn't tried to take hers.

Isla stepped away from the door and tiptoed back to bed. She'd seen enough.

She must keep a closer eye on Zach.

Chapter Twenty-Seven

Zach was sure he'd felt eyes on him.

He relaxed back in the chair, letting his eyelids gently close. He took some slow, deep breaths in and out. The meditation techniques he'd been using this past year really helped him to regain his composure in moments of uncertainty. During the times when stress threatened to consume him. When everything seemed bleak, or when his back was against the wall, it would be all too easy to lose control – and he had, on previous occasions. But not so much recently. While he concentrated on his breathing, Zach allowed his mind to wander freely. If negative thoughts came to him, he acknowledged them, then let them float away again.

It didn't matter if Isla had been watching him, seen him putting files into his briefcase. She'd assume he couldn't sleep so had decided to do some work. He could explain his nocturnal actions away easily enough. He was becoming well practised at getting out of tight corners. But what if Isla was beginning to recall more details from before her attack? If she was, then it wouldn't be long before she remembered what she'd found when archiving the files.

Why couldn't she just have left well alone?

It wasn't her business to go snooping in past deals. His father would go ballistic if he found out. Like Kenneth Biggins needed any excuse to bring him down. Christ, the times when he was growing up that he'd fly off the handle at the slightest mistake or slip-up Zach made. But he'd worked so bloody hard to prove to his father he was worthy of being the heir to the business. It would be a disaster for that to come toppling down. If the truth was uncovered now, he could kiss goodbye to any inheritance. And probably to his freedom, too.

Breathe in, hold for five, breathe out for a count of five.

It was fine. It wouldn't come to that. He could handle Isla. He just needed to keep an even closer eye on her. This was a reversible situation; all was not lost. Yet.

Zach slid in under the duvet beside Isla and wriggled towards her, pressing his body into hers. As he lay an arm over the gentle curve of her waist, he inhaled her. The smell of her skin filled his nostrils. A sweet scent greeted him rather than the sour one he was becoming accustomed to. Taking regular showers was a good sign. Although, that also meant she was feeling better. He'd have to be more vigilant from here on in.

Chapter Twenty-Eight

Christie's Crime Addicts – True Crime Podcast

Excerpt from Episode 163 – *The Couple on Maple Drive*

[ED] Ed here, giving you a quick update re the murder on our doorstep. We've been hearing from neighbours, friends and colleagues of the victim and the perpetrator. What are your thoughts so far? Do you believe they have the right person in custody? After some evidence-gathering of our own, we have reason to believe they have not.

Now, you may well ask how a bunch of armchair detectives can come to any reasonable conclusions about a murder case, but if you're a fan of the podcast and have been with us since the start, you'll know we don't always just sit back and wait for the eventual outcome, then record the findings so our listeners can hear the full case. Sometimes, we're a bit more active than that – more involved. We can do a spot of detecting too – it's our favourite thing to research and compile evidence.

Take the case four years ago – Episode forty-two – where a young woman was viciously assaulted following her twenty-first birthday bash. If you listen to that recording, you'll hear how her parents were fans of the show and her mum came to us in the hope we could help – and that's what we did. Using our own skills, we were able to uncover some key evidence, which we compiled and forwarded to the investigating officer. We're pleased it resulted in the arrest, and later conviction, of her on/off boyfriend.

We're already pretty involved in this case, too. And, because of our contacts and the additional help we receive from our listeners, I think we can uncover some evidence to prove they have the wrong person.

If you have any information you think would help, contact us in the usual ways.

That's it for today's live update. See you next time and be sure to check out our latest recorded podcast, which is available now.

In the meantime, Christie's Crime Addicts wish you a safe day in the bay.

Chapter Twenty-Nine

Isla listened intently to an episode where the Christie's Crime Addicts team were saying how they themselves had delved deeper into a case, uncovering their own evidence to support the claims made by the victim. The words: 'We also undertake our own research and compile evidence – it's our favourite thing to do,' echoed in her head.

Isla's pulse pounded. That was it – her way of figuring this mess out and fixing her life. What she needed to do was to contact the team and share her story – *the crime* – with them. Tell them her theories and the circumstantial evidence she believed she had. She could rope them in to help her gather solid proof needed to uncover the identity of her attacker. Surely she could successfully convince Christie's Crime Addicts hers was an interesting case and one they could use for their podcast? It was more likely they'd investigate further than the police currently were at any rate.

Isla scoured the podcasters' Facebook page to find their contact details, her adrenaline surging. If she got them onside and they managed to help her prove her attacker's identity, she could move on and put this whole incident behind her. Knowing the perpetrator was behind bars was the only way she'd feel safe again, because she had the awful feeling that what she knew – what she'd begun to uncover at Biggins & Co – was what led to her attack.

And he, or they, wouldn't want her to continue to delve into the files. Which meant they'd maybe try and finish what they started. Whether that was Simon, Graham or Zach, or another as yet unknown suspect, the end game was likely the same for Isla. The thought horrified her, and her logical mind fought against her instincts. But more and more, as painful as it was to admit, there was something niggling her about Zach's behaviour. She'd argued against her earlier negative thoughts, telling herself she was overthinking. All but ruling Zach out by convincing herself that it was the concussion making her paranoid. Now, ignoring those concerns and forcing herself to be impartial, she wrote a new list in her notebook – the one meant to be for keeping a journal of her online therapy sessions – with each of their names together with reasons they might want her out of the picture. Then she detailed what their actions were prior to that night, and where possible what they'd done, or were doing, since her attack. And with each stroke of her pen, with each action that led her to suspect them, as well as taking into account background, motive and opportunity, she knew Zach had to be considered as the most likely to have committed the act.

And he was the one perfectly placed to keep tabs on every move she made.

Maybe he didn't really want her to get better – or leave the house – because that meant he'd have to relinquish his control.

That final thought was enough to give Isla the push she needed. She was going to leave the house today.

Chapter Thirty

The fresh air blasted Isla's face as she opened the front door. She stood on the threshold, her heart beating wildly. This time, the wooziness, the dizzy feeling that hitting the air had caused, was due to anxiety, not alcohol.

The road wasn't busy, but enough cars were driving up and down to make her feel she wasn't alone. She swallowed and, taking a deep breath, stepped out of her house. Pausing at the bottom of the path, Isla glanced back and up at her neighbour's place. The banging noises had been forgotten once Nicci had turned up on her doorstep, but now she wondered if, before she ventured to the Crime Addicts' location, she should knock on the door and check her neighbours were all right. A shadow moved across their front downstairs window. Were they watching her? Isla shook her head. God's sake – she was the one staring up at their window. They were probably thinking: is she watching *me*? She turned away; now wasn't the time to stick her nose into their business – she had her own to worry about.

The details for the Christie's Crime Addicts team showed their location as central Torquay. Maybe it was one of their houses, or possibly they had premises like an office, or something, where they had an actual recording studio. Although they often came across as light-hearted, having a laugh between themselves, their set-up – the website and recordings, as well as their social media channels – did appear professional. Her research of them also revealed they each had a public services background. In addition, the podcast had sponsorships and advertising, plus an online store selling their own merchandise, so it wasn't out of the realms of possibility that it was a good moneymaker for them – that it was their full-time work. Isla was in the wrong career. They'd also mentioned helping out with some investigations, so maybe they even charged for private investigations.

Which was a concern, now, as Isla set out on her first journey since being attacked. What if she was wasting her time? She could get there and they might turn her away – or, agree to help, but for a fee. She didn't have spare money to offer a private investigator. She hadn't really thought it through. In all honesty, she'd assumed they'd just be grateful to help so they could have another case for their show. How naive was she being?

The thought stopped her in her tracks. She was being stupid, leaving the house on some wild notion that a group of people who ran a bloody podcast would be interested in helping her. They'd likely be polite but advise her to trust the police and go to them with her concerns. She *should* trust the police, but their handling of her case thus far hadn't filled her with confidence.

Isla delved into her bag, taking her phone out. The battery was already down to two bars. What if she had an anxiety attack and couldn't make her way home again? She should ring the number from their website, ask them for their help over the phone instead of wasting her time visiting without an appointment. But in person, maybe they'd be less inclined to turn her request for help down. Seeing her, her desperation, might tip the balance – make them feel obliged to offer their services.

As she put her phone back into her bag, her hand brushed against the hardbacked notebook inside. She'd written enough things down: observations of Zach's behaviour now, and as much as she could recall just prior to the attack, together with Simon's and Graham's, that would give the Crime Addicts an insight to whet their appetite. She'd listened to enough podcasts now to know they would, at the very least, be intrigued by her story.

This *had* to be worth the stress of the trip.

Re-energised, Isla pushed forward. She could do this. She had to.

Chapter Thirty-One

The Stagecoach bus appeared to be only half-full, she noted when it pulled up. That was a relief. Still, Isla's legs shook as she stepped up towards the driver and she had to grip the rail to steady herself as she boarded. She made sure to take notice of the driver, taking in as many details as she could in her nervous state. He was a thin, balding man with a kind face and he gave her a fleeting smile. She returned it, hesitantly. After an awkward moment, he raised his eyebrows and widened his eyes, and Isla realised she'd not asked for a ticket.

'Sorry,' she said. 'Er . . . um . . .' Her mind had gone blank. Which stop did she need again? She fumbled with her purse; her cast suddenly cumbersome. Taking a breath, Isla focused on pulling her debit card out, buying herself time to think which stop in the town centre she'd need.

'Where are you going?' the driver asked, his patience waning.

'Sorry,' Isla said. 'I need Union Street. I'm not sure what the stop is.'

'Castle Circus'll do you,' he said with a nod.

'Great, thank you. A return to Castle Circus then, please,' she said finally. She held her card to the reader, waited for the beep, then took the nearest empty seat without looking up. The other passengers were probably staring.

The bus rumbled off and Isla gazed out of the window at the passing scenery. It seemed like an age since she'd been outside, but everything was the same. Her world had altered, but her surroundings had remained constant. She tried to relax. It was a twenty-minute ride and she didn't want to be a tense, balled-up mess when she arrived. Isla looked at her hands, idle in her lap. Her nails were ragged on the hand with her cast, their pale, mottled appearance unsightly. She wished she'd made an effort before she left now. Isla pinched each fingertip checking for colour and sensation. They were fine. But she did it several more times to make sure. When the cast came off, she would treat herself to a manicure.

The bus stopped just up from the building Isla had as the location for Christie's Crime Addicts. She disembarked and walked back up the hill a little to the door to the side of the premises. The building was three-storey, next to an estate agent's, and on the outer door, there were three separate buzzers with bronze plaques beside them denoting names of the companies. CCA Investigates was the top floor. She assumed that was Christie's Crime Addicts. Presumably, having that on the door plaque would raise too many eyebrows so they'd gone for a more professional-sounding name. It boded well for Isla, in any case.

Now she was actually standing outside, her resolve weakened. Isla's pulse rate felt impossibly fast as she recalled the warning words of the neurological team at Derriford: *The effects of concussion could last for several months.* What if all of this, all of her suspicions, were in her head? If she were somehow delusional, could her mind be conjuring things like false memories? Accusing people she knew of wanting to kill her might sound completely far-fetched and verging on paranoia.

Ring the fucking bell, Isla.

She looked over her shoulder at the people walking by. No one was taking notice of her; no one was staring. No one would know she was here. If they dismissed her out of hand, the worst of it would be she'd made the trip for nothing. Caused herself undue stress leaving the house. But that in itself meant she'd made progress, so all wouldn't be lost – it wouldn't have been a complete waste of time. She'd just be no further forward than she'd been first thing this morning.

She pressed the button quickly, before the voice in her head told her to run.

After a few seconds' waiting, the door clicked open. *Shit.* She hadn't expected that; she assumed she'd hear a voice through an intercom or something, asking what she wanted first. This was good, then, she supposed. She had her foot in the door without having to stand outside trying to explain what she'd come for.

Inside the long, narrow hallway it was dim, with the only light source coming from one round ceiling light. Immediately, Isla's nerves were on edge. She hadn't told anyone where she was going. She'd entered an unknown property, alone, and without any real idea of who these people were. Or if they were who they said they were.

You're doing it again.

If she wanted them to take her seriously, she had to stop with the catastrophising and quash the paranoid thoughts. They wouldn't list their location if they were dodgy. Footsteps bounded down the stairs in front of her. Isla froze, waiting for the owner of them to come into view, her heart pounding.

'Hey there, can I help?'

She immediately recognised the voice. Jase. And when her eyes adjusted to the low-level light, she recognised his face, too, from the video recordings. He was in his forties, she supposed, his hair short, spiky and a dark grey. His slightly weathered face was relaxed; friendly, with longer-style stubble that looked soft rather than prickly – he was carefully groomed. While remaining at the foot of the stairs, dressed in blue stone-washed jeans and black T-shirt, Jase thrust an arm out, his hand flat awaiting her to reciprocate with a handshake. Cautiously, she moved towards him, offering her good hand. 'Hi. I'm Isla McKenzie,' she said. 'And I really hope so.'

'Well, you've already gained my interest, Isla McKenzie.' He smiled. It was strange, seeing him in real life – having listened to him speak, and sometimes watching him in the recorded videos on Facebook and YouTube, she felt as though she knew him. The vague sense of familiarity helped; her muscles, which had been rigid with nerves, now relaxed. She was able to return the smile and it didn't feel like a tight, fake response.

'I know turning up like this is a bit out of the ordinary—'

Jase gave a short laugh. 'Ahh . . . you'd be surprised. Although, I will just check – it is Christie's Crime Addicts you're after, isn't it? Only sometimes people get confused with the bells . . .' Jase indicated towards the door.

Isla gave a nervous laugh. 'Yep – it's definitely you guys I'm after. I realise I should've called or something first. It was kind of spur-of-the-moment.' It hadn't been, but she didn't want him to know she'd been contemplating it for days before plucking up the courage to go through with it.

'Don't worry, you're here now and I'm free to chat.'

'Thanks, Jase. I'm really grateful.'

'Come on up to our lair,' Jase said, turning and taking two steps at a time. For a split second, Isla hesitated, his choice of words unsettling her. But as she watched him disappear around the bend in the stairwell, she knew she must follow because despite any misgivings, these people were her best hope.

Chapter Thirty-Two

As soon as he stepped through the front door, Zach sensed Isla wasn't home.

There were no tell-tale sounds of activity and the TV screen was blank, the laptop screen closed. He stood at the bottom of the stairs, straining to hear a running shower. Nothing. She hadn't been outside of these four walls for weeks, so where was she now? Unconvinced she'd suddenly become brave and left the safety of the house, he walked from room to room, opening and closing doors, checking each one, just in case. Would she have nipped to the neighbours? Maybe she was friendlier with them than she'd let on and went around for daily chats and coffee.

Leaving the door on the latch, Zach darted down Isla's path and up the neighbours and rang their bell. He was sure he detected movement, a noise, but no one came to the door. Frustrated, he jogged back to Isla's, slamming the door behind him. A rising panic began in the pit of his stomach, spreading rapidly.

If it wasn't for the fact he'd just spoken to Nicci at her desk as he left work, he'd assume she'd convinced Isla to go out with her. Cajole her into getting back into the real world. But he'd left early, saying he had paperwork to collect, so Nicci would have a few hours left before she could leave. Plus, she would've run it past him first, like she had with her surprise visit. They'd talked several times about Isla's current state of anxiety, her inability to leave the house – Nicci was his ally.

He wondered what he should do – this was the first time he'd been faced with her leaving. Could she have attempted to walk to the closest shop maybe? She didn't have a car, so anywhere further would require her to get a taxi, or a bus, and he couldn't see her managing that.

Someone has been and taken her.

The thought was as ridiculous as some of Isla's. No, there had to be an obvious reason. It was sunny – a balmy day for April. She'd probably just gone for a short walk, maybe testing the waters by taking small steps. He *had* been encouraging her to move forwards, after all. But now it appeared she had, it unsettled him. Taking his keys from the hall table, Zach ran to his car.

She couldn't have gone far. He'd find her.

Chapter Thirty-Three

'Ed and Doug are recording and Christie's out meeting a new sponsor – she's in charge of the business end of things, so, it's just me for the minute,' Jase explained as they passed a large, glass-walled room with a red light above the door. A flurry of excitement rippled through her as she glimpsed Ed and Doug, headphones on, their movements animated, but conversation muted. She paused, curious.

'We've got a great set-up here,' Jase said. 'The soundproofing is top-notch.'

'It's so professional,' Isla said. 'I'm really impressed.'

'Were you expecting this place to be one of our houses, and the podcasts done in our basement, or a bedroom?' He said it with good humour, but Isla blushed.

'Oh, sorry – no. I didn't really know what to expect if I'm honest.'

Jase beamed. 'I know – we come across as big kids I guess, but we are very serious about what we do.'

'That's good,' Isla said. 'It makes my reason for turning up today more appropriate.'

Jase showed her into a small but bright room with a coffee table, a red two-seater sofa and a couple of mismatched armchairs. She took the seat closest to the door, popping her bag down beside her on the floor.

'Can I get you something to drink?'

Her mouth was parched. What with the bus ride and her nerves, all moisture had evaporated. 'Yes, please. Got anything cold?'

'We're die-hard Diet Coke fans here, so that's pretty much all our fridge contains. Will a can of that do you?'

'Perfect, thanks.'

While waiting for him to return, Isla stood up and walked to the window for something to take her mind off her rising anxiety. They were on the top floor, overlooking the top end of the town centre. To her right she could see the spire of St Mags Church and in front were views of rooftops. Below, people ambled along the pavements and she watched them, wondering what was going on in their lives. Before her thoughts became too deep, she backed away from the window. On the far wall, framed prints, photos and newspaper clippings covered it like wallpaper. Isla stood in front of it, amazed by the number of crime stories, solved and unsolved, and the articles where Christie's Crime Addicts themselves were the main story. Isla was surprised she'd only recently heard of them.

'Our wall of fame,' Jase said, returning with a can in each hand.

Isla turned sharply. 'You're quite the quartet, aren't you?'

'Hah! Yes, and trust me, some of the names we brainstormed for our podcast tried very hard to get that in somewhere. But, you know – the fab four was already taken and the fantastic foursome seemed a little . . . cheesy. So, given we're all from the bay and Christie was actually named after the greatest crime writer of all time, we decided on our current name.'

'Yes, it would've been mad not to capitalise on that,' Isla said.

'That one was where it all blew up for us,' Jase said, pointing to an article from 2016 titled 'The Body in the Suitcase'. 'And by that, I mean we got big quickly due to that coverage. What the millennials, or whoever, would today refer to as *going viral*. Our involvement, and subsequent podcast was downloaded and watched over ten thousand times in a matter of days, which is amazing for long-form content. It generated a lot of interest and a huge spike in advertising revenue, which really was the springboard for us. We were able to go from doing this as a second job – more of a hobby – to full-time.' The way Jase spoke with such enthusiasm was reassuring. He was very much invested in the business.

Isla remembered the coverage – how everyone was interested, talking about the Exeter case. 'I did listen to your episode on that, actually. I'm so glad they got him.' It had been an interesting case, but Isla had been mostly focusing on unsolved crimes. She could see how it had been a success for them – made their show popular. Would her story be interesting enough for them? Although Jase had managed to put her mind at ease a bit, Isla was still aware her posture, her outward appearance as a whole, must seem uptight. She had to tell him now; explain what had brought her to their door before going into great detail of what she hoped she could gain from them – and before she bottled it.

'Here. Sorry, I've been holding it so long I'll have made it warm.' Jase handed her a can. It was far from warm – the ice-cold metal made her shiver. 'Oh, sorry. I should've brought a glass . . .'

'Oh, I'm fine with cans. Shame it's not my usual G&T, though.' She forced a laugh, then took the armchair by the door again. Jase chose the sofa, and leaned back, crossing his legs by resting one ankle on the other knee at a right angle. Isla thought this was a typical macho position and would usually take it as a sign of power play, but Jase didn't strike her like that at all, and she decided this was his relaxed, open posture – intended to make her feel comfortable in his presence. She began to speak, slowly at first, giving the basic facts, then, finding her confidence, her words flowed out of her.

Jase sipped from his can of Diet Coke every now and then, but otherwise didn't take his eyes from Isla as she rattled off her story, detailing everything she remembered prior to the attack, and the fleeting memories she'd recovered since. She didn't leave a thing out – even telling him the names of the three most likely suspects. It felt like a betrayal to give them Zach's name. Vocalising her concerns about him made it real – not just a series of thoughts in her mind which, for a time, she'd managed to talk herself out of. She only spoke of them now because she wanted to be as thorough as possible. Tell Jase everything, no holds barred. She'd intended to be brief, but once she'd started talking about it, she couldn't stop. When she finally came up for air, she noticed Jase was now literally on the edge of his seat, his mouth slightly open, his eyes wide.

'You think I'm delusional, don't you?' she said, her voice filled with defeat.

'God, no,' Jase said, shaking his head. 'No, I don't.' He stood up abruptly and walked to the window. He stared straight out with his arms partly crossed, one hand up to his face and his finger over his lips. A classic 'thinking' pose. Isla waited. He was clearly trying to process what she'd told him; she wanted to give him that time without interrupting. It was like watching Columbo mentally work through a case. She almost smiled at her comparison, but the moment was too tense to allow such a light-hearted reaction.

Isla shuffled into a different position in the armchair. The noise of the movement appeared to break Jase's trance-like state and he turned back to face her.

'Right. I'll need to consult with the others first, but from what you've said, I think we can certainly help in some way.'

'Really?' Isla's throat constricted and her eyes filled with tears. It was the response she'd hoped for, but one she wasn't expecting; she hadn't got to the part where she actually stated what she wanted from them.

Jase got down onto his knees in front of her, then took her hand in his.

'Christ, you're not proposing, are you?' she said. Somehow, the seriousness of the moment had triggered the coping mechanism she'd often employed prior to the attack: humour.

'Bit premature for that,' Jase said, laughing. 'Not to mention the age difference.' He winked, but then his face took on a serious expression. 'Listen, let's get some of this recorded – if you can bear to go through it again – and by then, the guys should be finished, and I can get their input straight away. If you've got time?'

Isla checked her phone. Dead again. 'What time is it?'

'Two-forty.'

She had at least a few more hours before Zach was due home, and he'd been late the last two nights, so she might have even longer. 'Yeah, should be fine.'

'Good. I'll grab the stuff we need, then we'll get the ball properly rolling.'

It was a positive step forward. Not the type Zach had encouraged her to take, but one she knew would allow her an element of control. And that felt good. The crushing weight she'd experienced since this thing had happened to her was going to be removed, or at least become a shared burden. Already, there was a sensation of being a little lighter now than the moment she stepped inside the building. It might take a while but, bit by bit, the old Isla would return.

Chapter Thirty-Four

THEN – In hospital

Her wrist hurt; her head throbbed. But she was alive. And although she'd now been told several times how lucky she was to be, it had been the nurses overheard words that had resonated with Isla. The police themselves were more convinced it had been a simple mugging, not attempted murder. But they'd said if she'd fallen at a different angle, her head might've collided with the stones running along the pathway. As it was, she'd apparently missed them by mere centimetres and her head had, thankfully, made contact with the flat grassed area instead. The blow to the back of her head had been deemed 'non-life-threatening' and they'd concluded she'd been hit in order to debilitate her, not as an intention to kill.

For some reason, Isla was inclined to believe the nurses' appraisal. The realisation she'd come that close to simply ceasing to exist hit hard. Life was so precarious. Something as minor as a centimetre had been the determining factor between life and death. But then, her decision to walk home from the party, not get a taxi, could also be thought of in the same way. Isla felt sure, in that moment, that she wouldn't be able to make simple decisions without considering the implications to her life ever again. Every single action had a consequence, and from now, she'd likely overanalyse each of them.

'You're looking a little livelier this morning, Isla.' Heather walked into the room with a mug in her hand and placed it on Isla's table. 'You've managed to eat too, I see. That's good.'

'I'm more with it today,' Isla said. She shuffled up the bed, using her good arm to push back.

'How's the pain?'

'About a six.'

'Okay, love.' Heather checked the paperwork at the end of the bed, and scribbled some notes. 'Meds trolley will be round shortly. Once you've had your painkillers hopefully you'll be down to a more manageable three or below.' She smiled, replaced the clipboard and turned to walk back out.

'Heather, can I ask you something?'

'Of course.' She turned back and walked up to Isla's bedside.

'The police said I'd been brought in after being found unconscious and I was on my own, that no one came into the hospital with me.'

'Yeah, that's right, love.'

'But I was wondering who the first person to visit was?'

'Oh, now then.' Heather looked up to her left as she took a few moments to recall. 'There was a woman, your friend who was here yesterday too.'

'Nicci. Yes, it had been her who threw the party for me. Was anyone with her?'

'She came in alone, but then that fella of yours followed soon after.'

'That'd be Zach.' At least he'd bothered to come fairly quickly to make sure she was all right. If Heather had said he hadn't come until much later, that would've hurt. 'Okay, thank you,' Isla said, and put her head back on her pillow. Her head was painful still, but more like a dull headache now – the tail end of a migraine. She just wished it didn't feel so fuzzy, the line between the things she was being told and what she remembered blurring. Isla realised that Heather was still in her room.

'Sorry, didn't mean to keep you. You must be so busy.'

'Not at all. Well, I am busy, but you're not keeping me. And I just remembered something.'

'Oh?' Isla's interest was piqued.

'Those were the first people to visit, but it was your brother who was first on the phone,' Heather said.

'Really! That surprises me,' Isla said, slightly perplexed by hearing this. She lifted the mug and took a sip of coffee to lubricate her mouth. Her hand trembled slightly, causing the liquid to sway inside the mug. Good job it wasn't filled to the top.

'You not particularly close then?' Heather frowned.

'Well, we are, sort of.' Isla screwed up her face. She didn't want to give the wrong impression now, so she added, 'As much as most siblings, I guess. I just haven't seen him in ages – he lives in Glasgow, near our mam. In fact, I think I was about to call her before . . . this happened.'

'Maybe explains how he knew, then,' Heather said.

'What do you mean?'

'Well, he called within minutes of your admission. Before anyone had had chance to contact your next of kin.'

Isla's brows knitted together. 'And it definitely wasn't my mother who called?'

'No, love. He didn't mention your mum but maybe he was with her at the time. I took the call – I remember the conversation quite clearly. He said he was your brother, Fraser then asked if you were conscious. I said I wasn't able to give information out over the phone – but to allay his fears, I did say you were in a stable condition. He thanked me and hung up.'

'Seems a bit strange.' Isla's insides churned. 'Isn't that an odd thing to ask?'

'People ask all sorts of strange things when they're under stress, or worried about their loved ones. He was abrupt, I remember thinking that – and being surprised he hadn't asked me to send his love. That's usually what relatives want in those kinds of situations: reassurance and then to pass on a message of some sort.'

Yes, that would make sense and would be her request too if she were calling the hospital about someone who'd been attacked. Something didn't sit right with Isla about what Heather was saying about Fraser. Her brother would've wanted to know more – it wasn't his nature to be easily placated or fobbed off. He would've pushed for details, so only asking if she were conscious and nothing else seemed unlikely.

'Would you do me a favour, Heather?'

'If I can, yes.'

'Can you get me to the phone so I can make a call?'

'Of course. I'm sorry, love,' Heather said, her arms raised in apology. 'I should've offered that already. Forgot about you not having a mobile. These days patients who are able are usually texting and making calls all the time. I'll sort that right away.'

'Thank you.' Isla needed to speak with her mam. Not having a mobile was horrible – she was so used to being able to send a quick text or WhatsApp and now she felt cut off from everyone. The nurse on shift last night had said her mam had been calling regularly for updates, but Isla hadn't spoken with her directly – just passed on messages. And she hadn't asked about Fraser's call because until now, she hadn't known about it.

Her gut was telling her the new information from Heather was important; significant, even. She just wasn't sure why.

Chapter Thirty-Five

The streets around Isla's house were practically empty: Zach observed a few people walking the pavements here and there; a group of teenagers hanging around, likely bunking off school – but no Isla. He swung around the roundabout and headed off towards the road leading into Torquay town. He cast his eyes frantically this way and that, scanning the area as thoroughly as he could without making it look as though he were kerb-crawling. He was driving down Union Street now, but highly doubted she'd come this far. The thought of mingling with people in a crowded shopping precinct would horrify her; there was no way she'd consider walking into the town centre.

He drove back around the one-way system to get to the road taking him to the seafront. Isla enjoyed being near the sea; maybe that was a better bet. The day was bright, and it'd drawn many people to the harbour and beach: cars littered the spaces and there were too many people milling about for Zach to tell if Isla was one of them. He couldn't find a parking space, so with his pulse banging, his head throbbing with the beginnings of a migraine, he decided to head back home to Isla's. He could be overthinking everything.

You didn't even look in the back garden.

Zach groaned. For God's sake. He'd been so panicked not seeing Isla in her usual spot on the sofa he hadn't thought about looking out the back, preoccupied instead with searching the rooms. He'd probably worked himself up over nothing.

Parking outside, Zach sprang from the car and ran up the steps, thrusting his key in the door and swinging it open. Inside was still silent. He rushed to the back door and out into the yard. The rear of the property was layered – the lower level laid to gravel, the second was grassed with flower borders and the upper one – the one with views to the sea – was patioed with a border of small trees and shrubs and had a pergola. In summer, it would be the perfect spot to spend an evening with a glass of wine in hand.

After checking each level, Zach concluded she wasn't there and that she must've either been taken out by someone he didn't know, or that she'd remembered something important about the night of her attack and had ventured to the police station.

He wiped the sweat from his forehead. He needed to know.

Back inside, Zach dashed up the stairs and into the spare bedroom. He opened his laptop and found the spyware file. The last location Isla's phone showed her at was somewhere along Babbacombe Road and that was three hours ago. He sat back in the chair, pondering why she'd be there. No one he knew lived in that area, and he thought it was therefore unlikely Isla did either. It was a long road but nothing of interest really – a couple of shops maybe. But if she'd been to one of those, she'd have returned home by now.

A lack of a text message, phone call or even a note was completely thoughtless. He clasped his hands together as he fought to keep his frustration from tipping over into anger. Where *was* she?

Chapter Thirty-Six

Isla got off the bus one stop earlier than hers. She wanted a bit of time to think before going back inside her four walls. Part of her was afraid knowing she now had to continue pushing forwards, making brave decisions and choices despite worrying what the consequences might be. But she was proud of what she'd achieved today. She'd not only made it past the threshold of her house, but she'd also managed to get public transport and venture into town. And meet with new people. They were all massive steps and a complete turnaround from the previous two weeks.

She thought about her conversation with Jase and the other members of Christie's Crime Addicts. She'd really hit it off with them, particularly Jase, and felt reassured by their genuine interest and keenness to help her. They, however, weren't reassured to know that she was living with one of the people she'd listed as a suspect. Whether she believed him to be responsible for having carried out the attack on her, or being involved in some way, both options were bad news as far as they were concerned.

Since the smell of Zach's aftershave had caused a fleeting memory, more unwanted thoughts about him being involved had flooded her mind, but she'd done a good job of talking herself out of the fear that Zach was responsible. She'd pushed out her dark thoughts, convincing herself the memory must be from when he came to the hospital shortly after she'd been admitted. That was before she'd looked at it more objectively and made her new list. And before she'd spoken to the Christie's team. They added weight to her own suspicions by saying that a lot of perpetrators of violent crime were known to the victim. She knew this, of course – had come to that conclusion herself. But she'd fought against the idea Zach was anything but good and certainly didn't want to suspect him after all he'd done for her.

She'd put more emphasis on Simon and Graham as they were known to her, too. But the team had reminded her that Simon and Graham weren't in the same position Zach was – that he was now uniquely placed to know straight away if she recalled anything, and he would be able to tell by her behaviour if she were beginning to suspect him. And they'd delicately pointed out that Zach would therefore be in an equally good position to do something about it. To silence her permanently.

They put Zach firmly at the top of the list.

Isla heard Jase's voice in her head: 'Get him out of there, Isla.'

But, despite it all, she'd still argued against it – making a last-ditch attempt to take Zach back off the list. 'I see what you guys are saying, but my mind is still veering towards his innocence; that my memories, his behaviour, can all be explained away – that he can't be the person who attacked me.'

'That's natural, Isla. You've trusted this man; he's your boyfriend. We have no emotional investment, so it's easier for us to look at the hard facts. We have a lot of work to do before we can say he's the culprit. What we're saying to you now is be careful. Assume guilt to keep yourself safe.'

Having accepted their words, Isla knew she had to put her

trust in them now. But she wasn't going to be the one to back away; leave her own house. She did want to get to the bottom of this and gain the evidence to prove who was responsible for the attack. Which, in her mind meant it was better to have Zach where she could keep her eye on him, too. They don't say keep your friends close, but your enemies closer for no reason. She'd put up a good argument backing up her reasoning – the final conversation played out again in her head . . .

'I'll just make sure not to give anything away. I did drama in secondary school. I got an "A". I can do this. Maybe a little misdirection is in order.'

'Agatha would be proud,' Jase said.

'Would it offend you if I told you I'd never read any of Agatha Christie's books?'

Jase slammed his hand dramatically against his chest and loudly sucked in his breath. 'I'm mortally wounded by this admission. How can you *not* have read Agatha?'

'I'm sorry.' Isla smiled and put her hands up. 'It's remiss of me – I'm ashamed. Perhaps I should start. I might get some hints and tips.'

'You're a fan of our show – I think you've probably picked up a fair few of those already – even if you're not aware of it yet.'

It was a light-hearted moment – something she hadn't experienced for several weeks. It felt good, like a positive move towards the old Isla. It gave her a lift.

'I can't thank you enough, Jase. Really. Speaking to you and the gang has given me hope and a reason to pull myself together. The therapist whose online sessions I've been listening to has been saying to look forward, be proactive and to not merely muddle along allowing things to happen to me – I needed to take action and be a participant in my own life – in my own story. I don't think this is quite what the therapist had in mind,

143

but I'm already feeling more motivated, less fearful by taking these steps and taking control. Which is all very weird as I hadn't even been actively listening to the poor woman,' Isla said, giving a mock grimace.

'You clearly took in more than you realised,' Jase said. 'See!' he added enthusiastically. 'You didn't even need us. You've done this yourself. It's only because someone has agreed with you – validated your concerns – that you feel better. You're stronger than you think.'

'And braver than you believe . . .' Isla said, smiling. 'Winnie-the-Pooh said something similar.'

'There you go then. If Pooh said it . . .'

Isla brought her mind back to now. To how she should progress; how she should approach the next few days. Although she'd confidently said to the Crime Addicts that she could act the part, the reality of what lay ahead was more daunting and, as she neared her house, Isla's nerves tingled. She was walking back into a situation that might possibly be dangerous. Asking Zach to leave, or even leaving herself for a while, would probably be the more sensible course of action. But don't people watch a snake, keeping their focus on its movements so that they might know when it was about to strike and deliver a life-threatening dose of venom? You don't turn your back on it, or try to run. No, she felt sure the only way to find out, then deal with, the person who attacked her was to face the threat head-on. She wasn't going to be attacked from behind again; blindsided by some coward. She wanted to see who was doing it, wanted to know what was coming. Facing the fear was the only way to overcome it.

This absoluteness and determination faded as Isla opened the front door and was confronted by Zach, his face red and expression set.

Chapter Thirty-Seven

'Where the hell have you been?' Zach said, his voice strained, his eyes wide. 'I've been worried – scouring the bloody streets looking everywhere for you. Why didn't you let me know you were going out and where?'

Isla clenched one fist while raising her plastered arm in apology – an immediate defensive move. She was annoyed with herself. 'I didn't let you know because it was a spur-of-the-moment decision and you were at work.' She spoke slowly, calmly as she stepped over the threshold and carried on into the lounge.

'I came home early to spend time with you,' Zach said, his words sounding defensive, but his tone more controlled now as he followed her.

'I didn't know that. If you'd texted me to let me know, then obviously I'd have waited. It would've been nice to go out together.' She smiled and added: 'You've been late the last couple of nights, disappearing into the spare room to work, so I thought you must be really busy at the office and might be late again.'

'Sorry, you're right,' he mumbled. 'I guess I assumed you'd be here, that's all. Didn't think to text.' His apologetic words tumbled out, and Isla was surprised how quickly he'd calmed down. She thought he might push this into an argument for some reason. 'So, where did you go?' he said with a false lightness. Isla knew he was trying to come across as interested, rather than nosy. The effort was obvious – or was she reading too much into it because of what Jase had said?

'Oh, only a little way.' Isla hadn't prepared for Zach being home when she got back, so hadn't thought up an alternative route to the one she'd actually taken. She needed to think on her feet now. 'I wasn't aiming on going anywhere in particular – just outside of the house. To be honest, it was a bit stressful, and I can't even remember which direction I set off in, let alone where I ended up.'

'*Really?*' He dropped his curious tone, swapping it out for sarcasm and disbelief.

'Yes, Zach. Really. What's the matter with you?'

'I told you. I was worried. Walking somewhere you hadn't even intended – and now not even being able to remember where – that's more than a bit alarming, Isla.'

'I thought you'd be over the moon I'd been out. You've been harping on at me, pushing me to move forwards for days. Now I have, it's like I've done something wrong!'

'I'm sorry. I didn't mean to come across that way.' He exhaled, running his fingers through his thick, wavy hair. 'I had some irrational fear that someone had taken you . . .'

'Wow. Reassuring to know you think my attacker will come back.' Isla narrowed her eyes.

An uncomfortable silence settled until Zach let out a loud sigh, breaking the spell. He sat down on the sofa, leaning his elbows on his knees. 'Shit, you're right – I'm not helping, am I?'

Smoothing things over with Zach so as not to raise his concern didn't seem as though it was going to be as big a problem as she'd first thought. To Isla's relief, he was already appearing to back down. She allowed herself to relax; she'd been holding her muscles in a rigid position and now felt them give a little. She was about to tell Zach not to worry, that she appreciated his concern, was glad he cared enough to show his feelings, but he cut in before the words left her lips.

'I wondered if you'd remembered something . . .' he said, his eyes averted from hers. His words stole her breath, and for a few seconds she froze. Her fingertips tingled. She didn't know how to take what he'd said, but the fact he wasn't even looking at her when he said it prompted her to believe he was afraid of what she might see in them. Guilt?

She inhaled deeply, quickly, trying to regain composure. 'Like what?' she said, her voice hoarse. She coughed to clear her throat.

'Oh, you know . . . something vital about that night. Perhaps?'

Isla pushed her lips together in a pout, shaking her head at the same time – not trusting herself to speak. Now *she* was the one avoiding eye contact.

'You can tell me, Isla. The doctor did say memories might return, but I'm sure they'll be muddled and it'll be confusing, and you might feel overwhelmed. It would be better for you if you talked to me about them. Don't you think?'

Isla's pulse picked up speed. Jase's words filled her mind: 'He's now uniquely placed to know straight away if you recall anything.' Maybe he was right, and Zach was digging for information.

She nodded. 'Of course. But it wasn't that,' she said. 'I honestly just wanted to make an effort to leave the house. That's all.' Isla's legs trembled – she sat quickly in the hope Zach wouldn't notice.

They were sitting at opposite ends of the sofa, giving each other cautious stares for what felt like minutes, but was only seconds. But those few seconds held in them the truth each didn't want to confront. Zach broke eye contact, got up and walked out towards the kitchen. 'You must be hungry, out all this time and missing lunch. I'll start tea,' he said over his shoulder as he disappeared.

How had he known she'd missed lunch? She'd assumed he'd only got back a little earlier than usual but now he made it sound like he'd been back for hours. She really thought she'd get away with her visit to the Christie's team, but maybe she hadn't. What if he already knew where she'd been and he was playing this game with her, seeing if she would tell the truth? If that was the case, and he suspected her of keeping something from him, she'd have to be careful. She certainly didn't want him to realise she was suspicious of his involvement in her attack. Not until she had evidence to prove or disprove it.

The only way she could see of putting him off the trail was to actively point the finger at someone else. Simon seemed a good candidate. And before her trip to Christie's Crime Addicts he'd been high on her list of suspects, so she shouldn't strike him off it yet anyway. Not until there was proof to categorically dismiss *him* as her attacker. However – it was a dangerous move to tell Zach about Simon being the last to see her, and that she thought it could have been him. Because *if* Zach had no involvement in the attack – then he might fly off the handle and take matters into his own hands, paying Simon a visit to unleash his anger.

Was she playing with fire by participating in a game over her head? She'd told the Christie's team she would gain further info – and something was telling her that perhaps rather than vocalising her suspicions about Simon to Zach, the hospital would be a good place to start. In the back of her mind, Isla had a hazy memory of the nurse, Heather, talking about who had visited and called. Hadn't there been something about someone phoning the ward before anyone else knew she was there? Isla pushed her fingertips into her temples, trying to remember what Heather had said, but couldn't. She only had the vague sense that learning about the call had unnerved her for some reason. But why?

The period of time immediately after the attack, her hospital stay, was almost one big blur, with only snippets of memories making some sense – the main one being the fact she'd heard nurses talking about her being left for dead. Even that she had to question; there was a possibility she'd dreamt it. Going there, speaking with Heather, could help straighten her thoughts out. Isla had to begin by making an accurate timeline of events. Only thing was, Derriford Hospital was miles away. She'd have to catch a train and she wasn't sure she was mentally strong enough for that yet.

Chapter Thirty-Eight

Every step of the way to the station, Isla's eyes had searched for strangers in front of her, behind her – around every corner, behind every wall – afraid someone was concealed there, crouching, waiting to pounce on her like she was their prey. She tried talking to herself. Tried to dismiss her irrational thoughts and instead turn them around – making the voice a positive one, congratulating Isla on her bravery. It told her she was safe, that there was no reason to be afraid. She imagined those who passed by her were thinking she was mad, because sometimes the inner voice escaped her head and she spoke the words aloud.

But it'd worked. She'd reached the station, bought a ticket, and boarded the train.

Isla felt as though she were about to go to an interview; her nerves were jittery, her palms sweating. She was on the second train now, having had to make a change at Newton Abbot, and was sitting facing the direction of Plymouth – she couldn't bear to go backwards on trains; it made her queasy. And she could do without adding to her nervous stomach this morning. She'd called the ward she'd been on, checking that Heather would be on duty today. When it was confirmed that she was, a flurry of fearful thoughts swamped Isla's mind. There'd been a part of her that wanted the ward clerk to say Heather was on annual leave, or off sick, so she could give herself a pat on the back for trying, but remain safely in the house. Yesterday's trip had taken it out of her.

Maybe she was afraid of finding out something that would change everything; make everything worse.

Stop it, Isla. You can do this.

She *had* done it, she reminded herself. She'd taken another huge step. It was now merely a case of taking another, and another. One at a time. She would get there.

Unlike the initial train, there weren't many others in her carriage; she had the table seats to herself. Tilting her head, resting it against the window, Isla watched the green fields, then rows of houses all pass in a blur – their colours combining in a long smudge. Without warning, Lance's face came to her mind's eye. She hadn't hesitated to swipe right on his picture the moment it had popped up on the dating app last year. There'd been an honesty to his chosen image: no fake, wide smile showing a row of enhanced white teeth; no filters; no 'look at me with my backpack, climbing a mountain'; no gym shots with bulging biceps and not a cute dog in sight – all things she'd seen enough of in guys' pictures in their vain attempts to come across as alluring, fit, adventurous, sensitive. When underneath they were, in fact, shallow, conceited chancers. Men who wanted nothing more than sex. And just one night, thank you very much.

Lance's was a candid shot. He hadn't even been looking at the camera – it wasn't a selfie, but a snapshot that captured something different; something unique. She'd asked him, on their first date, who had taken the photo. He'd smiled, shyly, dipping his head. 'If I tell you, you're going to get up and leave.'

'No, of course I'm not,' Isla had said.

'My mum. It's just us, see. Dad left a long time ago.'

'Ah, I can relate.'

He'd looked Isla in the eye then, and she'd felt a jolt. Those eyes – like a deep pool of blue-green sea water – penetrated hers and she'd felt an immediate connection.

'I think you and I will relate to each other on every level,' he'd said.

Tears dampened her cheeks, now. They'd had a few weeks of near-perfect dates, mind-blowing sex, but more than that, they did experience a deep connection. She'd felt it; it had consumed her.

She thought he'd felt the same.

'Excuse me, mind if I sit here?' The voice startled Isla. She sat upright, quickly swiping the tears away.

'Er . . . yeah, sure.' Despite not meaning it, there was nothing she could do. It wasn't as though she could say no, not when there were three spare seats. The man, tall and willowy, threw his rucksack in the seat by the window, then folded himself into the aisle one. Isla unconsciously shrank, folding her own body into the seat too, her arms tight against her sides, her legs squashed up against the seat. She glanced out the corner of her eye, catching sight of the man's feet, Nike trainers flat against the seat next to her.

Isla turned her attention back outside, watching as her breath huffed the window in large circles. Nothing could happen on a train, she reminded herself. No one would attack her in a carriage where there would be many witnesses.

But he could follow her off the train, walk behind her, wait until there was a quiet spot and grab her.

She sucked in a lungful of air. *Stop it.*

Isla sneaked a look at her unwelcome travel companion. His head was lowered, his attention immersed in a book. He wasn't taking a blind bit of notice of her. She hoped it stayed that way. She rested her head against the window again, the cool glass making her temple tingle, and closed her eyes against the speeding scenery. Wouldn't be much longer – they'd reach Plymouth within the next hour.

Isla hadn't let Zach know she was leaving the house again today. But she had left a note this time, in case he popped home to check on her. She didn't want him searching for her like he had yesterday. She'd simply written 'gone for a walk' on a Post-it note and stuck it to the fridge. With luck, she'd be home before him and then she could put it in the bin, and he'd never know.

Chapter Thirty-Nine

Christie's Crime Addicts – True Crime Podcast

Excerpt from Episode 164 – *The Couple on Maple Drive*

Phone-in with people who knew the victim/perpetrator.

[ED] We're lucky to have some people willing to talk about their experiences of the couple on Maple Drive. We had a phone-in recently and recorded them with the participants' permission, so we'll be sharing those as well as discussing the case as it stands today in a live add-on at the end of this episode.

Excerpt from the recorded show:

[GUEST: call-in interviewee] Like others have said, I'd heard them sometimes. I don't even live directly next to them but their loud arguing travelled to mine. I'd walked past the evening before, actually; heard raised voices. Couldn't hear detail, it was muffled, but saw movement in the downstairs window. The curtains were parted enough to be able to see two figures.

[ED] And what were they doing?

[GUEST] Ah, it was hard to tell. It's not like I was going to stand outside and gawp – although I wish I had now, like.

[ED] Hindsight is a wonderful thing.

[GUEST] Yeah. Anyway, as I carried on past, I heard some

banging. Not like shots, or anything – more heavy, thudding noises. But, I'm afraid to say I put my head down, kept going, running into my place as quickly as I could. I guess I didn't want to get involved. A few of us have said that . . .

[ED] What? That you didn't do anything about it because you didn't want to poke your nose in?

[GUEST] Yeah, that sort of thing. Me and the other neighbours, you know . . . we'd obviously talked about it. And now it's all *anyone*'s talking about, really. Only, we're all feeling rubbish about it and saying the same thing.

[ED] Which is?

[GUEST] What if we'd done something before? If just *one* of us had called the police, reported a domestic disturbance or something. Maybe . . . [coughs] we might have stopped it. [Silence] It's like we all knew, but not one of us did anything.

[ED] There was a famous case, New York . . . 1964 – a woman, Kitty Genovese her name was. She was stabbed to death in plain sight of a block of apartments – and apparently thirty-eight people had either seen or heard it going on, but it was claimed that not one of them intervened or even so much as called the police. Why? Because each one assumed that someone else must've already put in the call, or that they would, so they didn't think they needed to. The case sparked a load of research and one theory that came out of it was called the bystander effect. I mean, it's since been questioned because the original reports about so many witnesses to Kitty's murder were incorrect, but the theory itself is an interesting one. And what you're saying would appear to back it up.

[GUEST] I'm not sure if that makes me feel better or worse.

[ED] I'm just saying . . . don't be hard on yourself. Hearing other people argue, banging and stuff, it's pretty normal most of the time. You're not to have known it was more than that. We've heard from other people who can recall raised voices,

156

but say they've never really spoken to the couple. Is that your experience?

[GUEST] Oh, no. I've had a few short conversations. With her, mainly. It was like she didn't really want to stop and chat though, was keen to wrap it up and get going. She appeared . . . I want to say scared. But that's not quite right. Wary, maybe. In her own world. Almost like she was drugged and unaware of the words I was speaking – you know what I mean? Spaced out. Yeah, that's it. She was spaced out. And him – I think our paths crossed once or twice, but all I got was a polite nod of the head and a good morning. Was always in a rush. Weird, though because he was always rushing into the house, not out of it. Maybe he just didn't want to get caught speaking to me. [Laughs]

Chapter Forty

Derriford Hospital was like a rabbit warren – numerous corridors, so many wards and different departments on so many floors – it was overwhelming. None of it seemed familiar to Isla as she stumbled through the throng of people. After managing to stop a person in a blue uniform among various others who skittered across the corridor, Isla confirmed the ward she needed was on the eighth floor. Standing in the lift, her muscles bunched up with tension, she considered what information she needed from Heather.

The lift pinged, opening to another white corridor. She stepped out, the smell immediately triggering. The fresh clinical aroma mixed with illness was vomit-inducing. Isla breathed through her mouth, not daring to allow the smell to invade her nostrils. Her legs were shaky as she took a left and finally faced the door with the large sign above. Burrator Ward. Isla pressed the buzzer on the wall and the door released with a loud clunk.

Isla hesitated, then stepped inside.

'Oh, hello, love!' a familiar, Plymothian accent greeted her. She knew straight away it was Heather's voice.

Isla attempted a smile, but was overcome with tears. 'Heather . . .'

'Oh, lovely. Right, give me a minute,' Heather said, putting a hand on Isla's shoulder and guiding her into a side room. 'Wait there, I'll be two secs.'

She returned a few minutes later, armed with two mugs and a packet of biscuits under one arm. 'Here we go, my love. Now, sit.'

She dragged a chair from one side of the bed closer to the one she'd indicated Isla should sit in. 'I was so delighted to hear you were popping in to see me. But concerned too.'

'Oh? Why?'

'I suppose I knew it wasn't a visit just to say thanks.'

'I'm not sure I follow,' Isla said, frowning.

'I'd had a bad feeling that your attacker was someone close to you. But at the time, of course, due to your head injury, you couldn't remember anything. Now, I'm assuming you have . . .'

Isla bowed her head and fiddled with the edge of her cast at her palm. She'd had some memories return, but she wasn't sure she should trust them; she had questions about the night she was admitted and was now hoping Heather could fill in some of the gaps her memory had failed to. The fact Heather even suspected Isla's attacker was someone known to her set her nerves on edge. Despite hearing it from Jase as well as believing it herself, Heather saying it too shocked her. But she'd wanted her fears validated, hadn't she?

'I've recalled a little, yes,' Isla said. 'But my memory is still hit and miss about it, *and* about my stay here. I'm scared I'm muddling different events up, misremembering certain things. Now it's been a few weeks, I admit I'm wondering if my brain is filling in missing information with false memories. If that's possible?' Isla paused. Heather leaned forward, readying herself to answer, but Isla realised she didn't really want to detract from the purpose of her visit by discussing head injuries, the after-effects or the likelihood of false memories, so she jumped in quickly before Heather could begin speaking. 'Did I say anything to you, that night, or in the following days?' She saw Heather relax back into the chair again.

'You were concussed, love – not making much sense at all, really, in those first hours. Just repeating the same phrases over and over. Nothing to do with the attack though as far as I remember. You were pretty incoherent that entire day if I'm honest.'

It was what she expected the response to be, but she was disappointed she hadn't spoken sense. She might've got a clue to the identity of her attacker if she was told now that she'd been uttering the same name over and over or something. Although, even then, if she'd been repeating Zach's name, that might have been because she was asking for him, not accusing him. No, she was wasting her time thinking about what she might have said. She needed to think about something more solid. 'What about visitors?'

'Oh, yes – I remember that,' Heather said, smiling, appearing pleased she could offer firm information. 'Your friend, then boyfriend, they were your first two. Er . . . maybe a couple of other colleagues, I think, a few days after your admission.' She closed her eyes for a second. 'One was called Alex? Came with flowers and I had to ask him to take them back home with him. Don't allow them on the wards anymore, I'm afraid.'

'I don't remember that . . .' Isla felt momentarily lifted that Alex had been to visit. He had sent the odd text message, but she hadn't spoken with him. Or, she may have, but she didn't recall it.

'It was the phone call you seemed concerned about,' Heather said. 'Do you remember that?'

'Nope. God – I've clearly forgotten most of the first days following the attack!'

161

'It's okay. It's normal with head trauma.' Heather reached across and laid a hand on Isla's. 'When you came around, you asked who'd been with you – the first to reach the hospital. You didn't seem surprised when I told you. But then I informed you about your brother's phone call – how he'd phoned the ward immediately after you were brought in. And I remarked how he must've known about the attack because the police hadn't even contacted your next of kin at that point. I suggested perhaps he knew because you'd been on the phone to your mum at the moment you were mugged. But you seemed adamant that wasn't the case. You asked to be taken to the phone so you could make a call.'

It was so odd being told things she'd said and done without the benefit of being able to remember them herself. It was like Heather was telling her a story about someone else's experience. 'Do you know who I called?'

'Your mum, so far as I could make out, love.'

'Okay.' Isla chewed the inside of her lip. 'Well, I've been speaking to my mam practically every day and I'm sure she said she hadn't told Fraser, my brother, until the next day because she hadn't been able to get hold of him before that. His mobile kept going to answerphone.' Confusion clouded her mind. 'I don't think it could've been him.'

Isla's gut twisted. Since getting back from hospital she'd been a bit hurt that Fraser hadn't bothered to give her a call – he'd passed on messages through her mam, but nothing personal. They'd grown apart as adults, having been close growing up – particularly in their teenage years, both wreaking havoc for their parents by going out drinking, getting high, and having a few brushes with the law in his case. But once Isla left Scotland to go to Exeter uni, their bond had weakened as they both got on with their own lives. He didn't contact her often, and it was only through Rowan that she found out anything about his life: his engagement to Sarah being the latest development. Fraser had become distant, a ghost of what she'd known when she lived at home.

Which is why she was almost certain Fraser wasn't the one to enquire about her moments after her arrival on the ward. It wasn't consistent with his past communications with her. But to be sure, she asked: 'What did he sound like? Did he have an accent?'

'Nothing I could clearly identify.'

'Not Scottish then?'

'Definitely nothing strong like that, no.' Heather nodded. 'Ah, I see. Then no, you're right. It couldn't have been your brother – unless he purposely hid his accent?'

'That seems extremely unlikely.'

So, who *had* known she was at the hospital?

As though Heather was reading her mind, she gave a deep sigh and said, 'I think you have to consider the fact that the person who called pretended to be your brother to get information we wouldn't give out to a non-relative. And . . .' She seemed hesitant to carry on, but took a deep breath. 'And that he was the one who attacked you. He asked if you were conscious, which at the time struck me as an odd question, but now, this makes sense. Maybe when he left you he thought you were dead, and then panicked when he realised you were still alive and being taken to hospital. And he needed to know if you were conscious and able to identify him?'

'That's my thinking too, Heather.' The fact Heather had just put her concerns into words gave Isla a strange kind of encouragement, like she was getting close and couldn't stop now. 'I'm sorry to go on, I feel like the police grilling you – but is there anything about the call, his voice, that stood out. Or that maybe you heard again?' She tilted her head to one side, seeing understanding dawn on Heather's face. She knew what Isla was implying. Isla was aware Heather had been on shift when Zach had visited, so she must've heard his voice. Did it seem familiar to her? She didn't want to put the thought into her mind, bias her – she hoped by talking about this it might jog Heather's own memory, help her reach the conclusion that Isla was beginning to reach herself.

Heather put both hands to her temples, closing her eyes and remained in that position for a minute or so. 'Sorry, Isla,' she said, bringing her hands back down. 'I'm struggling to remember his voice from the call, love. Apart from there being no discernible accent, I only remember he sounded anxious – his words all said in a rush – but that's about it, really.'

'Do hospitals record telephone calls?'

'I don't think so, love. There are thousands a day I expect.'

'What about a number though – do you reckon there's some kind of call log?'

'Possibly, if the call is put through to us by the switchboard.'

'And the police – did you tell them about the call?'

'No, I didn't.' Heather's shoulders slumped. 'Although it niggled at me, I didn't think to mention it when they were here. I'm sorry.'

'They were here?' Isla frowned.

'Oh yes, they waited until you were conscious to speak with them. But, obviously, they didn't gain a lot of info from you, love. They spoke to your friend and boyfriend though.'

Zach hadn't mentioned that to Isla. Neither had Nicci, although as they hadn't spoken much, that wasn't a great surprise. 'The police told me afterwards they'd spoken to most of the people at the party,' Isla said. 'But they didn't get any leads. I wonder if they even checked out Zach's alibi . . .'

'*Alibi?* You think he had something to do with it? Goodness.' Despite Heather appearing to have followed where Isla was going with her line of questioning, she seemed genuinely shocked that Isla was considering her own boyfriend as the suspect.

'I'm not ruling anyone out.'

'Blimey, love. I admit, that's a shocker.' Heather's face was pale and Isla half expected her to excuse herself now. Instead, she sat forward, quizzically. 'What did he tell you?'

'That he'd been at the office, working late. That's why he hadn't been with me to celebrate my promotion. He'd played it down, saying we could celebrate another night, just the two of us.'

'Hmm. Well, I'm sure the police would've been thorough. They must've checked he was where he said he was.'

Yes, Isla knew that, really. So why was she still questioning whether it was Zach?

'That's a good point.' Isla realised she'd gained as much as she was likely to and Heather had given her food for thought. She should leave her to work. 'Thanks for giving me the time today, Heather. I really appreciate it.'

'Oh, you're very welcome, love. I'm so glad you popped in – it's made me happy to see that you're recovering well.'

Isla got up and headed to the door.

'Do keep me posted, won't you?' Heather was leaning against the locker, scribbling something in her notebook. She tore a page out. 'Here's my number.'

'Thank you.' Isla pocketed the piece of paper. 'I'll send you a text so you have my number too. And if you remember anything – please will you message me? Anything at all – however small. It might help.'

'Of course. And actually, I'll have a word with my colleagues and see if any of them might have knowledge of other calls asking about you.'

'That'd be great.'

Isla was at the double doors leading back out of the ward when she heard quick footsteps behind her.

'Just had a thought,' Heather said, slightly out of breath. 'When I took that call, the man said he was your brother – but he didn't *say* what his name was. I remember now, I had been given the details of your next of kin. They were on the form brought with you from theatre and it had included Fraser McKenzie – that's why when you were properly awake I'd specified that it was Fraser who'd asked after you. But I think that had been my *assumption* because I knew you only had one brother. The man who made the call stumbled, changed the subject when I asked his name. I didn't think to question it, though – just put it down to him being worried. But now I think whoever it was, while they knew you had a brother, perhaps they didn't know his name.'

Isla sucked in a breath. Her pulse quickened. Obviously Zach knew her brother's name. If he'd been the one trying to get information falsely as Fraser, he would've given that name. Had she been wrong to concentrate her efforts on suspecting Zach was involved? He could be innocent after all.

But then, she was sure that both Simon and Graham also knew her brother's name. She'd spoken about him a number of times at work over the years, and Simon in particular had asked about her family in the past. Although, admittedly in the stress of the situation they might've been unable to recall it. As Christie's Crime Addicts would say often enough, most crimes are committed by those known to the victim, but muggings didn't fall into that category. They were often opportunistic and random. However, the fact was, her attack had been more personal, with a possible intention to kill. That was more likely to be a perpetrator known to her.

There was one person close to her who knew she had a brother in Scotland, but who wouldn't know his name.

Lance.

Maybe he wasn't as out of the picture as she believed. But why would Lance attack her? She'd heard absolutely nothing from him since he ghosted her.

He could've been in prison.

The thought sprung into her mind and back out again just as quickly. That was ridiculous.

Wasn't it?

Chapter Forty-One

Why had Isla been at the hospital?

Zach flung himself back in the chair. She didn't have a scheduled follow-up appointment today that he knew of. Her cast wasn't due off for another week. This was the second time in many days she'd ventured out of the house. She was getting braver.

'Hey, Zach, you got a minute?' His office door opened a crack, Graham's face, red as a beetroot, inched through. Zach reached forward, slamming the lid of his laptop down.

'Yes. What is it?'

Graham pushed the door open fully, and tentatively made his way to the chair opposite Zach's desk. He was so weird. He reminded Zach of the Wormtail character out of *Harry Potter*: the slithering, arse licker who sucked up to Lord Voldemort. That's what Graham was like with Kenneth. Zach didn't stand a chance at getting into his father's good books while this snivelling creep was around.

'Hate to add to your current situation . . . I know you're under some stress lately . . .' Graham turned away, his gaze directed to the window as he continued to speak. 'It's been brought to Kenneth's attention that you're not quite pulling your weight.'

'Oh. Right. It's been "brought to his attention" has it? Like by you, you mean?'

'You know your father thinks of me as his—'

'Second in fucking command – yes, Graham – I think you've mentioned it once or twice.'

'Sorry, mate. I have to report back to him. I can't show favouritism.'

'I'm not your mate. And trust me, that man has never showed me one ounce of favouritism. And you know it. Cut the crap. I'm not slacking. What is it I'm meant to have fallen behind with, Graham? Pray tell?'

'Well . . . you know . . . for starters there's the Fallon account.'

'Oh, go screw yourself. You and I both know that's your shortfall, not mine. But I guess you've been waiting for the perfect moment to bring me down, haven't you? No doubt you're trying to discredit me, make sure the old man cuts me from his will. Makes you the next head of the company.' Zach's hands motioned wildly in front of him.

'Don't be so stupid, Zach. Maybe it's your impetuousness, your propensity to fly off the handle that gives Kenneth reason to question your ability to carry this company. And your immaturity of course . . . That's always been an issue.'

'Fuck you.'

'Point made. You never let me down.' Graham gave a deep chuckle. Zach had to use all of his self-control to stop himself laying him out right there, in the office. Wipe the cocky smile off his face.

'Off you go, then. Run along to Kenneth,' Zach said, barely able to contain his rage.

Zach waited for him to leave, then stormed out, striding along the edge of the large open-plan floor under the glass dome, downstairs. He needed to get out, release the tension from his body. What with Isla and Graham both adding to his worry and frustration this morning, he could do with visiting a gym and punching the hell out of a boxing bag. As that wasn't an option, fresh air and a coffee would have to suffice.

As he approached Nicci's desk – her back to him – he heard her say: 'You need to stop this, Isla.' For a split second he froze. Then he edged closer, trying to listen in on the conversation. Nicci sounded astonished, and her words were staccato. She said something else he didn't catch, then turned suddenly. She jumped when she saw him, her hand flying to her chest, and she immediately ended the call.

'Christ, Zach. Sneaking up on me?' she said. Her eyes were wide, glaring. Like she'd been caught out. He knew that feeling.

'What was that about?' he said. He tried to make his tone curious, not accusatory, but his altercation with Graham just now meant his anger wasn't too far below the surface, and he wondered if he'd been too snappy.

'It was a private call – or are you monitoring those now?' she said it in a light, jokey manner and Zach wanted to push it, make her tell him what Isla had been saying. But that would come across as him being controlling and he didn't need that now; he needed Nicci to think the best of him – have her on his side.

'Sorry, no. Course not. Hey, was just about to pop out for some lunch. Want to join me?'

Nicci pursed her lips. 'I should tackle this . . .' She pointed at a stack of paperwork on her desk. 'Your dad wanted it finished ASAP.'

'Oh, nonsense. I'll tell the boss it's my fault – that I took you away from your desk. I could really do with a chat, Nicci. This place is getting to me and I'm so worried about Isla, it's affecting my work. Bloody Graham is on my back . . .' He cast his eyes skyward, towards the upper floor.

'The glass dome getting too much for you?'

'Like you wouldn't believe.'

Nicci fiddled with the pens on her desk, lining them up. 'I suppose I could spare a half-hour.'

'Great. I'll treat us to a meal deal from Boots.'

'Wow.' Nicci raised her eyebrows. 'I'm *so* honoured.'

Nicci locked her computer screen, got up and grabbed her jacket off the back of her chair.

'Don't ever say this company doesn't look after its employees.' Zach grinned, putting a hand on the small of her back as he guided her out. His goal was to cover several bases with this conversation.

Chapter Forty-Two

Due to lack of seating options on her train, Isla had been forced to travel backwards and was trying not to look out of the window at the scenery blazing past in the wrong direction. She was close to asking the woman opposite if she'd swap seats, but embarrassment prevented her. Instead, she pulled the piece of paper from her jeans pocket and texted Heather so that she had her number too. Then she called Nicci – one, to take her mind off the train journey, and two – to put her new fears into words and gain her friend's support. She wanted Nicci's reaction to what she'd just learned to be the same as hers had been. Needed confirmation she wasn't over-reacting or being paranoid. Being ridiculous.

'You need to think about it rationally, Isla,' Nicci said as soon as Isla finished recounting what Heather had told her.

As if she hadn't been.

'I am. The fact is, a man made a call to the ward moments after I'd been admitted, saying he was my brother. But unable to give a name? That's odd by anyone's standards.'

'Agreed. If it happened the way that nurse said.'

'Why would she lie?'

'I'm not saying that she'd lie, Isla. But she might have

muddled up the conversation – misremembered it? She must get so many stressed relatives calling every day.'

'Yes, true. But this stood out to her because they asked if I was conscious. She said the police hadn't even informed anyone I'd been attacked. So how could my brother – in Scotland – have known?'

The woman opposite Isla stared at her over the Kindle she was holding. Isla lowered her voice. Her conversation was probably more intriguing than the woman's ebook.

'So, immediately you've concluded that the man must've been your attacker?'

'Yes, because that's the most – in fact *only* – way he could've known. Surely you can see that?'

'Erm . . .' The woman opposite leaned towards Isla.

'Hang on a sec, Nicci.' Isla raised her eyebrows to the woman. 'Yes?'

The woman didn't say anything, but nodded her head sharply towards the window.

'Shit. Sorry.' Isla noted the sign: *Quiet carriage. No mobile phones.* So, the woman hadn't found her conversation more scintillating than her ebook – she'd merely been annoyed that Isla was ignoring the rules. She gave an apologetic smile and got out of the seat, making her way out of the carriage to stand by the window near the toilet. 'Sorry, Nicci, had to move. Go on.'

'I was going to say, if you're right, why would he risk phoning the hospital?'

'I suppose he didn't see it as a risk. However, leaving me alive *was.* He wanted to know if I was conscious because he was scared if I was, that I'd remember and identify him as my attacker.' Anxiety was causing Isla's voice to rise; even to her, it sounded screechy like the train's brakes.

'Where is this all heading, Isla?'

'I don't know.' She didn't want to divulge her plans, or the fact she'd roped in the Christie's Crime Addicts team to help her. 'I thought if I talked to you about it, it might make things clearer in my mind. Plus, I was wondering if you might have the same immediate thought as me.'

'Which is?'

'That it was Lance?'

'The guy who *ghosted* you?' Nicci's incredulous tone shocked her. 'Why?'

'Oh, I don't know, really,' Isla conceded, feeling foolish. 'It came to me as soon as the nurse said he hadn't given his name in the call. Because, when Lance and I talked about family and stuff, I'd told him I had a brother, but I never mentioned what his name was.'

'And that's it? That's your evidence for Lance being the attacker? It's a bit flimsy, isn't it . . .'

'A bit, I guess.' Damn. Nicci thought she was jumping to conclusions. Maybe she was. The simplest explanation was usually the correct one. Wasn't that the saying? In which case, taking into account her suspicions and Jase's words, she was back to Zach. 'Nicci, could you do me a big favour?'

'Depends how big?'

'A week or so before my promotion, I was looking at the files in the room upstairs – in the glass dome – and I found something . . . out of place. Like in terms of accounts. Stuff that didn't add up.'

'My God, Isla. Really? Look, I obviously want to help you, but digging around at our place of work? That's dodgy, mate.'

'But I think something I found out may have led to my attack.'

'You think someone here is doing something illegal and you were on to them, therefore they wanted you dead? Even for you, that's out there. You've been watching too many films!' Nicci laughed, but it sounded hollow; forced.

'It's a motive. Okay, don't snoop around the files if it makes you uncomfortable. But would you look into who was working the night of the party? The police reckoned everyone was where they said they were, but I'm not so sure about that. I need to know if Zach left—'

'For Christ's sake, Isla – you're not suggesting your own boyfriend is behind this, are you?' Nicci whispered.

'I'm not ruling it out just yet.' Isla bit hard on her lower lip. She'd shared too much.

'You're playing with fire. Come on. You can't really believe he'd hurt you? And I suppose you think he's up to no good within the company too then? Why? His dad is the boss – he's going to inherit all of this, his father's pissing fortune, when he croaks it. Zach wouldn't jeopardise all of that. You're barking up the wrong tree.'

'Am I?'

'Yes. I realise not knowing the identity of someone who almost killed you must be really hard, and I know you're scared he might . . . well, try again. I don't know – maybe that's normal for victims to have those thoughts; those fears. But you can't get hung up on them or you're never going to get better.'

'Please, Nicci. Just be open to it. It won't hurt you to keep an ear out, look for odd behaviour. That sort of thing. And ask around – see who else was working that night. Please? For me.'

'You need to stop this, Isla.'

'I can't. I have to know.'

'I can't see this ending well,' Nicci said. Her hushed words were barely audible and Isla was about to ask her to expand on her comment, but Nicci spoke again.

'Gotta go.' The line went dead. She'd hung up on her.

Isla stayed beside the open window, the air rushing in, hitting against her face and making her catch her breath. She checked her mobile. One bar of battery, and no signal now. Perhaps she'd lost signal and Nicci hadn't just hung up then.

There were only ten minutes of the journey left before she'd need to change trains at Newton Abbot, so she decided to wait by the door rather than go back to her seat. She liked to be prepared to disembark the second it was unlocked. Her fear of being stuck on a train, unable to reach the exit before it set off for the next stop was one she'd always had, long before being a nervous wreck because of the attack. It had stemmed from a family trip they'd taken to Inverness to visit her aunt and uncle when she was ten. Her father had been struggling to get the suitcases from the rack, blocking the gangway in the process, so none of them could get off. To this day, Rowan insisted he'd done it on purpose to ruin the holiday. He'd never got on with Auntie Flo and had only agreed to the visit because Rowan had pushed and pushed. She'd even got Isla and Fraser to beg him, and he'd eventually agreed. Because of the missed stop, they'd reached their destination a few hours late, with her parents stressed and arguing. Isla didn't remember anything else about that visit, but the fear of not being able to reach the train door in time for her stop had remained.

She was first off the train, and first onto the connecting one. Ten minutes later, she was at Torquay station, her anxiety rescinding. Isla checked her watch. The walk home would take too long. She saw the number 22 bus pulling in at the stop opposite. The thought of getting on it made her stomach clench. With no time to consider her anxiety, Isla ran across and jumped on. At least she'd be home within the next twenty minutes – then she could relax.

Only, she knew that wouldn't be the case.

She wouldn't relax until she discovered the identity of the man who had attacked her, and if it did turn out to be Zach, then she'd have to deal with the repercussions, whatever they might be. Isla took her mobile from her bag. She'd message Jase now, see if Christie's Crime Addicts had come up with anything. Isla stared at the black screen. It'd died. When she got back home, she'd ping an email to Jase, tell him all about her trip to Derriford, and what Heather had told her.

The evidence might not be compelling yet – but she had a direction to go in now. And maybe, with Nicci's help, she could shine a spotlight on Zach's supposed alibi.

Chapter Forty-Three

Isla gave a cursory glance to the house next door as she rushed up her front path. While she had now managed two trips outside the house, the anxiety hadn't diminished as much as she'd have liked. She still felt as though she were somehow 'on show' and by being out she was making herself an easier target. It would get easier the more she did it. Hadn't Dr Emile Forrester mentioned something about exposing yourself to your fears as a way of overcoming them? So, the more she went out, the less anxious she'd feel about it. That was the theory, anyway.

Inside the house, Isla immediately felt safer. For a moment, she leaned against the door, breathing slowly and deeply. Was she wrong to feel safe? She might well have invited inside the one person she *should* be afraid of. She held her breath to listen for sounds. Just the usual electrical noises. Zach wasn't home.

After sending Jase an email detailing her visit with Heather, Isla sat at the kitchen table with a coffee and a packet of Rich Tea biscuits, scrolling through podcast episodes on her laptop. Within minutes a new email appeared from Jase, asking if he could call her on the landline, which surprised her; she hadn't told him her mobile battery was dead. She abandoned her coffee and went into the lounge to wait by the telephone.

The initial conversation centred on what she'd said in her email, with Jase being more than a little concerned and still suggesting she should ask Zach to move out, or that she should even leave herself, go and stay with friends for a while. But, as Isla pointed out, that would only serve to raise Zach's awareness that she was suspicious of him, and wouldn't *that* put her at increased risk of him hurting her? Jase seemed uptight, stressed about her plan to stay, keep an eye on him. Because, he said, Zach would be doing the exact same thing.

Isla closed her eyes gently, trying to block out Jase's assertion that her boyfriend was staying close, watching her, keeping tabs.

'He's watching every step you take, Isla.' Jase's voice was almost a whisper now.

'Not really, he's at work for the majority of—'

'No,' Jase interrupted. 'I don't want to frighten you, but I need you to take this seriously.'

'Riiiight . . .' Isla sucked in her breath. 'I am, Jase. That's why I came to you guys, remember?'

'And that's great – I'm glad we can help in some way. But we aren't the police; we have zero powers. We can't save you, Isla.'

Her blood ran cold at Jase's words. Wasn't he being a little overdramatic? It wasn't one of his podcast shows. Not yet, at any rate.

But then, he dropped a bombshell. 'Your mobile battery's dead again, isn't it?'

'Yeah . . . how—'

'You know what drains a battery that quickly?' He waited a beat before delivering his own answer. 'Spyware.'

'Shit.' Isla swallowed hard, not wanting to even give head-space to this, but at the same time her gut was telling her he could be right. 'You really think he'd be able to do that?'

'It's easier than you imagine. And the mobile – he gave it to you, right?'

'Yes. A temporary one while I wait for a new iPhone.' Isla's throat tightened as tears threatened. She knew where he was going with this, and suddenly the situation took a different turn.

'You could've got a replacement iPhone immediately, Isla.'

'I'm not so sure, Jase. Zach said the company's insurance department were being awkward. When I called the other day it took forever to get through, then the incompetent idiots couldn't find the original claim . . .' Isla's words trailed, her heartbeat pounding in her ears. Oh, God. She hadn't considered that maybe there was no claim in the first place, and that's why they had no record.

'And you made the original call to the phone company? Don't answer that, Isla. Zach told you he had, didn't he?'

'Yes. He sorted it all. He was being kind, taking the pressure off me having to deal with any of it.'

'No, he needed to take control of it for his own reasons – a replacement iPhone wouldn't have served his purposes; you can easily disable the find my friends feature. He wanted you to have that particular phone because it was more than likely loaded with the spyware enabling him to track your movements.'

As much as she didn't want it to, it all made sense. 'That's why he came home early the day I came to see you.' She said it quietly, more to herself, but Jase carried on the conversation.

'Which means he knows what you're up to. It's not safe for you to be with him. Please, you have to get out of there. There's no telling what he'll do.'

'So, you believe categorically it's him, then? Zach is the person who attacked me? Wanted me dead?'

'I'm not certain, no. I'm going on the information available right now – we obviously need more evidence. The other suspects *are* plausible, and you mentioned in your email that your brother supposedly called the ward but was unable to give his name, which doesn't fit with it being Zach.' Jase gave a long sigh before continuing. 'But, to be honest, that could've been a purposeful omission. That way, if anyone became suspicious later down the line they would be querying it just like we are.' It seemed to Isla that Jase was in the middle of what would usually be an inner monologue – only he was sharing his thoughts out loud. She didn't interrupt his flow. 'But spyware? It doesn't look good. Unless Zach's just ultra-concerned for your wellbeing, afraid for you or thinks the assailant will strike again, why would he need that?' Jase finally fell silent for more than a few seconds. Isla took this as her cue to speak.

'He was worried when he came home and I wasn't here. Said it crossed his mind I'd been taken. It's a possibility he *is* purely looking out for me, making sure I'm safe. Surely, if he had access to my phone through spyware then he'd have seen I was in Torquay town centre and known precisely where to find me,' she said, pacing the lounge, her thoughts coming thick and fast just as Jase's had done. 'But the battery had already drained before I got to you,' she added, before Jase did. She'd yet to mention the sudden thought she'd had earlier that it might have been Lance. She should share everything to make sure they weren't missing something important. As she was about to tell Jase she withdrew the phone from her ear, looked at it, then put it back. 'Could the landline be bugged?' She felt stupid saying it, but given the entire conversation was complete madness, the question wasn't exactly extreme.

'If he's managed to put in place a way to track you then yes,

I guess it's a possibility he's gone further. He could've even placed a listening device somewhere in the room.'

'God . . . Like where?' Isla's eyes darted around the lounge.

'I don't know. Er . . . Has he bought anything new into the house recently?'

'No, not that I can recall.'

'Any parcels delivered? That sort of thing?'

Isla shook her head. 'No.' Then it hit her. 'My mate from work, Nicci – she brought me a gift.'

'And when was that?'

'A few days ago. I haven't even opened it. I left it—'

God. Surely not?

'Hang on a sec,' Isla said, placing the receiver on the table. She rushed to the bookcase, searching for the small box that Nicci had handed to her. She pulled at the spines of books, looking behind the stacks, and found it wedged between the case and the wall. That wasn't where she'd put it. Ripping open the parcel, Isla found two cans of G&T, a bar of Dairy Milk, some wax candle melts and a gift card. Nothing untoward. 'We've jumped to conclusions, I think. It's just a few bits and a gift card,' Isla said, picking the phone back up.

'What sort of gift card?'

Isla studied it back and front. 'The usual plastic kind, size of a credit card. Doesn't have a store name specified. It's just got a generic pink pattern on it. Why?'

'Isla, don't say anything else about it, okay? You can get listening devices that look just like gift cards. He's probably been eavesdropping. Put it somewhere out of range of the phone.'

'Okay, will do.' Isla had to force her words out, her mouth had become so dry – this was unbelievable. Surely Nicci wouldn't purposely give her something containing a bug? 'And if it's just a gift card?'

'A generic-looking card sounds suspicious to me. Especially if there's no other detail on it. Wouldn't your friend be more likely to get you a gift card you can use at a well-known store? And I wouldn't stop looking, either. Honestly, you can get listening devices and bugs so easily off the internet. There are voice-activated air fresheners, extension plugs, pens, calculators, you name it. If someone wants to know everything you say, every move you make, trust me, there's a way.'

The song 'Every Breath You Take' started playing in her mind. Isla shook her head, forcing it back out. 'Do you know that bit about not wanting to frighten me . . .'

'Sorry. Ditch that mobile, don't use your laptop, don't say anything incriminating on the landline. Although I suspect he can only hear your end of the conversation you must play it safe. Got it?'

'Yes.' Her voice quivered. The hand holding the phone trembled so much she struggled to keep hold of it. She hadn't told him about Lance, but now didn't seem like the best time. She didn't want to alert Zach to any of her suspicions, about him or anyone else. It would give him too much power.

'Tomorrow, we'll meet. Don't come to our studio. I'll get a message to you about the location.'

'Thank you.'

The front door slammed. Isla's stomach flipped. 'He's back,' she whispered into the phone.

'Be careful.'

The line went dead.

Isla quickly replaced it and assumed her usual position on the sofa. Every muscle in her body tensed up as she heard Zach's footsteps approach her.

'Hey, babe. How's your day been?' His face loomed over the top of the sofa as she looked up.

'Oh, the usual,' she said, trying to sound casual. Trying to hide the quiver in her voice. Zach lowered his head and gave her a kiss. 'How about yours?'

'Much the same,' he said. Did his voice sound different? She wondered how much of her conversation with Jase had been overheard. Had he also been listening in on her conversation with Nicci? Her mam? Off the top of her head, she couldn't remember if she'd spoken about anything that might warrant Zach to conclude she was looking at him as a suspect.

She'd have to tread really carefully from now on.

Zach placed a plate of food in front of Isla, then turned back to the worktop to get his. He sat down opposite her, lifting his fork, but before beginning to eat his dinner, he paused. Isla was aware of his eyes on her. She looked up.

'Thank you,' she said. 'This looks delicious.' And it did – chilli prawn pasta bake was one of her favourite dishes. He'd made an effort, rather than phone for a takeaway.

'Was the easiest meal I could think of that you can eat with one hand,' he said with a half-smile. 'Not long now though, eh? Cast is coming off in a week, isn't it?'

'Yes. Six days to go,' Isla said, with a fake brightness.

'And you have to go back to Derriford for that I presume?'

Isla nodded, her mouth filled with pasta. It stuck in her throat as she swallowed, so she had to gulp her water to make it slide down her gullet.

'That'll be the first real trip out, then. Won't it? I mean, that far. It'll be a bit of a challenge. But I'll make sure I'm with you. For that first big step.'

Isla forced herself to make eye contact with him; only liars avoided it. 'Thank you. I really appreciate that.' She held his gaze, but was afraid he'd sense her wariness; *see* that she was lying. She needed to change the subject because if he carried on like this, she was afraid she'd let slip she'd been to Derriford already.

But then, maybe he knew that.

An awkward silence stretched between them. Isla knew she had to at least try to act normally around Zach, despite her growing suspicions of him. 'You okay?' he asked, his mouth filled with food.

'Tired.' Acting normally was proving more challenging than she thought. It was difficult even looking at him with the knowledge he was likely spying on her. Maybe Jase was right: she should get out.

But this was *her* home. Her *safe* place.

'I thought we could do something tomorrow. Together. I'm going to take the day off.'

Isla's heart sank, her blood running cold in her veins. Why had he chosen tomorrow of all days?

Because he knows.

She gripped her fork so tightly her knuckles turned white. Zach reached his hand across, laying it on hers.

'You don't have other plans, do you?' he said.

Isla stared at his hand on hers. 'Other than the counselling session . . .' Her voice was tight. Cracking.

Zach smiled. Nodded.

Christ. Did he know she wasn't doing them as well? Did he know absolutely everything?

'After that, then,' he said finally. 'We'll have the afternoon out. It'll be fun.'

Isla knew it would be far from fun. In this moment, her brain ceased to process and she couldn't think of any way to get out of it. She'd have to say yes. She had no choice.

Somehow, she'd have to put off meeting Jase.

And she had a feeling that would be a huge mistake.

Chapter Forty-Four

The pain filled her head, overcoming her. Isla fell to the ground. Bone crunched. Darkness drowned her. Her nostrils filled with the smell of iron. She gasped, then pushed against the weight on her body. Turning, she stared into his eyes. Zach's eyes. She tried to scream, but a gloved hand muffled her attempts. Simon, his teeth clenched in anger, pressed his fist into her mouth, his knuckles knocking against her teeth. She gagged, began choking. Graham's voice erupted from Simon's lips. Isla couldn't breathe as she watched Simon's features morph into Graham's, then Lance's. Her chest tightened; ribs crushed. Noise came from somewhere to her right: yelling, running; feet pounding – then, suddenly the weight lifted. She sucked all the available air into her lungs. Jase's face was above hers. 'I've got you.'

He'd saved her.

Isla bolted upright, dragging the duvet off Zach as she sprung forwards, clasping one hand to her mouth. But the scream had already escaped.

'What's the matter?' Zach's sleepy voice asked.

'Noth . . . ing . . .' Her breaths were fast, ragged. 'Go back . . . to sleep.'

Zach's breathing settled back into its normal sleeping pattern within seconds; hers did not. Her pulse pounded violently and sweat trickled down her back, the remnants of the nightmare still with her, fear gripping her heart.

The dreams were becoming more vivid – the attack itself more detailed – but at the same time, the assailant's identity was less clear. Seeing the faces change and merge didn't help her memory; it clouded it further. But that was the first time Jase had appeared. Is that how she saw Christie's Crime Addicts? As her saviour? She wanted, *needed*, their help, but she also wanted to be strong enough to deal with this on her own. She was fed up with the vulnerable woman label – she wanted to take control. Yes, the game she was playing might be a dangerous one, but why should she bow down – cower in fear – just because she was female? It was horseshit. She wasn't running away, or backing down. Let Zach think he was winning, that he was the one controlling her. She'd show him. It was her who was calling the shots. Her who would be the one to gather enough evidence to bury him.

She wasn't weak. As much as he may want her to be. She was going to take him down.

The rational part of Isla's brain wanted to put the brakes on this thinking. The voice of reason telling her that, as yet, she didn't *know* it was Zach. She should still look at other suspects, not narrow her focus at this point, as she could still be wrong. Blinded by her own bias. Maybe he really *was* trying to look after her.

It was five a.m. No way she'd go back to sleep now, and even if she did, she'd feel like shit in a few hours. She slipped out of bed, leaving Zach's soft snores behind her. Downstairs, she began to look around, checking every household appliance, every light switch. Jase telling her about the array of listening devices available had shocked her. The stuff you could buy simply and quickly off the internet was mind-boggling. How easy it was to invade someone's privacy. So wrong.

But, having now looked, Isla couldn't see anything new or out of place. She spent most of her days in the lounge, on the sofa. If Zach wanted to listen to what she was saying, doing, then that would be where she'd try and put a device if she were him. With her good arm, she shifted the sofa away from the end wall so she could get a good look down the side. It was where she kept the knitting needle and where the remote often fell. There was nothing there but two empty sockets. Could the actual socket be hiding something?

'What are you doing?'

Isla jumped back. 'Oh, morning.' Heat flushed her face. She felt as though she'd just been caught out doing something she shouldn't. She hadn't heard any movements from upstairs, and now Zach was in the doorway, his dressing gown gaping, his mouth opening in a yawn. 'I was looking for an extension cable.'

'What for?'

Her mind leaped into action, seeking an appropriate response. 'Bloody mobile keeps losing charge,' she said, shrugging. 'I was going to plug it in so I could use it while it charged. Wanted it closer to the sofa, though, and the lead isn't long enough.' She smiled, inwardly impressed with her quick thinking.

'I've got one in the office, hang on.'

She breathed a sigh of relief when he turned and went back upstairs. This was going to be more stressful than she'd imagined. How would she keep this up? He came back into the lounge, his arm outstretched.

'Thanks.' Isla wanted to study the extension cable, but he was still standing, watching her. She plugged it in to the mains socket, got her mobile and pushed the plug into it.

'Sorry I got you such a crap phone. Shouldn't be much longer before you get the proper replacement.'

Isla smiled, but didn't say anything. He turned, saying he was going to get ready, that she should eat breakfast and get a head start on today's counselling session. Isla left it a minute then went to the bottom of the stairs. The shower was running; music blared. He'd be at least ten minutes – that would give her plenty of time.

Unplugging the cable again, Isla gave it a quick once-over. These days, most plugs and extension cables were moulded, not intended to be taken apart – but this one looked different. An older style. Her pulse quickened and she rushed to the kitchen. Sliding the paring knife from the wooden block in the kitchen, Isla took it back into the lounge and ran the tip of the knife along the seam of the plastic casing. It was awkward with one hand. Sitting on the sofa, balancing it on her lap, she managed to force the knife into the gap. It split open with a snap. Isla glanced at the lounge doorway, pausing to listen for movement. She could still hear the water splashing the shower screen. With the extension lead now in two, she scanned the insides. The wires looked normal enough and were positioned where she supposed they should be – not that she could be certain; she hadn't even looked inside a plug for years. Just as she thought she'd jumped to the wrong conclusion, that this was, in fact, a standard extension lead and she was being paranoid, she spotted a small card – like a SIM card.

Frowning, she pinched it between her thumb and forefinger, releasing it from the casing, and turned it over in her hand. It *was* a SIM card. Oh, my, God. She dropped the cable to the floor, sitting back in horror. Jase was right. Zach had planted listening devices in her house. He must somehow link his phone with this SIM, enabling him to listen in. Her mouth watered;

she felt sick. He said he'd got this one from the office, though. She didn't go in there, so why would he place one there?

Because she'd been outside it the other night, watching him.

She must've been close to catching him out with something and once he realised she'd possibly seen, he put the extension cable in the room in case Isla went in there snooping. Isla reached down to pick the device up, she'd have to put it back together and pretend she'd never seen inside it.

Soft padding noises – footsteps on the stairs – caught her attention.

Shit.

She fumbled, dropping the SIM card.

Panic swept over her. She couldn't see it on the floor.

The creak of the last stair.

For fuck's sake.

She quickly snapped the two halves of the cable back together, plugging it into the wall socket just as Zach walked into the lounge.

Heart hammering, Isla smiled up at him. 'Good shower?'

'Refreshing. Next time you should join me.'

She lifted her plastered arm. 'Yeah, when this is off.'

Isla looked down, her gaze falling on the carpet. The SIM card was red against the cream-coloured pile. He'd see it. But if she reached forward now, it'd draw attention to it. Zach moved towards her.

'Where do you fancy going today?' he said brightly. As he turned his body slightly to take a seated position beside her on the sofa, Isla swiped her foot out, covering the SIM and dragging it back. Now all she had to do was keep her foot on it.

'I'm not sure I feel up to much. I didn't sleep well.'

'See how you feel when you've finished your session.' He looked at her, unblinking. 'Why haven't you started it?'

'I was going to eat first,' she said.

'I said to do that while I showered.' Although his voice was slow and calm, he managed to sound almost angry, intimidating.

'I was fiddling with my phone. *Sorry*.' Her response was intentionally sharp. She didn't care for his tone.

'I'll fix you something.' His face lightened, like a dark veil had been lifted. 'You crack on.'

Isla waited for Zach to leave, then removed her foot from the SIM card, picked it up and slipped it in her dressing gown pocket. Now she had actual evidence her boyfriend was spying on her. And to her mind, there was only one reason he would do that.

He needed to find out how much she knew, what she was remembering.

And if she'd remembered that Zach was the one who had attempted to kill her.

Chapter Forty-Five

Isla stared, unseeing, at the laptop, unaware of the words the counsellor was saying – her mind was already far too occupied with thinking about how she could get a message to Jase. She was afraid to even use her phone now – and even though the SIM was removed from the one extension cable, there were likely more. The landline could even be bugged. She was trapped.

'Isla?'

Jase had said he'd get a message to her. But how? Now Zach was hovering over her every second, it'd be near impossible. He hadn't even left the lounge, clearly keen to keep tabs on her.

'Isla!' Zach's raised voice brought her out of her thoughts.

'Yes?'

'You're staring at a blank screen. The session finished five minutes ago.'

'Oh, did it? Was lost there for a bit.'

'Obviously. Why? Did it help you remember something?' He spoke in a nonchalant, curious manner as though it was a question he only vaguely wanted an answer to – but now, given Isla's findings, she read more into it and was sure he was attempting to disguise his desperation to know.

'No,' she said honestly. 'I was just thinking about it, that's all. Letting it sink in, you know.'

'Sounded like a positive session. I mean, from where I'm sitting. She advocates future goals too, like I've been saying. That you shouldn't focus on the past.'

'Yep. She says that in every session, Zach. And that's what I'm trying to do.'

'Good. That's good. Right, now how do you feel about getting out for a bit? For some fresh air.' He closed the newspaper he'd been reading, jumped up and clapped his hands together. 'I've been looking forward to this all morning.'

As Isla opened her mouth to offer another excuse, the doorbell rang.

Before she could even get up from the chair, Zach was out of the lounge.

'Delivery. For Isla McKenzie – need her signature, please.'

The voice drifted into Isla and she rushed out into the hallway before Zach offered to sign it for her.

'Thanks, I'll sort it,' she said, nudging Zach aside. She positioned herself so she took up the doorway space and waited until she heard Zach's footsteps retreat.

Isla's eyes widened, her smile faltering as she looked up at the delivery man. Despite a cap tilted low over his face, she recognised him. It was Doug from Christie's Crime Addicts. A small gasp escaped her open mouth. He put a finger to his lips, gently shaking his head.

'Okay, madam, I need to get your signature on a couple of forms here if you don't mind,' he said loudly. Isla took the clipboard he offered, and when she looked at the paperwork, it wasn't something awaiting her signature. The paper was blank apart from one sentence written in block capitals.

1 P.M. MEADFOOT BEACH CAFÉ.

Isla looked back over her shoulder into the hallway, then

back to Doug. 'I can't,' she mouthed, slowly shaking her head. Doug shot her a questioning look. 'He knows,' she whispered.

'What's taking so long, love?' Zach's voice came from the kitchen. He was getting suspicious.

Isla took the pen from Doug, scribbling a message on the paper. She smiled, said thank you and goodbye, loudly enough for Zach to hear, then closed the door.

'What is it?' Zach asked, walking through to the lounge, a plate in each hand. 'I've done crumpets for elevenses.'

'Can't a girl have any secrets?' she said, giving a coy look.

For a moment, Zach glared at her, and she expected him to say no, that actually she couldn't have secrets from him. His lips curled into a smile, though, and he just winked. 'I see. Must be a gift for your amazing boyfriend, then.'

'Oh? You know him too? I didn't realise you'd met.'

'Oh, ha-ha. Now, come. Sit. Let's eat. Then we can decide where to go.'

Isla put the parcel on the floor. She was itching to know what it was. Jase was surely taking a risk sending her anything. Maybe it was something random, something she could explain away if Zach queried it. Perhaps, it was merely a cover for getting the message about meeting to her without alerting Zach. But now, she'd had to let Jase know she wouldn't be able to get there, because it seemed Zach was on to her.

Isla bit into the crumpet, a sense of defeat filling her more than the food would.

She had no idea what her next step was going to be.

Chapter Forty-Six

'I'm going to change into jeans,' Isla said. She glanced back as she walked towards the hall, and when she was sure Zach's attention was on his newspaper, she took the parcel and went upstairs. She rummaged in her wardrobe, banged some drawers in her dressing table, then quickly opened the cardboard box. Inside was a wicker basket filled with pamper products: a rejuvenating face mask, eye mask, a moisturising foot pack, two bath bombs and a candle. Isla smiled. Nice of Jase to make up such a thoughtful parcel – one she could easily explain away as a 'recovery gift' from a friend or relative in Scotland. Clever. But pretty over the top, considering the entire thing was merely a decoy for the one-sentence message. He could've put something far less extravagant in the parcel. A warm sensation flooded her. It was like he'd really thought about it. Perhaps he somehow felt responsible for her, now they'd agreed to help; protective of her, like a father would be. Not that he was *that* old, she reminded herself. Isla carefully replaced everything and pushed the box underneath her bed.

She wondered if Jase would be at the meeting point anyway, regardless of her message. Just in case she managed to make it. She had two hours in which to figure out how she could give Zach the slip and get to the café for one p.m. Her best bet would be to orchestrate the afternoon so she and Zach visited the beach for a leisurely walk along the sand. He knew she found the sea calming, and Meadfoot Beach had been a huge part of his upbringing too – he'd often told her how his family had spent every day there during his summers growing up. She could tell him to wait on the beach while she popped to the toilet, quickly meeting Jase. At least she'd be able to pass him the SIM card if nothing else. And, if Zach insisted they go to the café together, Jase would see and know she'd been unable to go alone. It might still be possible to covertly hand him the evidence.

It was a plan of sorts. And the only one she had. In order not to arouse Zach's suspicion, though, she needed to ensure he felt it was his idea to go to Meadfoot Beach, not hers.

'You look nice,' Zach said, sauntering over to her as she entered the lounge. 'Pretty darn hot, in fact.'

'Get over. I'm in jeans and a baggy jumper – not what I'd call sexy.'

'Well.' He put his head on one side, and with a wink added, 'Better than those stinky pyjamas, babe.'

Isla swiped at him with her plastered arm. 'Watch it, Zachy – I can do serious damage with this.' The light, carefree laughing that followed reminded Isla why she had fallen for him. And it made her question her assumptions. Could this man *really* be responsible for hurting her? In this moment, no matter what she'd found out so far, it seemed utterly far-fetched he'd go to such horrendous lengths. If this were playing out on the screen, Isla would be yelling at her character, saying: 'It's not him, stupid!'

Yet, here she was. Trying to compile evidence to prove it was.

If she was wrong about him, the worst outcome would be

that he'd be heartbroken she'd even suspected him and their relationship would end – possibly her career at the firm too. But, if she turned out to be right . . .

'Ahh, it's good to see you smile – to hear that squealy laughter,' he said, mocking her then suddenly drawing her in close, enveloping her in a tight hug. How could he make her feel fearful in one moment, then safe in another? 'I love you, Isla,' he said quietly into her hair.

Her heart skipped. He'd never said that before. She held on to him, keeping her face burrowed into his chest. The words she should be able to say back lodged in her throat. She pulled away, speaking before the silence became even more awkward. 'Where shall we go, then? I'd prefer somewhere quiet if that's okay with you. Breezy would be good, too – to blow the cobwebs away.' She smiled, hoping he'd choose the beach.

'The seafront then?'

Isla screwed her nose up. 'It's maybe a little bit further than I'd feel comfortable with, really. And if we get there and it's crowded . . .'

'Meadfoot's the closest, then. And it has a café so you can have a breather before the return walk.'

Isla purposely paused, rather than immediately agreeing, then nodded slowly. 'Yeah, okay. That's your favourite beach, isn't it?'

'It's the one I know best, yes. Spent sooo much time there as a kid and teenager. Not so much lately.'

'Great. Sorted.' She smiled and kissed him on the cheek.

She was so relieved it had gone the way she wanted.

Over one hurdle – on to the next.

Chapter Forty-Seven

It was undeniably wonderful to be by the sea. The breeze deposited tiny drops of sea water on Isla's lips, leaving a residue of salt, which she licked every few minutes.

'Are you sure you wouldn't prefer an ice cream?' Zach said, watching her.

She laughed, running her tongue over her lips again. 'No, I love it. When I first came to Torquay the beaches were my number-one place to while away the hours. I'd bring my textbooks and sit on the front, sipping a Costa and listening to the rhythmic crashing of the waves on the rocks. Perfection.'

'We don't do enough of it now. Work seems to take up way too much time and effort. These simple things have been set aside.' Zach sounded as though he genuinely regretted his choice to put work first all the time. Even slightly resentful.

A seagull swooped over their heads and Isla's eyes followed it as it glided towards the café.

'Bloody things,' Zach said, ducking. 'And I bet some idiot feeds it their leftover chips!'

'Yep – there's always one.' Isla was looking towards the tables set up outside the café. Under a blue and white striped umbrella, a man sitting alone, reading a newspaper, caught her attention.

She couldn't make out any detail from where she was, but she felt certain it was Jase. Her stomach flipped.

'Talking of chips,' she said.

'You must've read my mind.' Zach grabbed Isla's hand and began guiding her towards the steps.

As they reached the top step, Isla sneaked a look to her left before Zach ushered her inside. It was Jase, without doubt. He had a hoody on, and a black baseball cap. At first glance he looked like a teenager. But as he lifted his gaze, clocking Isla, she noted his greying stubble. Good, he knew she was there.

'You want to stay in here? Best not give the seagulls any reason to attack you.' His eyes widened. 'Shit, Isla – I didn't mean—'

'It's fine, really. You don't have to edit what you say. Yes. I'll grab a table; you get the chips.'

Isla walked to the furthest table by the window, unsure what her plan was, but knowing the toilets were at the back of the café. She could easily pop to the loo and hopefully Jase would see and follow her. Gazing outside, she caught Jase's eye and she gave a discreet nod. Turning away again, she watched Zach as he queued. His posture was relaxed, like he didn't have a care in the world. It seemed so implausible that he was her assailant. She'd fought against it, explaining away the memory of the smell of his aftershave, but once she'd recalled the discrepancies in the files at work, it was more difficult to dismiss it. Maybe, if the smell hadn't prompted the memory, she wouldn't have suspected him at all. Not enough to have sought help from Jase; not enough to sneak around the house looking for listening devices.

She shuddered as an ice-cold shiver tracked down her back.

If she hadn't begun to question Zach's motives, how long would it have taken her to realise she might well be living with the very person who'd attacked her? Isla was glad she hadn't confided in her mam about it all. There was no benefit in sharing her fears because there was nothing Rowan could do from over six hundred miles away. All that would've accomplished was to cause her mam undue stress. And, equally, she didn't feel comfortable in telling Nicci every detail – she'd confided enough and hadn't gained the response she'd wanted. Despite her being the best friend Isla had in Devon, the fact she worked for Biggins & Co, too, meant she couldn't fully trust her friend not to pass on what she'd been saying. Maybe she had already – she might very well be complicit in planting a listening device disguised as a gift card in her lounge. Isla had to play it safe.

The thought made her laugh to herself. Play it safe? Like she was doing now?

The irony was not lost on her.

Isla struggled to eat the chips, her knotted stomach preventing enjoyment. The voice in her head constantly asked when she should make her move. Zach was quiet, and Isla was aware he was looking at her as he shovelled his chips in his mouth.

'Been ages since I came to this beach,' she said, attempting to engage him in conversation.

'Me too. Mixed memories here.'

'Oh?' Isla looked up, shooting him a questioning glance. When he'd spoken of Meadfoot before it had always been fond memories he'd shared.

'Just . . . you know – families, eh? Some of the times we came here weren't as . . .' he paused, reaching for the word '. . . *pleasant* as they could've been.'

'But wasn't it just the three of you?'

'Exactly. As always, the pressure was on me. No siblings to share the fun, no one to share the burden of success.'

'Success?' Isla frowned.

'Oh, yeah. Even on the beach one could fail, you know?' His voice was edged with bitterness. 'You're not using enough water, Zachary. You're not patting it down properly. Put some effort behind it, boy!' Zach put on a voice that was clearly meant to be his father's. So, even when Zach was a child, Kenneth Biggins had expected much from him.

'I'm sorry – that must've been awful for you as a kid. Doesn't exactly instil confidence.'

'No. It didn't. Not much has changed, eh? Anyway, let's not focus on the bad times. I've been telling you enough that you should be looking forward.' He smiled and raised his can of 7Up. 'Here's to moving forward, and not ever looking back.'

Isla lifted her mug of coffee, clinking it against the can. 'Here's to the future,' she said. Out the corner of her eye, she caught movement outside. Jase was getting up, heading to the café door.

'Well, all this liquid . . . must visit the ladies'.' Isla squeezed Zach's hand. 'See you in a sec.' She stood up, but Zach grasped her hand.

'Will you be okay? I mean, on your own?' he said.

For a horrifying moment, Isla thought he was going to get up, too, and accompany her to the toilet. She almost snapped at him to stop being so overprotective, that she didn't require supervision. But it was possible he really was being thoughtful, supportive, so she gave a reassuring smile instead. 'I'm sure. I know you're right here, waiting. I'll be fine. Thanks, though.' She slipped her hand from his.

Isla reached the door to the toilet just before Jase did and hovered inside the corridor leading to the two separate stalls.

'Hey, you made it.' Jase looked around furtively and checked inside the toilets. Both were vacant. 'Right, we'll have to make this quick. I don't want to put you at risk.'

'I found this.' Isla popped the SIM card from her jeans pocket and handed it over. 'In an extension cable.'

'So, he has multiple devices by the looks of it,' he said, studying it briefly before putting it in his own jeans pocket.

'It's definitely him, then, isn't it.' Isla's voice shook.

'Everything is pointing to him, yes. And my gut is telling me it's very likely to be Zach who's behind your attack – *but* we have to be careful, Isla. It's easy to fit the evidence to the person we suspect the most. I've seen it often enough in bodged police inquiries – the investigating team being so focused on the one they're sure did it, they fail to see the evidence could also fit with a completely different person. We mustn't overlook other potential suspects.'

'Okay, that makes sense. I don't know where to go from—'

The door flung open. Both Isla and Jase's heads snapped around. Isla held her breath.

'Is there a queue?' A woman with a toddler walked into the corridor.

'No – go ahead,' Jase said, standing back to let them pass.

'Look, Zach might be next through that door. In the box I sent, there's a candle in a glass holder. Take out the candle, underneath is a small, black device. Try and attach it to something of Zach's he always carries with him.'

'We're *bugging* him?'

'It's not a bug, it's a tracker. Any info, or possible evidence we get from a bug, seeing as we're not police, won't hold up. But a tracker will help us gather further intel we could use. You okay with that?'

'Yes,' Isla said. 'Oh, and there's someone else to add to the list. I told you what the nurse, Heather, said about my brother calling straight after I'd been admitted the night of the attack, but that it wasn't Fraser?'

'Yes, in the email you sent.'

'Right. And it might not be relevant, but the only other person I haven't told you about is the bloke who ghosted me last year. If we're going on the theory it was someone I know, and that we shouldn't rule people out . . .'

Jase took out his mobile. 'Name?'

'Lance. Gave his surname as Walker, but that was probably fake.' Isla leaned back against the wall, the sudden realisation she'd likely been taken in by a bunch of lies hitting her. 'God, maybe Lance isn't even his name.'

'Focus, Isla.'

'Sorry, yes. I met him through a dating app. He knew I had a brother, but I never mentioned him by name.'

Jase tapped these details in. 'Okay. I'll check it out.'

'How will I contact you again?'

'There's something else in the box of goodies I gave you that'll help with that,' Jase said, smiling for the first time during this encounter. 'Be careful, Isla.' He looked into her eyes, touched his hand to her cheek, then turned and walked out.

Chapter Forty-Eight

It had been such a wonderful afternoon, Zach dared to believe everything would work out as he'd hoped. Now, walking hand in hand with Isla as they headed back to her house, the sun warming his skin, his mind was calm, his muscles relaxed. For the first time in ages, he felt great.

It can't last.

Nothing good ever did.

If he could wipe the past year from his consciousness, maybe he stood a chance. But then, it wasn't just this time period that had defined him. If he had to erase that year, he'd also have to go back further, blotting out huge chunks of his life. He sighed.

'You okay? You're very quiet?' Isla said. Zach paused, turning to face her. She was naturally beautiful, didn't require make-up to enhance her features and embodied everything he found attractive in a woman. Yet, he'd messed it up. *Was* messing it up. His actions had gone too far now, though. There was no turning back.

'Yep, fine,' he said, tipping up her chin with his fingers and kissing her soft lips. 'Just being in the moment.'

She leaned into him, and for a few precious seconds nothing

else mattered. Then, as he pulled back, he caught the uncertainty in her eyes. And something else too.

He was kidding himself if he thought she didn't know. Or at least suspect him. He'd been so afraid she'd remember, had been doing all he could to prevent it – yet, she'd been afraid she wouldn't remember, and was doing all she could to ensure it. Everything now pointed to the inevitable: she knew he was the guilty one. He had to give it to her, she was playing it well. There hadn't been any obvious clues. Had he not been listening in, watching her every move, he wouldn't have realised; she was good at deceiving him. And if she definitely knew, then she was allowing him to stay with her, in her house, being with him, making love to him, all to keep him close. Maybe she was watching his every move too. Waiting for the opportune moment to confront him. Or report him to the police. Whatever way, it seemed for the moment they were trapped in a horror of their own making.

Their opposing needs meant there was no happy ending for them both.

One of them had to lose.

Chapter Forty-Nine

Since their return home, Zach had closed himself away in the second bedroom. Taking the day off to spend time with Isla apparently had its consequences, and now he was catching up on work before settling down for the evening. It suited Isla because she wanted to check out the pamper gifts Jase had sent. She'd been so curious after he told her to look inside the candle it'd been all she could think about. As she snuck past the bedroom Zach's office now occupied, she stopped short. Had Zach just mentioned her name?

Isla strained to hear what was obviously a phone call.

'I think it would be better coming from you,' Zach said. With Isla's interest now piqued, she continued to hover outside the room.

'Look, I'm not in the best position here. I'm trying to keep her positive, help her move forwards.'

Isla's breath caught. He was definitely talking about her. She placed her ear to the door. She didn't want to misinterpret his words.

'This will set her back – you know that,' Zach said. Isla thought she heard concern in his voice, but then his tone shifted. 'It was your decision – you tell her.' He practically hissed the words. A few seconds went by, then Isla realised he'd ended the call. Whoever it'd been, he was not happy with them. Sounded as though he was annoyed for being put in an awkward situation. How would she find out who he'd been speaking with and what it was he assumed would set her back?

Confused, but wanting to know more, Isla carried on into the bedroom. Getting down on her knees, she dragged the gift basket from Jase out from underneath the bed, then removed the candle as he instructed. A door banged. Isla froze. Shit – was Zach going to come in and catch her? She heard him stomping down the stairs. She had to be quick, he'd probably come back up looking for her any minute. Isla took out the tiny tracking device, shoved the basket back under the bed, and sneaked into the office. There was no time to dawdle, she needed to find something to attach the device to.

'Isla? Where are you, love?' She heard Zach's muffled words. He'd be up the stairs within seconds. The briefcase. It was lying open on the desk. Perfect. She rushed over to it, pushing the urge to rifle through the papers aside. She had to get it done, and get out.

'Hey, babe? You okay?' Zach's voice was closer. He was calling from the bottom of the stairs. If she answered now, he'd realise she was in the office.

Quick, quick.

In her haste she handled it clumsily, dropping the tiny device on the floor.

Fuck!

She should abandon this attempt. She was pushing her luck. Footsteps on the stairs.

She tried to think up a lie as to why she was in the office, but her mind went blank. Finally, she placed the tracker in the briefcase and stepped away from it, casting her eyes around for a reason she could tell Zach she was in there. God, he was almost there.

The sound of the doorbell made her jump.

A rush of air expelled from her lungs as she heard Zach's steps retreating and the front door open. She slipped out the office and was halfway down the stairs before Zach looked up.

'Were you calling me?' she asked, smiling.

'Yes. Just wondering where you'd got to.' Zach was standing holding a huge bouquet of flowers. 'These just came for you,' he said, thrusting the flowers towards her.

Isla took them from him awkwardly. They were heavy. 'Oh, these are gorgeous, Zach. Thank you. Can you take them though?'

'They aren't from me,' he said, turning away. 'They're from your brother.'

The atmosphere was thick with unspoken doubts, accusations and hidden lies. That's how it felt to Isla, anyway – but paranoia had a part to play in that. She was sitting at one end of the sofa, Zach the other, the six o'clock news blaring loudly from the telly to cover the awkward silence.

It was in stark contrast to their walk at the beach, when, for a moment in time, it seemed maybe she'd imagined everything. That Zach was the good man she'd believed him to be just a few days ago. That their relationship would blossom; be stronger because of what had happened, not weakened due to it. When he'd kissed her on the way home her doubts and worries briefly melted away. Until the reality of what Jase had said minutes before hit her.

Zach's phone conversation, whoever it was with, was clearly about her. Now, she wanted nothing more than to ask him outright who he'd been speaking with and exactly what they were talking about. But if she did, then he'd know she'd been listening. Did it even matter at this point, though? What was an overheard conversation in comparison to a bugged one? Zach could hardly take the moral high ground on this.

In for a penny . . .

'You're very distant tonight,' she said. Zach turned sharply, as if jolted out of a trance.

'Sorry . . . I—' He gave a deep sigh, not going any further. Isla waited a few seconds, but when it appeared he wasn't going to expand, she decided to come straight out with it.

'I heard you. Earlier, on the phone.' She kept her voice steady, but her insides quivered. It was all very well beginning this, but she had no idea which direction it would take; how it would end. She paused, waiting for a reaction. Zach stared blankly ahead. 'Zach? Did you hear me?'

'Yeah, I heard.' His voice was flat.

'It was about me. That was obvious from what you were saying. So, who was it and what is it that you're afraid will set me back?'

'I don't want to talk about it. You shouldn't have been listening.' He got up, and without looking at her, left the room.

Anger flooded her body. *She* shouldn't have been listening? How had he managed to turn this back on her when he was the one stalking her every move, recording her every phone call? Isla flew off the sofa and up the stairs after him.

'How dare you!' she said, bursting into his office.

Zach put his hands up. 'Okay, okay. I'm sorry. I just didn't want to be the one to tell you, that's all. You got my back up, trying to force my hand.'

'Tell me now, or you can leave,' she said slowly. 'It's up to you.' It was the first time Isla had even come close to telling Zach to move out. Despite what Jase and the team had advised her, she'd been adamant to stay put, and have Zach remain in her house, so she could keep an eye on him. But giving this ultimatum felt good; released some of the pent-up stress and emotions she'd been holding on to and covering up. Looking at Zach's shocked expression, Isla knew it had hit home. It had become clear he also wanted to maintain his surveillance of her, so the last thing he'd want is to be thrown out.

'Isla,' he said gently. 'Come on, love.' He walked towards her, but she took a step back to show him she was serious. She wasn't going to be easily placated.

'It can't be that bad, Zach. I'm not a child, I don't need protecting. What is it?'

'I was talking to Nicci!' His words erupted in a shout. His face reddened as he put the palm of his hand to his head then swept his fingertips roughly through his hair. 'And this has nothing to do with me. I'm the last to know, all right?'

'Well, that isn't true, now is it? I'm obviously the last to know! But what, Zach? Last to know *what*?' Isla's voice raised an octave, her frustration growing. The room was charged with their respective sparks of emotion. It was almost too much to bear. But Isla stood her ground. Waited for an explanation.

'She got your promotion,' he said. 'I'm sorry.'

Confusion stormed her mind. It was as if all the oxygen had been sucked from the atmosphere and her brain was being starved of it. She gasped. 'I . . . I don't understand. What do you mean she *got* my promotion?'

'Dad decided you'd been off for long enough, and that when you returned you wouldn't be . . . fit . . . to take on the extra responsibilities—'

'He can't *take away* my promotion, Zach. That's not by the book. I'll take it up with . . .' In that moment, hot tears and anger combining, she couldn't think who she'd be able to take it up with, but she knew he couldn't get away with it. There were employment laws to protect people in this situation – there had to be. 'Whoever I need to. A solicitor if I have to,' she said, waving her arms.

'I knew this would be upsetting. It's why I didn't want to be the one to tell you.'

'Ah, I see.' Isla took further steps away from Zach, her back slamming against the wall. 'So, you'd rather Nicci tell me she's stolen my job? Not have to deal with me having a meltdown.' This was not what Isla had expected to hear and on top of everything else, it was too much; a stab in the back. 'I've worked for years to get this promotion, and some *low-life* –' Isla lurched forwards, getting right up to Zach's face as she said those words '–attacked me and *I'm* the one who gets punished? That's great. Thanks for not wanting to support me in this.'

'I do want to support you. I will . . .'

'But you weren't even going to tell me. You wanted to be a coward and avoid the fallout. That's not being supportive.'

'I moved in with you to support you. Now you're making me out to be the bad person.'

'Well, aren't you?'

They stared wide-eyed at each other. And it felt as though they'd crossed a line somehow – that one was daring the other.

Isla wanted to scream: *Go on. Be honest. Tell me what you did.* And at the same time, she imagined Zach was thinking: *Go on, accuse me. Tell me what you know.*

'I'm not going to listen to any more of this. Take it up with Nicci. My dad. Get a solicitor onto it. Whatever you goddamn please. But I'm out.' He turned and grabbed his suit jacket from the back of the chair, then closed and picked up his briefcase. His jaw clenched, Zach stared at her and she thought he was going to say something else. Instead, he pushed past her. Isla stood, rooted to the spot. She heard his footsteps pounding the stairs. As he was leaving, Isla heard him shout back up the stairs.

'You're on your own. Good luck with that.'

The front door slammed shut.

Chapter Fifty

Isla didn't know whether to be more shocked about her friend taking her job from her, or Zach upping and leaving in the way he'd just done. Maybe it was the reaction he wanted. She couldn't grill him, blame him, if he weren't there. She wasn't sure if it was a show of frustration or a manipulative move: set her up by telling her something potentially explosive, then leave her on her own to stew – or to act. He might well watch from afar to see what she did next. The likelihood he wasn't coming back, though, was slim. She couldn't imagine he'd leave her to it, allow her to go 'unchecked'. He must now know she was gathering evidence about who her assailant was and without him being at close hand, he wouldn't be privy to what she was remembering. Listening to her calls, tracking her movements would only tell him so much. She felt it was what was *inside* her mind that concerned him most.

Isla hadn't seen this latest bombshell coming; hadn't imagined Nicci would go behind her back, undermine her and steal her promotion. There was a creeping sensation making her skin itch – a question lying beneath the surface that Isla didn't want to consider: were they in this together? Nicci had been so pleased for her when she'd finally gained the recognition for her hard work and skills. To think she'd snatch that away from her, stepping into her shoes within weeks of being brutally attacked was utterly gut-wrenching. It seemed as though slipping into her role had come easy to Nicci, and that hurt. Should she believe Zach's word on it, though? Admittedly, believing Kenneth Biggins and the senior team would allow it wasn't as hard. Isla had been replaced.

Had it been the plan all along?

It had been, after all, Nicci's idea to throw a promotion party for her. She chose her place as the venue, arranged the date and time, and invited the people. Now she was the one with the promotion. Anger bubbled; there was increased energy as adrenaline forced its way through her. Isla was close to erupting. She had to move, stomp around the house, anything to release it.

She had to call Nicci. This couldn't wait.

Isla snatched up the landline, then slammed it back down. Of course, Zach had thought of everything. She couldn't use this phone without fear of him listening in. Although, maybe she could play it to her advantage. Ranting at Nicci would be what Zach would expect from her. Its absence might rouse suspicion. And if she knew Zach would be hearing her every word, she could use that knowledge to detract attention and hoodwink Zach: lead him to think she didn't suspect him at all. Let him believe he'd won this particular battle.

She dialled Nicci.

The mobile went to voicemail. She tried again. Within a few rings Nicci's voice cut in with her impossibly cheery recorded message: 'I've got more interesting things to do than talk to you right now. Let me know what you want and I'll get back to you when I'm bored.' It ended with a girly giggle. After several more tries, Isla launched the phone across the lounge. It hit the wall with a cracking sound, then thudded to the ground near the bookcase. After pacing up and down some more, Isla ran upstairs and slammed her bedroom door. In an attempt to neutralise her anger, she yanked the box back out from under the bed and looked through the rest of the items in the pamper basket. Jase had mentioned there was something in there to help her communicate.

Prodding the packets containing the face mask, then foot mask, Isla was amazed to feel a small, hard object. Curiosity building, she tore it open and a little black plastic item dropped into her lap. She picked it up, frowning as she turned it over in her palm. What was she meant to do with this? On closer examination, she realised it was hinged. She flipped it open and gasped. It was a mobile phone. It was about two inches long. Surely it wasn't real? The buttons were tiny, she had to really focus her eyes, but she guessed for the intended purpose, it would suffice. Was this phone even legal? She imagined it would be used for purposes that weren't, that was for sure; she didn't want to think too hard about how something this small could be smuggled into prisons and used for unlawful means.

Isla switched it on; it was fully charged with one contact number stored. She picked up the other packets from the gift basket and opened the face mask. Curled inside that was the USB cable to charge it. Jase really had thought of everything. Nicci might not be answering the home phone because her phone had caller ID. She wouldn't know this number.

But, what if Zach was with Nicci?

If Isla called, on an unrecognisable number, it would alert Zach to her having another source of communication. Unable to safely call Nicci to rant at her, Isla took the only other option open to her. She called Jase.

Chapter Fifty-One

Christie's Crime Addicts – True Crime Podcast

Excerpt from recorded episode – *The Body on the Beach: Update*

[DOUG] Not everything is as clear-cut as it seems – which is certainly the case with the recent murder investigation in the bay. We've covered a number of angles in our podcasts, interviewed people, had phone-ins – and of course, the Christie's team have been delving into the circumstances too – because that's what we love to do. We'd gathered solid background information, as well as some exclusive material along the way and, rest assured, anything relevant will be handed over to the investigating team. But, as regular listeners will know, if we've covered a true-life crime, we will always come back to it if new evidence comes to light – if an unsolved case reopens, or if there are updates to inform you of.

With that in mind – for today's podcast – Ed, Jase, Christie and I will be bringing you the latest development in a previously featured case. That of the body on the beach. Jase, you were the one to revisit this and investigate a little yourself – tell us what you found.

[JASE] Sure. To recap, back in March last year, the body of a man was found washed up on Meadfoot Beach early one morning and investigating officers struggled to ID him. At the time, the reason given for this was that he'd been in the water a fair while and had no forms of identification, no distinguishing marks and no one matching his description had been reported as missing. It went quiet in the media after the initial flurry of attention and most reports concluded he was a homeless guy who'd maybe taken his own life. However, what wasn't being reported was that another reason they'd been unable to identify him was because his fingers had been severed and his teeth removed. So, it didn't look like drowning, or suicide, or any other natural causes. It was murder. Following a number of dead ends and false leads, the trail went cold, along with the case.

[DOUG] And now? What's the update on this case?

[JASE] Well, someone came forward. A woman who'd been reluctant to mention her partner had gone missing.

[DOUG] And was the victim her partner?

[CHRISTIE] Presumably, only that wasn't confirmed. However, it was the best lead the police had received. We'd also tracked down the investigator responsible for the case and offered up what *we* knew of course – and together with the new information, they were able to make a positive identification.

[JASE] Obviously a result. The downside being the evidence just wasn't there to link the murder with a suspect.

[CHRISTIE] Unless it was the girlfriend who had something to do with it. Would certainly explain the reason she didn't report him missing sooner.

[ED] Well, that's where it became interesting.

[DOUG] Thought you'd been a bit quiet today, Ed!

[ED] I bide my time. [Laughs] With a positive ID and with

what we'd given the police, a few things dropped into place. And today, we can give you the victim's name.

[Interval music]

[DOUG] Be sure to keep listening. We'll be back following this short advertisement.

Chapter Fifty-Two

Isla took the mini mobile and went outside into the back garden, away from anywhere she thought might have recording devices. A few solar lights illuminated the path up to the highest tier of the garden, and she perched on the top stone step, cold seeping through her jeans. She struggled to hold the phone as the shivering fingertips of her casted hand attempted to hit the right numbers on the tiny keypad. It took several tries before the call connected and she finally heard the trilling of the ringtone. Despite the cold, Isla was clammy with sweat.

'You found it. Are you okay?'

Hearing Jase's soft, calm voice on the other end brought tears to her eyes, the sudden awareness of her situation over-whelming her. She swallowed hard to dispel the lump in her throat.

'He stormed out about twenty minutes ago,' she said. Isla turned her head, checking all around her in case someone was in earshot. There was no movement from the neighbouring house. In fact, she'd not heard any noises coming from them the past few days. Her earlier memory of the banging noises came back to her now, but she had no time to consider them. Zach might well turn up again at any moment.

'What happened?'

'He told me Nicci's taken my role at work – snapped up the opportunity to have *my* promotion. Now I'm seriously beginning to question her involvement in all of this. I don't know who to trust anymore, Jase.'

'I know – it must seem like everyone and everything is working against you right now. But we'll figure it all out, keep you safe. I . . .'

The line went quiet, and Isla took the phone from her ear to check she hadn't accidentally disconnected him. 'You still there?'

'Yes, sorry. I want to promise I'll keep you safe, Isla. But, you have to help, too. It's not safe for you to be with Zach. I'm glad he's stormed out, but he'll be back. One way or another, he has to finish what he's started.'

Isla's heart thudded. Hearing Jase state what she already knew, but had been avoiding putting into words for fear of making it real, was a wake-up call.

'What about gaining proof? We haven't got enough to link him with my attack yet. All we have is evidence of him tracking and listening to me, but he could explain that away by saying *he* was fearful for my safety. By the way, I placed the little tracker in his briefcase. He took it with him. Can you see where he is?'

'*Christ.*' There was rustling and some clattering over the line. 'I wish you'd mentioned that at the outset . . .' Jase said. 'Hang on, I'll access the software.'

Isla waited as Jase checked his computer. After a minute or so, he spoke again.

'He's close by. Ilsham Marine Drive – isn't that where his parents live?'

'Yes. Typical. He's run back to Mummy and Daddy.' Isla had thought she was falling in love with Zach, but the more she thought about him, his background, his family – the more she disliked him. Had she been blindly going along with the relationship prior to this? And, thinking about it, why had he still been living at home anyway? All the money they had, and he chose to remain in the family home until his recent offer to stay with her. He'd told Isla he was there for ease, although admitted that working *and* living with his father had been a struggle. Isla couldn't think of many worse things than spending twenty-four hours a day with Scrooge.

She'd watched Zach carefully since he'd moved in with her – weighing up whether he was like his father or not – and she'd concluded that while he did have some of his father's traits, he appeared to take after his mother. The harsher edges were rounded off. Not as sharp and spiky as Kenneth Biggins. Not on the exterior, anyway.

Now, it seemed, she'd made a mistake to think he was any better. She was beginning to realise Zach's bad traits were under the surface – not as obvious as his father's – but maybe worse. More dangerous. There was something to be said for being able to see someone's bad side – the fact they made it so obvious offered a safety net of sorts. You could choose whether to 'sign up' for it, or walk away. But with Zach, what he'd kept hidden meant Isla had been sucked in by his charm like a fish being deliberately, carefully reeled in before being wrenched from the water and killed.

'Come to mine. I'll send over a taxi,' Jase said. 'Together we'll figure out our next move.'

'Oh, I don't know . . .' Isla hesitated. 'I mean, thanks for the offer, but that seems a little hasty. He's at his parents'. He won't come back now tonight I shouldn't think. And despite what we have so far, his actions don't *prove* he's behind my attack. I need more.'

'I'll come to you, then. I have something I need to tell you and I'd prefer to do it in person.'

'Oh? Can't you just tell me now?'

'As I said, it'd be better if I was with you.'

'And if Zach does come back and finds you here?'

'I'll say I'm a concerned friend.'

'We both know if Zach is guilty of what I suspect him of, he's more than likely looked into where I was the other day and will have researched the Christie's Crime Addicts team by now. We know he's been keeping tabs on me one way or another. He could recognise you and our cover will be blown.'

'He didn't recognise Doug when he delivered the parcel.'

'Not that he let on, no. But don't forget, he's watching, waiting – and we can't be sure he's not just keeping things to himself, making his own plans what to do with what he finds out.'

'Okay, fair enough. I'm tracking him, though, don't forget. If I see he's on the move, I'll leave.'

Isla considered this for a moment. 'Okay. Come on over then.'

Chapter Fifty-Three

It was inevitable he would find himself in a compromising position at some point. The clock was ticking and he was becoming tangled up in the lies. How had he fucked up so badly? Trying to cover up one lie had led to the telling of others – each one bigger than the last, and all because of his father. Zach's stomach knotted; his fists balled as he watched Kenneth Biggins moving from room to room in his mansion. The studio was Zach's safe haven, always had been. He was out of sight, out of mind there.

Spending the past few weeks with Isla had been good in many ways. He'd glimpsed what a normal life could look like. But now the curtain was falling, and he had to act fast to limit the damage. Telling Isla about Nicci might have bought him some time; she would be focusing her anger and attention on her, not him. Soon enough, though, it would all piece together – her knowledge about him altering files to cover his tracks, accounts not adding up, the fact he'd not been at the office the time of her attack, would all come to light. She'd begun digging, and the only outcome was the unearthing of his lies.

The police hadn't looked at him as a suspect, or at least they hadn't questioned him as one. They believed him to be the caring, loving boyfriend who was distraught about Isla's attack. Her brush with death. It had been relatively easy to convince Nicci he'd been working late, and with the help of some fudged paperwork and a phone call putting him in the building – and thanks to one of his colleague's lapse of judgement when it came to telling the police what time he'd left – they didn't look into his alibi any further. It hadn't been warranted. But if Isla had figured it out, had help to check the facts and had gathered evidence to the contrary, he was in trouble.

He'd hoped it wouldn't come to this.

With the aid of his mobile's torchlight, Zach packed up a rucksack with everything he'd need.

It wasn't going to be easy. He really liked Isla – *loved* her – even thought she'd be the one. All of what he'd done up to the night of the attack had been to ensure it; Isla was part of his future plans. Or had been.

He hefted the bag onto his shoulder and as he was checking if the coast was clear, he saw another shadow cross the lounge inside the house. Larger, bulkier than his father.

Graham.

Zach huffed. Bloody creep was never far away. How he spoke to Zach the other day still angered him; he couldn't wait to be rid of the hulk of a sidekick. He'd always known there was a possibility his dad might hand the reins over to Graham instead of him. But if he did, it would be temporary. Bit by bit, Zach would ensure he was squeezed back out again. He was accruing enough money to buy the shares to the entire company. Then it wouldn't matter if Kenneth had him written out of the will. And by the time Kenneth was ready to stand down and hand over the company, he would have the funds. Fuck Kenneth and Graham. Biggins & Co would be his one way or another.

He gave a furtive glance around the darkened studio. He'd have to come back afterwards to deal with all the things that could link him to Isla's attack. Both of them. The fact she'd considered Simon as a suspect and relayed it to Nicci was perfect – he'd plant some damning evidence in his possession to divert the attention from himself. He'd go to Nicci's straight after he was done. She'd supply the alibi this time. After all, he knew how she'd managed to get the promotion and she wouldn't want that getting out.

Chapter Fifty-Four

Jase said he'd only be fifteen minutes. Why did it feel more like an hour had passed?

Isla stopped pacing as the ring of the house phone blared loudly in the hushed room. So, she hadn't broken it after all. Zach would probably listen in, but she picked it up anyway.

'I need to talk to you.' The voice sounded distant. 'About something I've done.'

'I wondered when you'd find the backbone to tell me you'd stolen my job while I've been recovering from a *brutal attack*.' Nicci's voice had triggered an overwhelming need to yell at her friend, blame her for everything that was happening; she didn't even care if Zach could hear her. 'You came to my house, bearing gifts and positivity, but then practically ignored me – I called you earlier and you couldn't even bother yourself to answer and you're meant to be my friend, Nicci. What else have you been hiding from me? Maybe you know more than you've told me about—'

'I've been having an affair with Ken!' Nicci cut in, her words ringing in Isla's ears.

'Who the fuck is Ken? And why is that even relev— Oh . . . Shit.' Isla's words stuck in her throat, the penny dropping. 'Ken as in Kenneth bloody Biggins? *Scrooge*?' Suddenly, this information took precedence over the fact Nicci had snatched her job from her.

'Yes. I know . . . I wouldn't believe me either. But it's true. It doesn't detract from the awful thing I've done accepting the opportunity to step into your shoes. I'm sorry.'

Isla was stunned into silence. She sat heavily on the sofa, the air in her lungs ejecting like wind whipped from a boat's sails.

'Isla? You still there?'

'Yeah . . . I don't know what to say.'

'About Ken, or the fact I took the promotion?'

'Both, Nicci. Obviously. Christ. Why? You never once said a word about Kenneth, not in *that* way. You always slated him, called him a misogynistic pig!' It was beyond incredible to think Nicci would want to be with that man. Isla hadn't even suspected anything. Maybe Nicci was lying about it, for reasons unclear at this time. Now she thought about it, she did remember seeing a new nickname in Nicci's phone contacts the night of the party, when she'd been trying to find her Spotify playlist. Perhaps it was Kenneth's. She felt physically sick. 'Were you sleeping with him to get promoted?'

'Sort of. I guess.' Nicci's voice was thick with tears. Isla realised it must all be true. This couldn't be an easy phone call for her to make. Nonetheless, she shouldn't be feeling bad about her colleague's actions. Nicci had made a clear decision to act in the way she had.

'Why bother telling me? Didn't Zach inform you he'd already spilled the beans? About the promotion, I mean. Not about my friend shagging the boss.'

Her words were likely to cause hurt. Knowing it didn't stop her from saying what was on her mind.

'No, he didn't – I spoke with him earlier and he told me *I* had to be the one to break the news to you. He's not who you think he is, Isla.'

'And Kenneth is who *you* think *he* is?'

'What you see is what you get with him. Zach, on the other hand, well – I think he's sneaky. Keeps his flaws well hidden; his true intentions are buried deeper and I don't think any of them are good. And from what Simon let slip the other day . . .'

'Simon's back to work?'

'He came in for a catch-up before he starts back next week. He took me to one side and asked after you. Wanted to know if you were still with Zach.'

'What's it got to do with him?' Despite the evidence stacking up high against Zach, Isla hadn't quite let go of her initial suspicions about Simon. An image shot into her mind. 'He tried to kiss me!'

'What?'

'God, I remember now. I was leaving yours and he tried it on with me. I pushed him away and walked off. He cornered me in the filing room the week before too.' Had she been too quick to stop digging into Simon? If he'd followed her from the party, then he could've easily been the one who'd jumped her.

'I can't believe he'd hurt you, Isla. A drunken pass is one thing; it's a huge leap to think he'd attack you. Besides, I actually think he's just concerned about you. He told me something to pass on to you. Said to be careful. That Zach "had form".'

'Really?' Isla had to balance any information from Simon against his possible reasons for disclosing it. What better way to take the focus off himself than to implicate Zach? Admittedly, though, she had a gut feeling Simon's intentions were good. 'For what?' she asked.

'According to him, Zach had a few – well – issues – with a

233

past relationship. Became fixated on this poor girl, wouldn't leave her alone. Said he was completely obsessive.'

'And he knows this how?'

'It was Simon's mate who was the unlucky recipient of Zach's jealous outrage. Had to file a restraining order after he beat the shit out of him.'

This bombshell struck a chord, and something in Isla's mind made a connection, but it was fleeting, her memory not able to assimilate all the information. She was about to question Nicci, ask her what else Simon had said, then remembered that Zach might be listening in. If this were all true, Jase was right – she wasn't safe here. She should leave with Jase.

'I have to go, Nicci. Speak soon.' Isla was watching out the window and, seeing Jase walking up the path, cut the call. She rushed to the front door. With her fingers to her lips, she slipped outside. 'Shouldn't alert him to the fact you're here.'

'Okay, but not sure here's the best place to chat, either.' Jase stepped back from the door, looking at the house next door. The curtains twitched.

'Back garden is more secluded. Come through, quietly.'

Sitting on the top tier of the garden as she had earlier, Isla relayed the conversation she'd just had with Nicci. Jase remained quiet while she spoke, but he was on edge, fidgety, his hands constantly moving.

'Are you cold?' Isla said.

'Not really. Look, I need to tell you something.'

'God, not you as well. What more is there?'

Jase gave a sympathetic smile. 'This might come as a shock . . .'

Isla braced herself for whatever new revelation she was about to hear. 'Go on.'

'As you're aware, we were looking into other potential

suspects. We needed to eliminate others in order to build stronger evidence pointing to Zach.' He paused.

'Yes,' Isla said, keen for him to get to the point.

'You gave me a name. Wondered if an ex might have been the man who'd called the hospital immediately after your admission.'

'Lance. Yes, I know it was a long shot . . .' Was Jase about to tell her he *had* been the one who'd called? Isla's mouth dried. If she'd been wrong about Zach, what did that say about her judgement?

'Lance Walker was the name he gave you. And that *was* his name.'

'Okay, so he told the truth and the fact he ghosted me was just bad luck for me, then.'

'Bad luck for him, actually.'

Isla squinted her eyes at Jase. 'What do you mean?'

'He didn't ghost you, Isla. Not in the way you thought. I'm sorry. Lance Walker has finally been identified as the body on the beach.'

Chapter Fifty-Five

Isla shook her head. 'No, that can't be right. You mean the man washed up on Meadfoot Beach last year? It can't have been Lance.'

'I'm afraid that after the team and I did further research, found some interesting links, I passed on some information to my contact in the force. That, together with a separate report from a woman who'd eventually reported Lance missing, helped them make an identification. The other woman, presumably his girlfriend or ex, hadn't come forward imme-diately; she'd waited for months for some undisclosed reason. But the timeline she gave appears to coincide with the last time he texted you.'

'I . . . I can't believe this.' Isla put her head in her hands; her chest was tight, her limbs weak. 'And all this time I've been slagging him off, telling everyone who'd listen what a shit he'd been – a coward who hadn't even been able to face me to ditch me.'

'You weren't to know.'

'But, if I'd reported him as missing right away . . .'

'Seems like you weren't alone in that. It might be he had a habit of starting new relationships then doing a disappearing act? You can't blame yourself as you barely knew him. Ghosting does happen – remarkably often these days. Your conclusion was the most obvious to make.'

'I appreciate you trying to make me feel better about it, but I won't. Poor man. Seems I was unlucky for him.' Or was it more than bad luck? Was there more to it than that? As if Jase were reading her thoughts, he piped in.

'The question bothering me is whether Lance's death and your attack are linked. It's why I don't want you to stay here. I know it's your house, I know you believe being here with Zach means you can keep a closer eye on him, but I think he's a very dangerous man. Walk away. We'll go to the police together—'

'With what *evidence*, though? I think what we have is stuff he could explain away. He might get arrested, but they wouldn't have enough to hold him. Then I'd be in more danger – he'd know I'd been the one to give his name to the police and he'd have even greater reason to get rid of me. Permanently. I want to gain enough evidence to ensure they can charge him and it sticks.'

'If he was responsible for your attack, I'd put money on him being the one who killed Lance.'

Isla spun around to face Jase. 'Are you serious?'

'It fits, Isla.'

Isla shot up from the step, adrenaline raging inside her. 'This just gets worse and worse,' she said, pacing as her mind scrabbled to make sense of it all. It was like a bad film playing out in real life. Zach – responsible for her attack *and* Lance's murder? But he'd never shown any hint of jealousy, no warning that he could be capable of hurting anyone. And all at once, Nicci's bombshell came to her. 'Oh, my God, Jase!' She sat back down, facing him as her words began spilling from her like cascading water. 'I'm not sure how long ago this happened, but Nicci has just told me that Zach received a restraining order against him. Something to do with beating up the boyfriend of an ex of his who he'd apparently become obsessed with following the break-up.'

'So, he has a record of violence?' There was a hint of excitement in Jase's tone.

'I guess so. And a history of obsessive behaviour. But I hadn't seen any evidence of it myself.' Isla thought for a moment. 'Also, I wasn't going out with Zach when Lance was on the scene. How could he have even known about me seeing Lance?'

'You never spoke about him at work?'

'Well, yes. But Zach wasn't part of those conversations.'

'But you and Zach *did* work together then?'

'Yeah – I mean he spent most of his time on the top floor, but our paths crossed a fair bit. He'd made various attempts to get me to go out with him, so I was definitely on his radar, so to speak.'

'Maybe he'd been watching you – listening to your conversations – for a lot longer than we thought.'

Isla shivered. Was Zach capable of murder? Nothing in his manner, none of his actions prior to her attack, had ever given her cause for concern. Had she simply not seen any of his abnormal behaviour? Or was he very good at keeping it hidden? Lance's death could've been an accident – maybe Zach *had* beaten him up, much the same way as he'd done to Simon's friend, and it went too far. His intention might not have been to kill him. Likewise, if he really was the man who'd attacked her, she only had Heather and the nurses at Derriford who'd spoken of their belief her attacker had meant to kill her – the police didn't frame it in the same way. He could've been trying to frighten her, or temporarily incapacitate her to keep her out of the way while he got rid of evidence of whatever he was up to with the company accounts. Whether it was covering for his father, or himself, he was involved deeply in some form of illegal activity; she felt certain.

Jase checked his mobile. 'Zach's still at his parents' – I've got the app running on my phone.'

'Good. I'm going to go over there now.' Isla got up from the step and brushed down her clothes with one hand. 'It'll be a safe environment – his parents will be close by if it gets nasty. I'll pretend I'm there to make it up with him, and at the same time try and get him to open up. Ask questions about when he first had feelings for me and maybe mention my previous boyfriends, see if it elicits a reaction. If I can get a better picture about his past actions, particularly around the time Lance disappeared, maybe we can link him to that . . .'

'I'll come with you.' Jase put his hand on Isla's arm. 'You're not going there alone.'

'No.' Isla shook her head. 'With his track record, and if we're right, he may target *you*. I'm not having your death on my conscience as well as Lance's.'

'I'm a big boy. I'm sure I can handle him.'

'Perhaps Simon's mate and Lance thought the very same thing.' Isla placed her hand over his. 'Look, I'll go into the main house, make sure his parents are close by when I talk to Zach. He's hardly going to do anything in front of them. His father would take him down. Verbally, of course. Seriously, Zach is afraid of Kenneth. I'm absolutely sure of that. Their relationship has been fractured since childhood – God only knows the extent of what went on.'

'Fine. But I'll be outside, in my car, just in case.'

'Or, you could gather up the Christie's team and put together what evidence we've got so far. I'll pack a bag now, then I'll head straight to your office when I'm done. I'll stay away from Zach. Let you protect me,' Isla said, smiling.

'You'll finally do what I asked? Good.'

'Yep. You're right, it's not worth taking the risk now this has all come to light.'

'Sounds like a plan. Although I'd still feel better driving you and waiting outside. I could park down the road, out of sight. I'll call Ed, Christie and Doug from the car, set the ball in motion.'

Isla knew she wasn't going to dissuade him, so gave in. 'Sure. Wait for me in your car then while I get some stuff together.'

Chapter Fifty-Six

Did they think it would be that easy to catch him out?

Zach had paused at the door to the studio to ring the home device, had listened in to the conversation Isla had with Nicci. And had clocked her reactions, feeling sure someone had come to the door. If he went there now, she might not be alone.

Fuck it.

He retreated back inside, sitting on the leather Chesterfield Kenneth had allowed him to take from the main house. He had to think this through carefully. The person at the door was obviously not Nicci. Given the lack of other possibilities, Zach concluded it would be one of the idiot podcast people she'd become obsessed with. He'd read her journal – seen her attempts at gathering evidence against him, Simon and Graham. He'd had to laugh about her suspecting Graham, but Simon was plausible. And to be fair, she'd been close to the mark with her observations about him, too.

It really cut deep to realise she'd turned against him so quickly. How could she betray him after all he'd done for her? It was her fault it had all gone so wrong in the first place. Such a shame it now had to come to this. The stuff she'd written down about him had been circumstantial, though – a tenuous link at best. As far as he could tell, she had nothing noteworthy; nothing concrete the police could take seriously enough to arrest him. But that could change. He had to act fast to nip all of this in the bud. But to get the timings right, to ensure he planted the best evidence at Simon's place at the opportune time, he had to get to Isla first. Do the deed, *then* go to Simon's.

He couldn't stay here: inactivity would spell disaster. But now he had another problem. He could no longer use Nicci as his alibi. The fact she'd chosen to come clean about her affair with Kenneth was a surprise. He hadn't seen it coming – had felt sure she'd do anything rather than risk that coming out. How wrong he'd been; he'd never understand women. He *had* to chance going back to Isla's now. Maybe by the time he got there, she'd be alone again. If not, he'd have to wait it out until the perfect opportunity. Getting Isla out of the picture was one thing; he couldn't afford to add another victim into the mix. Whichever member of the pathetic Christie's Crime Addicts it was, he couldn't feasibly get rid of him as well. There was absolutely no way of pinning *that* on Simon.

Zach got up, confident he could still pull this off. No one had ever suspected him of Lance's disappearance and the last time he'd checked, they hadn't even identified the body, still assuming it to be some homeless bloke. So he was safe there. He had an alibi for the time of Isla's attack and now, with his phone on and left in the studio, together with the briefcase with the tracking device Isla thought she'd covertly attached to it, he'd be placed here at the time of her death. It wasn't airtight, obviously – it could easily be said he'd gone to Isla's without both of those items, but with them finding clear-cut evidence at Simon's together with Isla's voiced concerns over him having followed her from the party, Zach thought it was enough to keep himself distanced from the case.

Having just heard Isla tell Nicci about Simon's failed attempt at making a move on her as she was leaving added weight, too. By the time he'd finished, Simon would undoubtedly be the one with the most solid evidence stacked against him. And it served him right for sticking his nose into *his* business and trying it on with *his* girlfriend. As if once hadn't been enough for him, the slimy prick. He'd allowed him to come out of the last situation unscathed, focusing his anger on his mate who'd started seeing his ex instead. This time Simon would pay.

His new plan was good as long as his bloody father didn't come knocking and realise the studio was empty. To make it more obvious he was there, he should really put a light on, have the telly on, music playing or something. That way, when asked, Kenneth, his mum – even Graham if he was still at the house – would tell the police that Zach was on the premises at the time of Isla's murder. But he ran the risk of one of them popping in to see him if there was a light on. And, finding him *not* there would be something they'd remember if the police came asking questions.

He sighed. This was more complicated than he thought. If it came to it, he'd just have to say he'd had a migraine, turned off all the lights and gone to bed. The CCTV would have captured his arrival at the house earlier and he was going to leave on foot now and he'd go around the side of the property, climb over the wall. It would bring him out the other side of Ilsham Marine Drive, and he could walk along the coastal path for a bit, away from any surveillance. He knew he would also be able to access Isla's from the rear to prevent witnesses seeing him.

Just for good measure, he shoved clothing inside his bed and covered it with the duvet. Might be something a teenager would do when sneaking out without their parents' permission, but it could work. Zach slipped out quietly, locked the studio door and glanced through the glass. He smiled. It did look as though someone was in the bed. The migraine story would work.

It was child's play.

The rest of the plan wouldn't be.

Chapter Fifty-Seven

The car, with Isla in it, drove out of sight as Zach turned the corner to the house. He'd caught a glimpse of her, pale and tired-looking, when she was briefly illuminated by the street-lamp when they passed underneath it. And he'd glimpsed *him*. He knew that face. Zach's heart pumped wildly, adrenaline shooting through his body. Isla was meant to be at the house. His plan was to get rid of her there; it didn't work if she were anywhere else. And especially not with *him* by her side.

Where the hell were they going? Zach cursed. Now he was on foot, there was no way of following. Isla wouldn't have her mobile with her either after she was told about the spyware. *Dammit.* The idea she might be going to stay with *him* swept through Zach's mind. He was screwed if that were the case. He'd have to wait. If she stayed away, though, was under some kind of protection, the opportunity to get to her, the likelihood of her being alone long enough, was drastically reduced.

Zach forced himself through the gap in the shrub-lined border at the back of the house, battling with the thin inter-twining greenery. Then, after checking no one was in the neighbouring garden, he ran down the steps to the back door. He let himself in.

How dare those podcast people push their way in, manipulating Isla while she was vulnerable the way they had. Who did they think they were? And that one who was clearly behind Isla's new-found bravery, the one who'd just driven her away, well, he had a lot to answer for.

'Thinks he's fucking Poirot,' Zach said, pulling off his rucksack, coat and hat, flinging them on the kitchen floor. He yanked the fridge door open, lifting out the bottle of wine. Grasping the neck, he tilted it to his dry lips and began gulping it down while he contemplated how to get around this latest hitch.

Chapter Fifty-Eight

Jase's car was parked right opposite the house. He was sitting, both hands gripping the steering wheel, his focus dead ahead as Isla locked the front door and dashed down the steps towards him, a backpack filled with a few days' worth of belongings. Her heart beat absurdly fast; she was afraid it was going to flip into an abnormal rhythm her anxiety was so high. There was no way of telling if what she was about to do was a good or bad idea. The proof was in the pudding, as her mam would say.

She should've called Rowan before taking this step. If something went wrong, if this decision turned out to be a dangerous one – possibly resulting in her death – her final conversation with her mam would be the hurried one Isla had been keen to close because she was busy trying to gather evidence against Zach. There'd been a rushed 'love you' ending, but no meaningful discussion between the hello and goodbye. Isla hadn't confided in her mam – she knew nothing of her suspicions about Zach, and now she hoped she wouldn't regret that.

'If something . . . bad happens. To me,' Isla said to Jase as she struggled with her seatbelt. 'Will you tell my mam I was planning to go home to Glasgow and spend some quality time with her please.'

Jase shot her a wary glance. 'I'm not going to let anything bad happen to you, Isla. You can tell your mum yourself when you get to Scotland.'

She smiled at him. 'Yeah, but, you know . . . in case. You'll fill her in on everything and tell her I love her, won't you?'

Jase sighed, taking his hands off the wheel and turning in his seat to face her. He took hold of the tops of her arms and gave a gentle squeeze. 'Everything will be fine. I've got your back. But if it makes you happy, then yes – of course I'll make sure she knows. Although I'm sure she already does.'

'I wouldn't be that sure. I did leave her, going to live at the other end of the UK – and I haven't seen her for so long and before the attack, I only spoke to her once a week, if that.' Isla felt tears prick her eyes. 'Right,' she said, turning away from him and sitting up straighter in an attempt to overcome the wash of emotion she'd suddenly experienced. 'Let's go.'

Jase switched on the ignition – the engine gave a brief splutter and Isla thought it wasn't going to start. That would be terrible timing. But, it rattled into life and Jase flashed her a wide smile.

'Had you there for a second, eh?' he said. 'She's a little temperamental sometimes, my ole Vanessa.'

'Vanessa?'

'After my mum.' He shrugged as he manoeuvred the car down the road to the junction. 'I think you and I may have something in common. I didn't tell my mum often enough that I loved her either.'

With Jase using the past tense, Isla concluded his mum had passed. 'So, you named your car after her to make up for it?'

Jase laughed. 'She'd have been *so* impressed I named a battered old Vauxhall after her. And a green one at that – she hated green.'

She examined Jase's profile as he drove. His chiselled jawline with close-trimmed stubble, long, straight nose and sleek neck with large Adam's apple were appealing. Being in his company felt safe, yet also alluring. 'Did you always do stuff to annoy her?' Isla said, hoping Jase hadn't realised she was staring at him.

'Bless her. Yep – right from the get-go, I think. My dad was only ever referred to as "The Sperm Donor" as he disappeared the moment Mum told him she was expecting. Then I was a breech birth, had numerous behavioural issues as a child, then – just when she thought life as a single mum was going to get easier – I decided to go into the army and she worried about me the entire time.'

'Wouldn't going into the army mean she'd worry less, though? I mean, if you were a bit . . . troublesome, surely getting some discipline and being part of a team was beneficial? If I was your mum, I'd have worried more had you *not* gone into the army.'

'There is that. I was likely headed for prison at some point otherwise,' he scoffed. 'It was more to do with fear of losing me, like, forever, though. When I went to Iraq she was a mess. She couldn't bear to think she might lose her only child at twenty-five.'

'Oh, I see. Yes, that must've been such a worrying time for her.' Isla did a quick calculation in her head. From what she remembered, UK troops went to Iraq in around 2003. If Jase was twenty-five then, he was now forty-two. So, there were sixteen years between them. That was quite a substantial age gap. *Why are you thinking about this now?* 'Do you miss the army?' she said, quickly sidestepping her own thoughts.

'Sometimes. My leg injury meant I couldn't continue and I was retired on medical grounds. I was gutted at the time, but I came to terms with it – and it could've been far worse, I mean, I didn't lose my life, or a limb like so many others. Just as luckily, I met Doug soon after and was introduced to true-crime podcasting. Found my niche and haven't looked back since. Shame Mum didn't live to see me more settled . . .'

Isla put her hand on Jase's shoulder. 'Hopefully, she knows.' She wanted to ask if he had a partner, or family of his own, but she didn't want to appear nosy.

'Do you believe in life after death?' He glanced at her before pulling over to the side of a road.

'I want to,' she said. 'Given my brush with death, I kind of need to.' She didn't expand. If she verbalised how she was scared her life might come to an end sooner rather than later, it would make what she was doing more real; more risky. The knowledge her own boyfriend might be capable of killing people who got in his way was too much to comprehend. The fact she was about to walk into the lion's den suddenly felt rash and stupid.

'We're here,' Jase said, killing the engine.

Isla's stomach knotted. Jase had parked far enough away from the Bigginses' place and avoided the streetlights so they wouldn't draw unwanted attention. The cover of darkness was both good and bad – the grip of anxiety was beginning to take hold and Isla had to fight it if she was to get out of the car and head to the house.

'Well, I guess I'll get on in there, then.' Her voice was filled with reluctance and her body seemed to be fighting against the notion too – her muscles freezing, refusing to move.

'Look, are you sure you want to? There are other ways we can gather evidence without putting you in the direct line of fire, as it were.'

Jase was giving her a get-out clause and the urge to snap it up was almost overwhelming. She wanted to say: *no, I'm not sure*, and *okay – let's leave and I'll come to yours and we'll think up a better plan*. But neither of those sentences left her lips. 'Are you afraid I'll balls this up?' Isla said instead. She stared into Jase's eyes, their blueness still striking even in the darkness of the car.

'No, Isla.' He shook his head. 'But, I *am* afraid for you – I can't help that. I don't think I should be letting you go in alone. It doesn't seem right. I said I'd protect you and this totally goes against that promise.'

She wondered if his concern was like the kind of worry he'd display if she were his little sister. She wondered why she cared. Heat blazed at her cheeks.

'I'll be back before you know it.' She tried to give a confident smile. Just in case it wasn't clear, and just in case this was the last time she spoke with him, she added: 'And then I'll go with you to yours and you can protect me from then on.' She laid her good hand on his, stroking the skin with her thumb. She was holding her breath as she waited for his response. He looked down at her hand. He didn't move his, but Isla saw his forehead crinkle into a frown and the horrifying thought she'd misread everything crashed into her mind. Embarrassment was hot in her belly as she quickly removed her hand and spun in her seat to get out.

Chapter Fifty-Nine

'Wait out of sight, and don't come in after me. I'll be as quick as I can, but it might take a while to soften him up,' Isla said just before closing the car door. She turned to look at Jase one final time before disappearing down the road that led to the Bigginses' mansion. She couldn't afford to be sidetracked by her mortifying faux pas; she had to focus on the task ahead of her.

On any other evening, Isla would've stopped to take in the cool evening air – relishing the airborne droplets of salty sea spray on her skin, and would like nothing more than to walk the short distance to the cliffs to appreciate the stunning night-time views across the bay. This wasn't like any other evening though. The Bigginses' huge property came into view, the top floor just visible behind the gates. She'd only ever been to it a couple of times before – the most recent being an invite to a social gathering from Kenneth's ever-attentive wife, Viola, after the company had won a best local business award. Even then, the imposing house, and its equally imposing inhabitants, had made her feel uneasy.

Money didn't afford you the right to superiority. And that's how the Biggins family had first come across to her. She'd altered her opinions as her perceptions had changed over the years, but now, as she pressed the buzzer on the wall beside the huge gates and heard the pompous voice of Kenneth demanding to know who she was and what business she had coming to his house this time of night, Isla's initial instincts returned twofold.

'Sorry to bother you, Mr Biggins. It's Isla. Isla McKenzie,' she said, wanting desperately to add: *you know, the woman who waited three years for a promotion that you then stripped from her behind her back, giving it to your secret lover instead?* 'I would really appreciate it if I could come in and talk to Zach.' There was a long pause, and Isla thought he would dismiss her, telling her to go home. Like a good little girl. 'It's about what he did,' she added, in the hope he'd be intrigued enough to open up. Without another word, the gate clicked, and each half began its slow, dramatic parting. Isla squeezed through the moment it was wide enough.

She didn't go straight to the entrance of the house; she wanted to know if Zach was inside his studio first. She hadn't seen it before, having only been invited to the main house and their previous dates had all ended back at hers, but he'd described it, saying it was situated in the grounds around the side and to the rear. She raised her eyebrows when it came into view – it was hardly what she'd consider a studio; it was the size of a bungalow. It was, however, in darkness, so he must be inside with Kenneth. Which also meant he probably heard her opening gambit over the intercom. Isla hoped Viola was home too; she'd feel more at ease knowing a woman was there to ensure nothing untoward happened. Kenneth wasn't exactly young and agile; it was highly unlikely he alone would prevent Zach harming her. But she felt sure that with his mother observing nothing bad would be allowed to happen.

'He's not here, Isla,' Kenneth said the second he opened the door. He had an old-fashioned-looking velvet dressing gown on, although Isla knew it was likely a new, expensive item. Kenneth enjoyed luxury at any cost.

Isla narrowed her eyes at him, contemplating his statement. The tracker placed Zach in this exact location. Was Kenneth lying to protect him?

'Oh, I assumed he was. But anyway, now I'm here . . .'

Kenneth appeared hesitant, but stepped aside to let her in. 'It's quite late. We weren't expecting company.'

Isla glimpsed the inside of a room she recalled was Kenneth's study – or office, in her language – as she walked towards the lounge, catching sight of two cut-glass, crystal tumblers filled with what looked to be whisky, before she was ushered past. Kenneth Biggins had company. Was the other person still in the study and had merely positioned themselves out of sight when she'd interrupted them? She'd never seen Zach drink whisky – but he would if his father poured it for him.

'What can I do for you, Isla?' Kenneth sat down on one of the two single, high-backed chairs, propping an elbow on each of the sculpted wooden arms, then he rested his chin on the knuckles of his interlocked hands. He regarded her without blinking. When she didn't move, or speak, he nodded towards the sofa.

Now she was confronted with Scrooge, she felt every bit as weak and pathetic as he would want her to feel. She straightened, pushing her shoulders back and directing her focus onto him. She wasn't going to let him intimidate her. She'd worked for him long enough, and before the attack stole her confidence she'd never succumbed to any of his bullying tactics. She refused to start now. And besides, he was in the wrong – she couldn't believe he was acting as though nothing had changed, like he hadn't just given her job to his lover.

Needing to get to the point of her visit, Isla explained Zach had left following a disagreement. She wasn't entirely confident Zach wasn't hiding around the corner, listening – but she had little choice but to broach the subject. She had to do it carefully though. Rocking the boat too violently by categorically stating she thought Zach was involved with underhand, illegal activities within the business probably wouldn't serve her well at this early juncture. But, she did want to ask about the fact Zach had a previous restraining order, *and* get Kenneth to open up about the details of the night of her attack. Zach had said it was his father who'd asked him to stay late, so this was her opportunity to get it straight from the horse's mouth. Any information around these subjects would be beneficial.

The shape of the conversation that had played out in her head before reaching there now eluded her. Everything was tense, her mind was stuttering around for the right things to say. She'd already furrowed a way in by mentioning an argument, so now she just needed to slip in the right things to ensure Kenneth's answers were able to give her clarity. He was looking to her, waiting for her to continue. The pressure was on.

'It's been difficult. Challenging. As you can expect, a near-death experience has lasting effects, good and bad. Zach's been amazing.' She smiled – wanting to get across her gratitude for her knight in shining armour, so Kenneth might shed his own armour. She laid both hands in her lap and began squeezing the parts of her fingers that were visible above her cast. 'But it's been hard for Zach, too. It wasn't exactly the fairy-tale beginning to a relationship, was it?'

'No. It was a terrible thing to happen.' Kenneth steepled his fingers again. 'Not sure why you've come to me about it though.'

She was losing him.

'Because he's not coping very well, I don't think – and I

suppose you being his father and boss, I wondered if it would help if I came by to speak with you. After all, this has a direct effect on your business, so . . .' Isla hoped by bringing it back to money, his successful business, she'd succeed in reeling him back in.

'You said you were here to see Zach, not me.'

'Yes, obviously I wanted to speak to him, smooth things over. But I hoped to talk to you too – kill two birds with one stone, as it were.' She inwardly cringed at her words and before he could question her further, she continued. 'Zach felt responsible in some ways, guilty even, that he'd not been with me the night of the attack. It was the party for my *promotion*,' Isla said, purposely accentuating promotion. 'It was important to me. So, when he said he wouldn't be there, I'd made it quite clear I was disappointed. You can imagine, then, how he felt when he learned I'd been viciously attacked while walking home afterwards.'

'Sure. I can imagine.' His expression was deadpan.

'I thought you might . . . er . . . help.'

Kenneth snorted air down his nose. 'How can I help with *his* guilt?'

'Well, you know he'd do anything to help make you see him in a good light, and I think that's why he couldn't exactly say no when you asked him to stay back late that evening – so, I thought maybe if you reiterated how he'd had no choice . . .'

A brief, yet unmistakable, expression of confusion passed over Kenneth's face, his features hardening before his skin colour reddened. Isla was afraid he was holding his breath like a toddler did when they were having a tantrum.

Zach had lied, and now Kenneth knew it too.

Maybe this was enough to plant the seed of suspicion in Kenneth's mind. If Zach was capable of that lie, and capable of beating someone up – which Isla felt sure Kenneth would have knowledge of – then it wasn't a huge jump to consider he'd been Isla's attacker.

'I give him a hard time because I want him to be more gutsy. More ambitious,' Kenneth said, the brief slip of his mask now corrected; his complexion more its usual colour. 'I don't suffer fools gladly, as you well know by now. And I won't have the good family name – the name of *my* business – affected because he can't make his own decisions. He needs to be up to the job, Isla. If the boy can't stand up for himself then I'm afraid he loses the little respect he's gained.'

His response skirted the issue of Zach's alibi; his disparaging remarks were maybe a cover – a way to shock Isla into silence, or put her off her flow. It was enough of a sign that he was now fully aware of what she might be trying to do here. Whatever his intention, Isla realised Zach was right about him – he really did love his bloody business more than him. Now wasn't the time to feel sorry for Zach, though.

'Yes, I understand, Mr Biggins. All I'm saying is due to that, maybe Zach wasn't able to say no to you.' She tried to engineer the conversation back to the topic of interest. 'Which isn't your fault of course,' Isla said quickly. 'I know your work ethic – it's one of the reasons I've stayed with your company since starting on the graduate scheme five years ago. It's about lifting some of the responsibility of the choice Zach made that night from him, that's all. Would only take a quick chat – a few words from you. I mean, obviously I don't *blame* you for asking him to work late, or him for doing it. Now I want him to feel the same way.'

Kenneth mumbled something inaudible. His feathers were clearly ruffled, and Isla knew she had him on the ropes. If he said, 'But I didn't ask him to work late,' he was essentially calling his son a liar – and a violent attacker – and despite what he'd just said to the contrary, he wouldn't want his only son to be labelled with those attributes. What would his peers think then? It would be extremely bad for business. No, he had to go along with what Isla was saying in this moment to save face, and his reputation, as well as his son's. She should probably back down, before she angered the man. But she was like a dog with a bone now.

'What had been so important that night, Mr Biggins? That Zach had to miss my promotion party?'

'My son is a good man!' Kenneth's voice bellowed. Was he trying to convince her or himself? He sucked in a huge breath, his chest rising up, almost touching his chin, before he exhaled it in a long huff. 'He moved in with you to protect you. How many men would do that? You hadn't even been dating for long.'

In that moment, Isla knew she was going to go around in an endless loop until one of them caved. He bad-mouthed Zach in one breath, then defended him in the next. It appeared he could think and say what he pleased about his son; others could not. She wasn't going to get the clear answer she sought about Zach's alibi tonight. Using what Kenneth said, Isla changed tack herself. 'Is that what he was doing before? When he beat up the new partner of his ex-girlfriend – he was *protecting* her?' Isla clenched the fist of her good hand, her nails digging into her palm. She may well have gone too far now. She watched with dread as Kenneth ejected himself from the chair, eyes wide, proving her assumption correct.

'How do you know about that?' he hissed, his face inches from hers as he stood in front of her, his head lowered.

Keep calm. He's not going to do anything to you.

'Simon.' Isla stated the name with as much conviction as she could muster. She felt bad naming him, but right now it seemed her only option.

'Well, we all have our moments where clarity is clouded. It was a lapse in judgement – that was all.'

'I think you'll find Zach's had rather too many of those, Mr Biggins.'

His nostrils flared, his cheeks colouring as he straightened and took several steps back from Isla. 'As Zach isn't here, I suggest you leave now. Take this up with him when you see him.'

'I'm not sure where he is. As I said, he left my place. Told me he was heading straight here.' It was only a small lie.

'Well, he isn't here.' A flicker of concern crossed his face. It was gone instantly, Kenneth's stern, controlled manner returning, but she'd glimpsed it. 'Anyway, you seem to be better, running around alone at night again.'

The change of subject caught her unaware. 'I'm stronger than you, or Zach, think,' she said, smiling, pleased with her swift comeback. Kenneth merely gave a silent nod. A noise to her left made Isla turn her attention to the doorway. Viola had been absent during the discussion, but came in now, her long cream-coloured silk dressing gown open, flowing as she walked purposefully towards the hearth. She turned, elegantly, taking a seat in the smaller leather chair opposite Kenneth's. Isla had always found Viola to be friendly, yet aloof. She wasn't nearly as intimidating as her husband, but she sensed there was more beneath the surface than the woman had ever let on. Zach's softer side had come from his mother; she felt certain.

'How are you, Isla?' Viola smiled, but it displayed no warmth. 'I'm so sorry to have heard about the awful attack.'

Isla would bet she'd been lurking outside the lounge waiting for the right moment to enter. She would've heard the entire conversation.

'Thank you, Mrs Biggins. I'm getting there. Slowly, but surely, I'm taking back control of my life.' Isla's smile was cool in return.

'Good to hear.' She paused, leaning forward slightly. 'They haven't caught your assailant though.'

Isla narrowed her eyes. It hadn't been phrased as a question. 'No. Not yet.'

'They will,' Viola said. 'Those like him will inevitably strike again.'

It was a weird thing to say. Her tone could be inferred as a warning. But then, Isla was oversensitive and drained from the conversation with Kenneth, and so possibly her reaction was a bit extreme. Viola may well have been stating a fact, not a premonition.

'I've taken up enough of your time. I'll leave you to it,' Isla said, rising from the sofa. 'Have a good evening – and sorry again to have disturbed you.'

As she was about to leave, she turned back to Kenneth. 'Oh, while I'm here can I grab some things from Zach's studio? He said he'd accidentally left a file of mine here when he popped in the other day.'

Kenneth frowned. 'You haven't had need to take work files out of the office, surely?' His voice was clipped and Isla sensed he was angry at the thought she'd removed anything pertaining to accounts from the premises. This might be the perfect opportunity to add fuel to the fire.

'No, no. My private admin, not yours,' Isla said. 'I'd had quite enough trying to go through the work files, Mr Biggins . . . finding – well, *anomalies* . . .' She raised her shoulders in a shrug and grimaced as if she'd accidentally revealed something she hadn't intended.

He shook his head, his cheeks wobbling. 'Anomalies? You didn't bring those to my attention.'

'No,' she said, pausing for dramatic tension. 'I was stopped.' Isla didn't dare say more; she'd given him enough food for thought. Even he should be able to see where she was going with her comment; what she was implying without directly accusing anyone of anything. *Yet.* 'Can I, then?' Isla asked, her hand outstretched.

Kenneth faltered, dithering on the step for a moment, then nodded. He disappeared into the hallway returning with a single Yale key. He held it up but with no attempt to lean forwards and drop it into her hand. He was going to make her reach for it. Such power play. She thanked him as she took it.

'When you're done,' he said, his voice abrupt, 'press the silver, square button to the right of the gatepost to get out.' He looked up and down the driveway, then, without further parting words, went back inside. The heavy wooden door clunked behind him.

Chapter Sixty

Isla cursed. As soon as she flicked the light switch on in the studio, she realised why Jase had been so sure Zach was here. His briefcase lay open on a round table to the side of a large, old-style leather sofa. Had he found her tracking device? It was a clumsy move on her part, but she'd hoped it would work. In her favour, not Zach's.

Now she had no idea where he was. The hairs bristled on her neck and she turned sharply, her eyes darting around, wondering if he was watching her right now. She had a sinking feeling she might've fallen into a trap. Her heart slammed against her ribcage; her eyes widened as her gaze fell on the double bed against the far wall.

Zach was in bed.

None of her muscles moved. She was standing, barely breathing, staring dead ahead at the body-shaped lump beneath the duvet cover. If it was Zach, though, why hadn't he jumped up when she first entered and whacked the light on? The room was still; hushed. There wasn't a single sound of breathing, not a single flinching movement from the body. She swallowed hard. Her mind raced to a conclusion she knew to be one born from fear.

The body, whoever it belonged to, was dead.

Inching towards it, her legs wobbly, Isla considered what she would do if it was a dead body. And, more to the point, who she expected it to be. She cautiously took the corner of the duvet in between her fingers and slowly pulled it back.

'For fuck's sake.' The words floated out on her hot breath. Her relief at seeing a bundle of clothes was immediate, but it didn't last. She was right: this had been some form of trap. Zach wanted her, or whoever came to the studio, to believe he was in the bed asleep, while he was elsewhere. Probably up to no good.

She might not have uncovered a body, but she may well have just uncovered Zach's alibi. Though for what? Isla replaced the duvet over the clothes. She'd have to search the studio quickly, then get back to Jase. To safety. Because whatever Zach had planned, she realised she was the most likely target.

After exploring the bedside table and units in the kitchenette, Isla moved to the oak wardrobe. She pulled clothes out, not caring now if she made a mess – time wasn't a luxury she had. She crouched down and then sat back on her knees, out of breath from her frenzied search. It was useless; there was nothing here she could use. She banged the flat of her hands on the bottom of the wardrobe. Something shifted. With a flurry of adrenaline, she realised the bottom was loose. Sticking her nails under the groove, Isla lifted the false panel and felt around inside the cavity below.

Her fingers made contact with a cool, slim object.

An iPhone. Hers.

In her shaking hand, she held irrefutable evidence linking Zach to her attack. As much as she'd known in her heart he was responsible, somehow the revelation still shocked her. Up until this point, there'd been the chance, albeit a slim one, she was wrong about him – that Simon or Graham, or even a random stranger, had meant her harm, not her own boyfriend. Any slight hope now shrivelled and died. Zach had wanted to silence her. Still did.

If Isla took the iPhone from here though, she'd have no way of proving it had been in Zach's place, that she hadn't simply found it elsewhere. It might have Zach's fingerprints on it, or it might not, but even then, it wouldn't prove anything. Unless it was found in his possession, this vital piece of evidence would be useless in a court case.

What to do, what to do? Isla's head swam. If she made an anonymous tip to the police, stating an exact location and giving them reason to believe Zach was someone they should look into, they would find it themselves. Discovering an additional link to Lance would be even better. Accusing him of murder was stronger than attack. Isla caught sight of something maroon-coloured in the back of the wardrobe she'd missed before; she pulled on it. Bile rose into her mouth. It was her handbag. Dizziness overcame her. He had both the stolen items. Isla couldn't understand why he'd kept them. Surely getting rid of the evidence, by burning it, throwing it into the sea, simply binning it, would've been the best way to ensure he got away with it?

The question of why he'd stopped the attack on her popped into her mind. One of the theories was that he'd been disturbed in the act. Thereby it looked like a mugging instead of attempted murder, which she felt sure was his real intention. This now cemented the thoughts she'd had originally, thinking he would come back to finish her off if needed. And as she'd begun to recall the events of that night, Zach's identity was at risk of being uncovered, and he must've realised the shocking reality of him being her attacker might soon be out in the open. And he couldn't afford that any more than he could've afforded Isla to continue delving into the past accounting records of Biggins

& Co. Fraud carried a hefty sentence, so committing murder to cover his tracks wasn't an altogether dumb move. If he could get away with both.

She hadn't found other evidence linking him to Lance's death. But she did have the mobile and handbag. Surely it would be adequate evidence for Zach to be arrested and charged, kept in custody. She'd be safe. With a sinking feeling, Isla realised it all hung on Zach not coming back to the studio and removing the evidence in the time it took her to even get out of there, call the police and for them to reach the Bigginses' property.

Taking her mini phone from inside her bra, where she'd kept it while it recorded her conversation with Kenneth, Isla pressed the speed-dial button for Jase. She needed to know what to do for the best. It could be possible to get the police here, with Jase watching out for Zach the whole time to make sure he didn't sneak back.

The ringtone went on and on. Jase didn't answer, nor did voicemail click in. Strange. She couldn't have got the wrong number because she'd carefully and deliberately keyed in the mobile digits on the tiny pad, saved it to contacts *and* tested it while she'd been in the car with Jase – for the sole purpose of being able to call him quickly and easily if she needed him.

Isla checked her watch. God – she'd taken so long with Kenneth and now in Zach's studio, she'd left Jase at risk. She tapped the button again.

A darkness descended. Was he *unable* to answer? What the hell could've happened?

She tried to slow down her ragged breathing. *Don't lose focus now.* But if Jase couldn't answer, there was a strong possibility it was because of Zach. He was there. Isla made a split-second decision. She grabbed an empty holdall from the top of the wardrobe and bundled her handbag and mobile into it. She couldn't chance Zach coming back and finding her here and finishing what he'd started *and* destroying the only evidence linking him to her attack.

Chapter Sixty-One

Isla raced down the road, around the bend to where she'd left Jase.

His car was gone.

Isla stopped and tried to regulate her breathing, her torso bent over, her hands on both thighs as she gasped for air.

No, no, no! She frantically searched along the pavements, checking each parked vehicle in case he'd had to drive to a different spot. Jase was nowhere close. And he hadn't answered his phone. Neither was a good sign.

Taking her mini phone, Isla tried his number again. Still nothing. A huge part of her wanted to dial 999. But what would she say? *My friend has gone missing and he's not answering his phone?* By the time she gave details and they realised she'd seen him only an hour ago, they'd probably conclude he'd got bored of waiting for her and had gone for a drive.

Which *might* be the case. She doubted it though – he'd been adamant about staying outside to wait for her. He'd promised to keep her safe. Leaving her was the direct opposite.

Standing in the middle of the street, feeling abandoned, Isla realised she only had Jase's number, not any of the other members of the Christie's team. *Stupid.* Isla pulled her fingers roughly through her hair, releasing a cry of frustration. He had said he'd call the rest of the team while he was waiting for her. With luck, they'd found something really important, and Jase had left to meet them. And, if something had come up, he would've been afraid to call her while she was in the mansion, potentially alerting Zach to the fact she had another form of communication and would assume she'd head home if he hadn't got back before her. As far as Jase was concerned, Zach was at the Bigginses' place. And if he checked again, he'd still be showing there thanks to the discarded briefcase. In which case, thinking all was safe at her house, he'd likely pick up with her there later. She realised she was giving him the benefit of the doubt, and also knew it was because the other option – that he'd merely let her down – hurt too much.

Whatever the reason, she couldn't stand around waiting for his return, or a call. Isla had no choice: she had to go back home.

Isla could make out one dimly lit downstairs window as she approached her house from the far side of the road. It was the single Tiffany-style lamp she'd left on in the lounge before she and Jase had headed to the mansion. So far, so good. She ducked out of view, waiting a moment as she took in each of the front windows, checking for signs of movement.

Nothing.

From her position, only part of the pathway leading to her front door and half the top step was visible, the neighbours' bushes obscuring a clear view. Jase wasn't there as far as she could tell, though. He didn't have a key, so he wouldn't be indoors. Unless he'd broken in. Isla had never attempted to gain entry from behind the house, maybe that was possible, but she thought it unlikely Jase would try. He wouldn't want to frighten her to death. Moving out of the shadows now, Isla ploughed on – the same confidence affording her the ability to walk home from the Bigginses' place alone in the dark now spilled over, allowing her to walk into her own home.

If Zach was there, she'd have to face the music. If she hid the holdall quickly before he clocked her, she could still pull off the innocent act so as not to alert him to her findings – the reason for her being out would be simple: she was worried about him after he left in such an abrupt way. Acting upset because of their argument wasn't going to be difficult to pull off, given how she was feeling about the knowledge he was definitely her attacker.

Before she'd even put the key in the lock, Isla had decided she would pack another bag, given the other one was in Jase's car and he'd gone AWOL. Then she'd go and buy a train ticket to get as far away from this place as possible – for the time being, at least. Making a trip home to Glasgow was way overdue – and there was nothing more comforting right now than the thought of being in the loving, protective arms of her mam.

Tomorrow, she could be far away from all the madness; she could be home.

The idea gave her a warm feeling and it spread throughout her tired, stressed body. An overwhelming need to sleep consumed her. She'd gone from sitting on the sofa twenty-four-seven, watching Netflix and scoffing junk food, to running around the streets of Torquay on some Jessica Fletcher escapade. Despite everything, a smile played on her lips. Watching *Murder, She Wrote* was the closest she was going to allow herself to get to real-life crime in future.

Isla slipped inside. It was quiet. She turned to bolt the front door – she didn't want Zach to be able to use his key to gain entry.

Hot pain flashed through her head like a lightning strike.

Isla stumbled, flinging her good hand to her scalp, touching something wet, viscous, before collapsing to the floor.

Chapter Sixty-Two

Christie's Crime Addicts – True Crime Podcast

Podcast – Live from the scene at Wellswood, continued . . .

[DOUG] Some onlookers have told us there's some movement outside a house . . . Can you see anything?

[CHRISTIE] A body perhaps . . . I'm trying to get closer. Looks like police are bringing someone out.

[DOUG] Do you guys think it could be a murder?

[ED] Forensics are on scene. Maybe. I'll leave you with Christie while I see if I can find a credible source.

[CHRISTIE] I'm at the cordon set up by police, watching as a covered stretcher is being brought out. The air is tense, people wondering what's just occurred in their neighbourhood. I'll get immediate reactions from those here with me. [Rustling sounds] You guys have been here since the first police unit arrived. What are your thoughts on this unfolding horror?

[ONLOOKER 1] It's shocking. First seeing them swarms of police, then to see them tents being erected. Teams of people going in and out in their white crime scene suits – looked like aliens invading. And now this!'

[ONLOOKER 2] It's surreal. All the times I've walked by,

with only a sideways glance at this house. You never know what goes on behind closed doors, do you? But murder. In Wellswood. Sends my blood cold.

[CHRISTIE] We don't know the details yet – might not be murder.

[ONLOOKER 2] Have you seen the police presence? Look around you, love. Of course it's murder. Or being treated as such, anyway. No accident. Wouldn't be receiving this much attention if it was just someone dying from natural causes, now would it?

[CHRISTIE] Tension is running high, here, Ed. Shock and fear is palpable. But the overwhelming thoughts at the moment are – who is the victim? Is it the woman who lived here? As we're still waiting for police to make any kind of statement, speculation is rife. Just who are the couple from Maple Drive? As yet, Ed, we haven't got names.

[ONLOOKER 3] I know who they are.

[CHRISTIE] Oh, hi, thanks for coming up to talk. You say you know who lives here?

[ONLOOKER 3] Yeah. I saw the guy a few times, but she lived here first. I think he'd only moved in recently.

[CHRISTIE] You know their names?

[ONLOOKER 3] She's called Isla. Always remember it because of Isla Fisher, my favourite actress. [Laughs] And the guy – he's called Jack, I think. Or, no – maybe *Zach*.

[CHRISTIE] Oh, wow. [Coughs] Okay, er, thank you. So, we have some possible names – not verified yet, of course, but it's the most info I've managed to get. It's not clear who the victim is, or who's the perpetrator. I couldn't see much from here – they were quick to bundle the stretcher into the waiting coroner's van, so no way of telling if it was male or female. Hang on, there's more movement.

[Shuffling noises, commotion, voices]

[CHRISTIE] They have someone. The suspect maybe . . . I'm trying to get closer. Looks like police are bringing someone out in cuffs.

Chapter Sixty-Three

The room was dim; quiet. Light from the lamp only illuminated a bright halo around the table it stood on, the rest of the room garnering a filtered, diluted glow. Isla's head ached. She was transported back to the moment she woke up in the hospital bed, dazed and sore following the first time she'd been struck over the head.

But waking up in a hospital bed with a nurse caring for her was far less fear-provoking than regaining consciousness with the face of her attacker looming over her. She wished this was a nightmare, as the ones she'd been experiencing since that night had been. In those terrifying dreams the face of her assailant morphed from one identity into the next. Now, though, just one remained in focus.

'Why, Zach? Why?' Her voice sounded small and inconsequential. To her ears, the sound was in the distance, emanating from a source other than her own mouth.

'You tell me, Isla.'

Isla stayed still. She was lying on the sofa, her head at the window end. Her fingers searched the back of her skull and found a lump and a clump of hair clogged with drying blood.

Zach straightened, taking a step back from her. He seemed even taller from her supine position.

'It's nothing. Just a small cut,' he said. 'Well? You must have something to say?'

'There's plenty to say,' Isla said, the strength beginning to return to her voice. 'Right now, though, I have a headache and I'm so utterly devastated I can't even bring myself to have a conversation with you.' She turned her face away, a sharp pain making her wince.

'Typical. Melodramatic as always, eh?'

'Oh, come on. If anyone deserves an Oscar for their perform-ance, it's you, Zach. Why didn't you finish me off? Would've been so easy to kill me while I was unconscious. Or isn't that fair game? Maybe you need me to be awake, have a chance at fighting back so you can feel better about it.'

'You do talk a load of shit sometimes.'

'You're the one who made me do the online psychobabble nonsense. You reap what you sow.'

'Humph. You always were too clever for your own good. If I were you, I'd shut up. You might live longer.'

'You just want longer to toy with me. Like a cat clawing at a mouse, tiring the poor little thing out before delivering the killer blow.'

'Maybe. Or, it could be because I want to explain.'

'No need to explain, Zach. I've got it pretty straight in my head. I found the dodgy files, saw your name and deduced you'd been committing fraud against your own father, and, to prevent me from whistle-blowing, you had to intervene and stop me. Did you really think I'd be the only one to pick up on discrepancies and delve deeper – finding incriminating evidence to allow the inevitable adding of two and two? What were you thinking? The execs must all know. You wouldn't have continued to get away with it. Even if I hadn't been the one to uncover your deception, someone else would've. *Will*. Trust me. I'm the least of your worries.'

'You're wrong. You *are* the only one who's ever unearthed those files. You are the *only* one to put two and two together. You think Graham is ever going to be arsed to sift through old documents? If it's not on the computer database, he isn't ever going to see it. I altered files over a year ago, signing *his* name as the one who'd overseen the deals, signed off on releasing money from the company account for fake transactions. He has absolutely no clue. And the other execs are too far up their own arses to notice what I'm doing. Thanks to my father, they all underestimate me.'

Zach believing no one else knew what he'd done wasn't good news. If he was right in his assumption, he only needed to get rid of her. It ruled out making a case that she wasn't the only one who knew, that his days were numbered even if *she* didn't say anything because someone else would. No amount of arguing to the contrary would sway him now. She had to try a different tack. 'I made a copy of the—'

Zach's sudden burst of laughter made her jump. 'No, you didn't, Isla. Sorry, but that won't work. And what was left in the archives has been . . . slightly altered . . . and – let's say – *redistributed*.' Zach smiled. 'Nicci's penchant for indiscretion came in very handy.' He walked backwards, not taking his eyes off her, then sat in the chair to the side of the sofa. In the dull light, Isla couldn't make out his face clearly, but what she could see, she no longer recognised. Being a true-crime buff, watching and listening to all the documentaries and podcasts, hadn't prepared her for this situation. No matter what she would've liked to think, she *was* out of her depth.

What would Jessica Fletcher do?

Isla began to cough. She doubled over, taking large, hiccuping gasps of air.

'Don't be stupid. Stop that.' Zach lurched forwards.

Isla started to make choking noises, her face turning redder, her eyes bulging with the effort to catch her breath. 'I—' Isla put her hand out to Zach. 'I . . . can't . . .' She pulled her hand back and grappled with the buttons on her top, ripping the material.

'Shit.' Zach sprang from the chair and knelt down in front of Isla. She pulled at his T-shirt as he attempted to calm her down. 'You're having a panic attack, Isla. Take slow, deep breaths.' He held on to her upper arms, but she shook him free. With one foot, she kicked into his chest, pushing him back. He lost his balance. 'For Christ's sake!'

While Zach repositioned himself, Isla quickly reached down the side of the sofa.

'Isla, please, calm down. You need to breathe more slowly; you're going to faint.'

Their eyes met. 'Oh, I see. Of course. Clever Isla. That was the plan. How long do you think you could prolong this game?'

'You'd be surprised,' Isla said, shrugging. She was exhausted from the pretend panic attack, but it had served its purpose. It'd given her the cover needed to push her bad arm down beside the sofa and slip the knitting needle she kept there up inside her cast without Zach realising. 'But you were concerned. I don't understand you, Zach. You want me dead, but you just tried to calm me down, stop me from hyperventilating and fainting. Why?'

'I didn't want *this*! All I wanted was to get out from the shadow my father had put me in. Show him I wasn't the push-over, the weak link, the useless idiot who disappointed him at every turn. It's him I'm wanting to make suffer, not you, Isla. You were meant to be . . .'

'What? I was meant to be what?'

'The one!' Zach flung his arms out, gesticulating frantically.

282

'You and me – I wanted us to be forever. First, that prick got in the way of us getting together. What a complete waste of space he was. You weren't right for each other. He didn't deserve you.' Zach paced, his movements jerky; uncontrolled. Isla was in a dangerous position. She knew what he was capable of, yet she couldn't stop herself pushing him. Fuelling his fire.

'So, you *killed* Lance? Can't you see how deranged that is?'

'Fuck you.' Zach grasped a handful of Isla's hair and yanking her into a standing position, began dragging her into the hallway, then up the stairs. To prevent her hair being torn from its roots, Isla made it easy for him – not daring to resist this heavy handling.

'You won't get away with this.' Fear mixed with anger as she was hauled towards her bedroom. 'You can't cover up two murders!'

'I won't have to,' he said. He was breathless from his efforts, but Isla could tell adrenaline was keeping him pumped. 'I've got it covered. The police won't spend much time considering me as a suspect, no matter what stupid shit those podcasters will spout about me, because they will find overwhelming evidence for your murder at Simon's.' He laughed. Outrage burst from Isla. Using all her available strength she twisted her body to pull away from him, yelling out to provide extra power – a technique she'd seen martial art students use on TV. But his grip on her hair was impossible to escape from. She heard a door being flung open, then slammed again. Her bedroom was going to be where she died.

Using his weight against her, he pushed her onto the bed and lay on top of her.

Isla's breath expelled rapidly with the compression; her lungs wrung out. *Is this all it takes to snub out a human life?* Her arms were splayed out at her sides – she had no way of reaching the hidden knitting needle. Now would be the time to give in to him.

Give up.

Fighting the inevitable was futile.

Chapter Sixty-Four

Isla heard her mother's voice inside her head; words of wisdom Rowan had imparted: 'Don't you ever give up, Isla – promise me? You must fight for what you want.'

As a teenager, Isla had mostly had a love-hate relationship with Rowan. She'd pushed the envelope on a daily basis, and it wasn't until she'd been living away for a while that she realised just how awkward she'd been. How difficult. Her poor mam. But she'd never given up on Isla, had always encouraged her to do something with her life, and secretly, Isla believed her mam was glad she'd moved away. She'd escaped the place Rowan had always been trapped in. Rowan hadn't lived her life the way she'd envisaged, hadn't chased her dreams – but she was dead proud Isla had.

Isla couldn't let her down. She had to fight now.

A renewed wave of determination forced its way through her. Isla brought her good arm up and slapped her hand against Zach's side like a wrestler tapping out to indicate they submit. She wasn't sure this approach would work, but her oxygen levels were dangerously low, her carbon dioxide increasing, making her woozy, so she had to try and save herself somehow. She didn't have the ability to fight hard. Zach's bodyweight shifted, giving her the space to breathe. Isla sucked in large lungfuls of air.

'Thank you.' Isla managed to say the words, despite his body still lying on top of hers. He'd given her a little reprieve, nothing more. 'Before you do what you have to do, can you tell me what happened?' She was breathless, the words like a gentle hiss of air from a deflating balloon.

'What do you mean, what happened? You *know* . . .' He pushed up from her, but straddled her lower half and held her arms so she was still pinned down.

'I mean to *you*. There's so much hatred and anger inside you. He must've done a real number on you.'

'You know what he's like to work for. Imagine living with him, being brought up by him. But none of it matters now. That part of my life is over. I'm getting the money, getting the business, and no one's going to stand in the way of that. Not him, not Graham, and not you. Don't think this doesn't pain me. At no point did I want to hurt you. You ruined what I thought was the perfect plan – ruined *everything* – with your digging around. But I thought you may still come through for me. Until you began your mission to take me down!' Zach's eyes were wide, his pupils dilated. Isla saw the hurt in them. He really did believe *she* was the one who'd betrayed *him*.

'I need to understand, Zach,' Isla said, her voice soft, pleading. 'From the moment I set eyes on you, we clicked. I thought you loved me. How can love make you kill? What will you do afterwards? Dump my body somewhere? Leave me here for the flies to feed off? And my iPhone and handbag? I assume you'll be getting rid of those?'

'Stop with the third degree. Jesus wept – you always have to grill me. Be the one in control. Well, not this time.'

'You don't think I deserve to know how you're going to dispose of me?'

Zach lifted his body fully from hers. She didn't want to chance leaping up straight away and be thrown back onto the bed, her opportunity to escape lost once and for all. She had to take it slowly. She stayed perfectly still, waiting for him to speak again.

'My father has belittled me for as long as I can remember. Making me feel worthless as my mother watched, helplessly from the sidelines, never quite brave enough to speak up – stand up for me. Do you know how that feels?'

'No, I don't.' Isla's father had been a let-down, and he had shouted and made her fearful as a child. But she'd always had Fraser; she was never alone. And Rowan had stuck up for her, even if at the time Isla hadn't been able to see it as such. She knew now. It was certainly a very different parenting style to what Zach had experienced. 'It must've been soul-destroying.' Isla knew if she could show she related to him, be empathetic and listen without coming across as condescending, she might buy herself some time here. She pushed herself up onto her elbows, and when she wasn't shoved back down went a step further and raised herself into a sitting position. 'You can have a different life now, though. Your past doesn't have to control you, your future decisions. You're part of Biggins & Co, Zach. Why go to such great lengths to embezzle money from the company you're going to inherit anyway?'

'Hah! You're not as clever as I gave you credit for if you think that's what's going to happen. You think that fat dick Graham is going to stand by and allow Kenneth to hand the business over to me? That snivelling creep has been waiting in the wings forever, just biding his time, ready to leap into action at the opportune moment to discredit me and ensure he gets everything.'

'I thought you said he was too lazy to do any digging around. Now you're saying he's looking for every opportunity to discredit you. If you ask me, that makes it sound like he'd go searching for a reason. Which is it?'

'I'm not asking you, though, am I? Don't confuse me!' Zach threw both his hands to his face, then grabbed at his hair. 'Shut up, now, Isla.'

'I'm not trying to confuse you, babe.' Isla lowered her voice; spoke more slowly and deliberately. She was aware he might think she was being patronising, but at this point, she had to try anything. 'I'm attempting to understand – that's what you want, isn't it? All I'm saying is, Graham is the one who is in your way, yet you're going to frame my murder on Simon. Why not Graham then? Wouldn't that kill two birds with one stone?' Despite her fear, the awful position she found herself in, Isla was genuinely baffled by Zach's actions. Keeping him talking also kept her alive a while longer. Maybe enough time for Jase to save her – like he'd done in her dream.

'Has to be a credible suspect, Isla. Think!' Zach jabbed a fingertip at his temple. 'Who's going to believe he managed to sneak up behind you, overpower you, attempt to kill you, and then run away before anyone witnessed it? Sweaty fat bastard would die himself. No. It has to be a *plausible* killer. The last person to see a victim is the one who makes the best suspect. It's what you thought too at first. The fact he tried it on with you adds credence. Nicci will testify to that because you told her! Simon *fits*.' Zach's face blazed, his eyes popping.

Rather than keeping Zach calm and buying herself time, Isla realised all she was accomplishing was to further agitate him and help him confirm his thinking was sound. Isla knew he was right about the last person to see a victim being high on the suspect list. She had to pull his plan to pieces, make him realise it was flawed and he wouldn't get away with it, for any hope of getting out of this situation alive.

'But he has no motive, Zach. The police aren't going to

believe he did it just because he tried to kiss me – they will look at the boyfriend as the key suspect. They always do. And didn't they check out where he was after the party? Surely he too had an alibi and—'

'Shut up, shut up, shut up!'

Isla flinched, blinking rapidly as his screaming echoed in her ears.

'Ahh, I'm so stupid letting you talk, Isla. I know what you're doing!' His arms grasped hers, yanking her up to her feet. 'You're setting me up even now, aren't you?' Zach patted her down roughly, tears streaking down his face.

'I haven't got anything,' Isla said, hoping he'd stop looking.

'Do you think I want to go through with this?' he asked. 'I'm not getting any enjoyment out of it – I'm not a bad person, Isla. Everything that happened, it's not my fault. Apart from this, here now, I hadn't planned to kill the others.'

The others. Plural. Isla's heart thudded. 'What do you mean . . . others? Lance. And who else?' Had she missed something? Had Zach killed before? Maybe it was to do with the relationship Simon had told Nicci about. Although, she wasn't aware anything further had happened following the beating Zach had given the boyfriend.

Zach's eyes clouded over, his stare reaching beyond the room. 'She was so beautiful. And kind. At first, anyway. But as with most people in my life, she lost interest. Made me feel worthless.'

'Who?' Isla had a terrible feeling she might know the answer already.

'It doesn't matter now. It was her fault. Why do women put themselves at risk walking alone in the dead of night? They're asking for trouble.'

Isla's jaw dropped; a knot grew in her stomach and her chest tightened. How had she fallen for this guy? Nicci had been right – he kept his flaws well hidden, his disturbing idealism under the surface, only showing what was socially acceptable to those around him. All the time she'd known him he'd been harbouring deeply destructive, antisocial thoughts and beliefs. Isla felt sick. But, now wasn't the time to get into a debate about it, as much as her anger and frustration warranted it. 'The Polish student. You killed her the same way you intended to kill me.' Tears welled in her eyes. That poor girl. Isla recalled how the podcast had caught her attention because of its similarity to her attack. Christie's Crime Addicts had said the case was unresolved. If she got out of here, she'd make sure Magdalena's family gained closure.

'I'm so sorry this is how it's ending between us. I really did love you.' Zach bent forward, lowering his lips to Isla's. His salty kisses were soft and gentle. So different to the actions he'd taken. Was about to take. His hand wandered upwards, to her chest. His fingers brushed against her breast, then he cupped it, squeezing hard.

Isla's heart juddered.

She looked into his face, watching as his expression turned to anger. He'd felt the hard lump in her bra. The tiny mobile phone. Zach tore at her shirt, exposing her bra. He plunged his fingers into the cup and pulled out the mobile.

The slap came hard, stinging her cheek. 'You underhanded, sneaky bitch!' he yelled. 'Must've got it off *him* – that bloody wannabe Poirot. Who the hell do they think they are? Thought you'd catch me out, recording me? Nah. I was always one step ahead, Isla. Everything's sorted, ready for Simon to take the fall. Your stupid stunt hasn't changed a thing.' Zach threw the mobile to the floor, stamping on it with the heel of his boot. He repeated the action several times, splintering and crushing the plastic casing.

Tears burned at the back of Isla's eyes. Her one chance at

calling for help was in a little heap of sharp shards on the carpet. Deflated, she sat back down on the bed. A realisation hit her. She'd helped Zach by playing right into his hands bringing the very things she thought would prove he'd attacked her to the house. Now he didn't even have to return to his studio to get them. He would kill her here and now, then plant all the evidence at Simon's. And she had no way of warning him. An awful thought crossed her mind. Zach had disposed of Lance because he'd come between them, without her knowledge even. Had he killed Jase too? Is that why he wasn't waiting for her in the car? She was afraid to ask.

There was a strong possibility no one was coming to her aid – that this time, there would be no one to disturb Zach: this attack would end the way he planned. If she didn't do something now, he would finish the job without fail.

'You're going to kill me tonight? You didn't do a good job the first time around, what makes you think you can succeed now?'

Zach looked at his watch. 'I'm going to have to do it now, Isla. Time is running out – it'll be light soon.'

Isla glanced towards the flimsy curtains – no light was seeping through yet. She wondered what time it was; for how long she'd been knocked unconscious when she entered the house. By her calculations, she'd got back around ten-thirty. If she'd been out cold for a few hours, then now would maybe be two, three-ish. He didn't have long to do the deed and get to Simon's to plant the evidence. She didn't have long to make her move.

Zach might've checked her clothing, but he was stupid enough not to look inside her cast.

Slowly, Isla began working the needle out of her cast with the fingers of her good hand, careful not to make any big movements. She needed to keep him talking.

'You don't have to do this,' she said. 'There's another way.'

'Oh, really? Pull the other one, Isla.'

'No, seriously – think about it – it's perfect.'

'What is?' Zach was either humouring her, or he was truly looking for an alternative way to get out of the mess he'd created.

'You're in a position where you could keep the money you've already . . . acquired . . . and could take even more with my help – then we could still be together, have the life we both want. Free of your father, free of Biggins & Co. We could have it all. Our cake and eat it, if you like.' Isla's eyes were wide, her tone excitable as she tried to sell her plan to Zach.

'Why would I trust you? You have never done anything illegal in your life, Isla – you think I believe you'd do something like this now?'

'I'm trying to give you a way out. I know you don't want to go through with killing me. You said yourself you love me. I'm proposing something that'll benefit both of us. I get to live; you get to have all the money *and* me.'

'And live in exile forever more. No thanks. My way, I get the money and the company, not to mention the respect – *without* being on the run. I just have to sacrifice the girl. Two out of three ain't bad.'

Zach turned and walked towards the door. Where was he going? If he was leaving her in the room, alive, then she still had a chance to get away. If she ran at the door the second he opened it, she may be able to overpower him long enough to run outside. If she screamed loud enough, or banged on the neighbour's door, she'd create enough of a commotion to make Zach think twice about harming her.

There were a lot of 'ifs', but it was better to try than admit defeat. She poised herself, ready to spring.

Zach turned back. 'You're going to try something, aren't

you?' He shook his head, tutting, then looked around the room. 'I'm going to have to tie you up.'

Hope plummeted along with her heart. Being bound would spell the end; she'd never escape. Isla had no choice. She had to act now.

She pulled the knitting needle all the way out of her cast and launched herself forwards. An animal-like scream ripped through the air as she plunged the needle into Zach.

Chapter Sixty-Five

Isla felt herself flying backwards. All the air was knocked from her lungs as she slammed against the far wall, the bloodied knitting needle still grasped in her hand. For a few seconds, she was stunned; confused at what had just happened. But, with adrenaline pumping, she recovered quickly, propelling herself forwards again, towards the open door. But Zach was too quick, moving to block her exit in a single stride.

'You fucking bitch!' He shouted as she lunged for him again. Tears streaked his face; blood soaked his T-shirt in a circular pattern. He kept one hand pressed to his side and with the other, he shoved Isla. She fell to the carpet, hard onto her bottom. She grappled on the floor, attempting to get back up quickly so she could ram the needle into him again. The first time hadn't hit the mark; she needed to disable him completely. Maybe even kill him. To her, this was one of those life-threatening situations she'd seen play out on the screen so many times, and it was clear she must kill or be killed.

Despite his injury, Zach was still quicker than her. He was out the door before she could reach him. Isla pulled at the handle, but it didn't open. She heard a key turn, locking it. She slammed her palm against it, the sting making it feel like a hundred needles penetrating her skin. 'Fuuuuuck!' she yelled through gritted teeth, her jaw clenched so tightly she wondered if they might crack under the pressure. The bastard had found where she kept the bedroom door keys. Isla hit her forehead against the wooden panel, then pushed against it again and again. Maybe she could smash through the wood? She knew the doors were thick. For it to work she'd need a hammer or something equally heavy. She rattled the door handle, frustration giving way to despair. An easier option would be to break the handle, then the door would surely open. But, she doubted breaking the handle itself would disengage the lock.

Climb out of the bedroom window.

Isla strode over to it, only half-believing this to be an option. She threw back the curtain to find it too was locked – and even if it wasn't, she knew it was too high. This room overlooked the back garden. If she screamed and was actually heard through the triple-glazing, she suspected her neighbours would ignore her. Isla wondered if they were even in. Having not heard any movement, there was a possibility they were staying somewhere else. Or the banging she'd heard the other day was something bad and they'd been silenced, or worse. She shook the thought from her mind. Zach knew he could only get away with so much, even he wouldn't push it that far. The body count was going to be bad enough without adding her neighbours to it.

How long did she have?

Zach would probably have to spend a bit of time patching himself up before coming back to finish her off. Unless he was too angry, adrenaline forcing him on. In which case he could be gathering his tools to kill her and be back within seconds.

Isla went back to the door and slouched against it, contemplating what to do. She was done for. She slid down until she was balled up on the floor, holding her knees tight up against her chest, her head tucked down so she was in a foetal-like position. There was nothing else she could do but wait to be handed her fate. Perhaps Jase would be waiting for her on the other side. It was strange, now she thought of it, how she'd connected with Jase. He was much older than any of the other men she'd ever fancied. It was possibly a father figure she craved – someone trustworthy, not like her own father. Whatever the underlying reasoning, she liked him and although she wasn't certain it was reciprocated, particularly after the awkward moment in the car, she'd experienced something – a spark of some description. Their brief time as friends had brought her warmth and a real sense of belonging and she really wanted to have the opportunity to see if, given the right circumstances, the spark would ignite. The thought that Zach had hurt him – and all because she'd involved him in her quest for the truth – made her heart ache.

What if Jase needed *her* now?

Isla looked up, her eyes drawn to the bloody knitting needle discarded beside her.

With a renewed energy, she took it and stuck the pointed end into the door lock. She remembered a scene in a crime show where the lock was picked – and although she didn't know if it was possible in real life without the expertise of a locksmith or burglar, it was worth a go. After a few wriggles of the needle, she stopped. It wasn't working – she was missing something. Blind panic was affecting her memory.

'Think, think.' She needed another tool. Jumping up, she rummaged in her bedside cabinet. Rifling through some old statements, she found a letter with a compliments slip attached to it with a paperclip.

'Yes!'

Isla steadied her good hand, the needle held to keep the tension on the top part of the lock as she tried to insert one end of the straightened paperclip into the bottom. It was fiddly with her cast and she dropped it several times. After a few failed attempts, Isla wondered if she had it the wrong way around. Using her casted arm, she placed the needle in the bottom of the lock, rotating it the same direction as she would the key, and held it there. Then, with her other hand, she inserted the paperclip to the top of the lock and wriggled it up and down.

Sweat trickled down her back, and a sheen of moisture formed on her upper lip. The fingertips of her hand in the cast became slick with it too, causing the needle to slip and, together with the paperclip, they fell to the floor. Isla wanted to scream. She listened at the door. She couldn't hear any movement. Had Zach collapsed? Maybe she'd done more damage than she thought. She still had to get out of the locked room though – alert the police.

Frustrated, Isla pulled at the cast. It was a week away from being removed, but right now the stupid thing was preventing her getting out of the room. There'd been scissors in the cabinet. Isla rushed to get them, and with her good hand hacked away at the plaster around her fingers.

A thudding noise stopped her cutting. She froze. She'd run out of time. He was coming back.

She'd had her chance, and now it was too late; she was going to die.

Just like Lance. Magdalena. Maybe like Jase.

But, she did have two weapons. She still had the needle, and now she had the scissors. Isla stood flat up against the wall to the side of the door. The second he opened it, she'd launch at him, plunging the needle *and* the scissors into him – and this time she'd make sure she hit major organs.

With her hands grasping the weapons, both arms raised to inflict maximum forward thrust, Isla waited.

There were no footsteps on the stairs. No sounds of his approach.

Silence now.

What was he *doing*?

Isla waited a while longer, then relaxed her arms. They ached with the tension she'd been maintaining. With no further noises, Isla continued to chop away at her cast, finally freeing her fingers enough for them to be useful. They felt weak, but after wriggling them and rubbing them with her other hand, she was able to grip the paperclip. Positioning the needle and clip as before, Isla fiddled with the lock. After anxious seconds passed with her thinking she'd have to give up, she heard a series of clicks and the needle suddenly rotated freely and unlocked the door.

The release of the door released the tension in Isla too, and for a moment she smiled and wanted nothing more than to collapse on the ground with relief.

But her work wasn't done yet.

Standing at the top of the stairs, Isla listened intently.

She couldn't hear anything other than the hum of the fridge coming from the kitchen. Had Zach left? She couldn't be that lucky. It was more likely she was about to walk right into her own death trap.

Armed with the scissors and knitting needle, Isla crept down the stairs.

Through the small, glass windowpane above the front door, Isla could tell dawn was breaking. She'd at least survived the night. If she could reach the door, run out into the road, she would be safe. The middle stair creaked as her weight shifted from it. Her foot hung, suspended between that step and the next, her breath held as she scrunched up her eyes, waiting for a sudden movement.

Still nothing.

She was four steps away from the foot of the stairs, another five strides from the front door. She could see the chain was linked across, so she'd have to allow a few extra seconds to unhook it before making her escape. Stress held all her muscles tight.

One more step.

Reaching the final stair, Isla ducked down. She didn't want Zach to see her until the absolute last possible second. Leaning forwards slightly, she edged her head around the end of the bannister to check where Zach was.

She retracted it quickly.

Shit.

He was right there. Sitting calmly in the kitchen, his back to her.

This could still work. By the time he heard her make her move, he wouldn't have time to get to her before she was outside. *He moved damn quick in the bedroom.* Isla ignored the negative voice in her head and peeked back around the bannister.

He was still.

Bright-red blood pooled on the floor beneath him.

Isla's heart raced. So much blood. From one puncture wound made by a knitting needle? Her internal voice now screamed 'run!', but another part of her needed to see. Like prodding something that appeared to be dead just to check if it moved. If he did move, would she get away from him in time? This could be his tactic. Straightening up, Isla took tentative steps towards the kitchen. As she got closer, she saw he was low in the chair, like he'd slipped. The puddle of blood continued to enlarge, the circular mass growing inch by inch. It didn't make sense.

Isla crept even closer, careful to avoid standing in the blood. She gasped as she got level with him, flinging a hand to her mouth to prevent a scream.

Zach's throat gaped. Blood pumped from his carotid artery. Although it was slow now, it had clearly gushed from the wound initially, sending huge spurts on to the table, up the wall to the side of him and had been steadily collecting on the floor. She stumbled back, away from the macabre sight, and collapsed on the hallway floor, all strength drained from her limbs.

Zach was dead.

And it wasn't by her hand.

Chapter Sixty-Six

Christie's Crime Addicts – True Crime Podcast

[CHRISTIE] A woman, mid to late twenties, petite – is being led out of number five Maple Drive by police. She's in handcuffs. No one else is being detained by the look of it.

[DOUG] She's the suspected murderer then?

[CHRISTIE] Looks that way at this time, Ed. News crews are here, the place is a hive of activity. Maybe we'll get a statement now. There's certain to be a media frenzy surrounding this one. Been a while since there was a serious crime in this area. The last was Lance Walker – the body on the beach whose identity was confirmed in the last few days. Makes you wonder if the two are linked – being that both are in such close proximity.

[DOUG] For the viewers listening in live right now – we'd not only been looking into the body on the beach case, but another developing story, too. One we'd been asked to advise on by the victim. I'm fairly sure the cases are linked. Jase was working on evidence-gathering. Shame he's gone AWOL today, as this latest news is key to his investigation.

[ED] I heard from him late last night, Doug – said he had new evidence to add to the file he'd been working on. No clue where he is now – I'm not sure this is the outcome he was expecting, though.

[DOUG] What do you mean?

[ED] The couple at number five are those he had under investigation. But it was the man, Zach – if the onlooker who named them is correct – who was under suspicion of trying to kill the woman. But the way this is playing out, it's the woman, Isla, who is the one now suspected of murder. Looks like Jase might've been duped.

Chapter Sixty-Seven

'It wasn't me. I didn't kill him.' Isla was exhausted. The night trapped inside her own house had been long; the morning was looking as though it would be even longer. Her main aim of escaping death had been successful, but she hadn't bargained on being the one accused of murder. Living the rest of her life in prison wasn't the outcome she'd envisaged. How many more times would she need to tell these detectives she wasn't the one who delivered the fatal wound to Zach?

Isla sat uncomfortably in the plastic chair, every one of her muscles aching. Her head wound had been cleaned and was only superficial, the doctor confirming she wasn't suffering with concussion after carrying out some basic tests. Not like the last time. But having been dragged by her hair up the stairs, her scalp still hurt all over. From being manhandled, to her attempts to escape, Isla's body had taken a battering. Mentally, emotionally, the damage was even worse. When she'd seen the police burst through her door, relief had flooded her. She'd done it. She'd survived. She thought that was the end of her traumatic experience. Now, having been stripped of her clothes – provided instead with a plain black T-shirt, grey jogging bottoms and nondescript black pumps – swabbed, and processed like a criminal, Isla was in shock and disbelief. She had to make them believe her. Inhaling deeply, she sat forwards, her eyes meeting the detective's.

'The puncture wound on Zach's left side was me. I admit that,' Isla said. Her aim to speak slowly and calmly failed, the sudden compulsion to get it all out overtaking. 'He'd trapped me in the bedroom, for God's sake, was going to *kill* me. Haven't you found his "kill bag"? Or my stolen mobile phone and handbag, which I found in his studio in the grounds of his parents' place?' Isla was aware she was rambling – it was as if her mouth was independent from her brain. Both detectives stared at her blankly, dispassionately, as if they didn't believe her – weren't bothered about what she was saying. They thought she was spinning them a story. They'd framed this as a 'you were the only one in the house; it must therefore be you' interview. When they'd repeatedly asked about the timeline of events, Isla was struck by the same problem. She herself was unable to comprehend what had happened; she hadn't *seen*. 'I was locked in the bedroom,' she'd told them again and again. She reiterated this again now.

'But you weren't, were you? When police entered the premises, you were standing over the dead body of your boyfriend,' the detective leading the interview said.

Had she been? That's not how she remembered it. 'I – I don't think I was . . .'

'You don't *think* you were . . .' The man, Detective Sergeant Armstrong, gave a sideways glance to the other, less talkative detective, then shuffled through some notes in front of him on the table. Isla watched but didn't really see. She felt separated from reality, like she was watching one of her documentaries play out on the screen – an actor in her place. 'According to your medical records, you recently sustained a more serious head injury and have been finding it difficult to recollect events, or recall memories, from that time.' He directed his dark, almost black eyes directly onto her now.

Oh, God. Isla realised where this was going.

'Yes, I had been suffering from post-traumatic amnesia and wasn't able to recall the night I was attacked. But things had been returning, and I remember *exactly* how last night went down. And I know I was not the person to cause the other . . . fatal injury . . . to Zach. I mean, come on – you saw the blood spatter, right? And did it look like I was in close proximity to the victim when that wound was inflicted?'

'Sounds like you've considered this quite carefully. Planned a good answer there, Miss McKenzie. I'm impressed.' DS Armstrong raised one eyebrow and smirked. Isla was close to losing her cool with his condescending tone.

'I didn't plan anything,' she said steadily. 'Other than to uncover the truth of who attacked me and why.' Her stomach was tense, her pulse rapid. She bit on her lower lip, but couldn't prevent her snarky comment escaping: 'Shame you lot didn't bother to do your jobs and find my assailant, eh? This would've had rather a different outcome if you had.'

Riling up detectives wasn't a bright move, and Isla knew she wasn't gaining anything by doing so. But frustration was bubbling, the tension increasing to such a level she felt she would erupt. And she'd be damned if she was going down for this.

'You mean you took matters into your own hands? Decided to play detective and bring the culprit to justice yourself?' Armstrong leaned back in his chair, crossing his arms. Isla glimpsed colourful tattoos on his dark-brown skin, ending at his wrists, as the sleeves of his shirt rode up a little. For a moment, her mind drifted, but she became aware his focus on her hadn't faltered and snapped her attention back. She sucked in her breath, readying herself to go on the defence, but she wasn't quick enough to respond.

'I'm calling for a break.' The duty solicitor Isla had been provided with, a woman in her late thirties, sharply dressed, stood abruptly. 'I need to speak to my client before we continue any further.' She began to usher Isla to the door of the interview room. Isla was grateful for the intervention; she was sure to have lost her patience in a dramatic fashion and say more things she would come to regret. Clearly Trinity Canmore had suspected the same and wanted to shut her up before she did any further damage.

'Taking a break at eleven-fifty-three,' DS Armstrong said before switching off the recording.

Isla turned back before leaving the room. 'You didn't answer my question. Did you find my iPhone and handbag that had been stolen the night I was attacked? And Zach's bag filled with stuff he was about to use to kill me? He was going to plant it on a colleague, Simon Frost.'

Isla caught a flash of uncertainty in Armstrong's expression, but he recovered quickly. 'We'll continue the interview once you've spoken to your solicitor, Miss McKenzie.'

'I hope you've not stopped looking, Detective. Because there's a killer out there. You're wasting time here with me.'

Chapter Sixty-Eight

Isla and her solicitor worked out a prepared statement. She'd allowed the solicitor to talk her into doing it, and, going forward, to only respond with no comment to any questions. Isla stared at the woman who she'd never met prior to this. She wore a serious expression, fitting for the circumstances she guessed – her hazel-green eyes popped against her olive skin, her deep-brown hair hung neatly to her shoulders in gentle waves. She was striking. And intimidating. If Isla had been able to choose a solicitor, she'd happily have picked Trinity Canmore.

Once her statement was read and recorded, Isla was returned to the custody suite. There were many burning questions she'd been unable to come up with an answer to, and now, alone in the confined, bare space of her cell, Isla turned them over in her mind.

Where the hell had Jase gone?

Didn't the police find the bag? Judging from the fleeting look of confusion on DS Armstrong's face when she mentioned it, she concluded they hadn't. So, whoever killed Zach must've taken it.

Had she been wrong in her assumption Zach had been acting alone in all of this?

One disturbing theory troubled her. As much as she didn't want to even entertain it, she knew she had to consider it – it was Jase who'd said not to allow focus on other suspects to narrow too soon. So, perhaps *he* had come to the house, interrupted Zach just after Isla had jabbed him with the knitting needle, an altercation followed and *Jase* slit Zach's throat . . . Isla breathed out heavily. It seemed ludicrous. But he'd disappeared. Left her at the Bigginses' mansion. As much as she'd tried to rationalise it, thinking he must've had a valid reason, now she had to question it.

Why? Why did you abandon me there, Jase?

Maybe he'd seen Zach leave. Yes, that was possible. Then he'd have realised Isla was safe, but he wasn't able to alert her to the fact he was going to follow Zach, so he just made a snap decision and did it.

If Jase had confronted Zach before Isla had even got to the house, Zach could've hurt *him*.

Oh, my God!

Isla launched herself at the cell door, banging both fists against it repeatedly. Pain shot up her wrist into her arm and shoulder. If she wasn't careful, she'd fracture it again. But she had to gain their attention; had to get them to search the rest of her house and garden, make sure Jase wasn't lying injured, or worse, dead, somewhere. Finally, she heard voices on the other side.

'You have to check something!'

'Miss McKenzie, you need to calm down.'

'No! You need to listen to me. Open the door, let me speak to DS Armstrong. Now.' Panic filled her voice. They wouldn't open the door if she was coming across as agitated. 'Please. I have information I need to tell him.' She spoke as calmly as she could given the adrenaline firing through her at a rate of knots. She waited, her breath held.

The door clanked and swung open. Armstrong strolled through.

'I'd gone to the Bigginses' place with someone called Jase – he's part of a true crime podcast team – Christie's Crime Addicts . . .'

Armstrong scoffed. 'Really?'

Isla ignored his scorn and continued, aware she had one chance to get this right; make sure he took her seriously enough to fully search the property and its surroundings. 'He was in the car down the road, waiting for me. I'd gone to Kenneth Biggins to extract information about Zach, gain evidence that would help my case—'

DS Armstrong flung both his arms up to stop her speaking. 'Oh, come on. What is this? Bloody Nancy Drew and the Hardy Boys stuff? Don't waste my time.' He turned away. She was losing him.

'Wait! I know how this probably looks. I was so sure Zach was behind my attack, but I didn't have any evidence to back up my suspicion. Knew you lot wouldn't listen. I had to get someone on my side, so I paid the Christie's team a visit and they agreed to help me. There was a tracker in Zach's briefcase. We knew it was at the Bigginses' place. But, after talking to Kenneth I went to Zach's studio and he wasn't there. The briefcase was. I don't know when he left, or why, but when I got back to where Jase had parked the car, it was gone.'

'The guy left you there? Nice.'

'He'd have only left if he thought I wasn't in any danger.' All at once. Isla knew this to be true. 'Which leads me to think he saw Zach leave and followed him.'

DS Armstrong drew in a long, steady breath through his nose, his nostrils flaring. He tilted his head, his lips pursed. Isla waited, her fingers curled in a tight ball. He was working it through in his mind; she didn't want to push it by interrupting his flow of thoughts.

He lowered his head and locked eyes with Isla. 'We'll look into it. Finding this *Jase* will be in our interest anyway.'

'Thank you,' Isla said. Her legs were weak; she collapsed onto the hard counter-bench running alongside the far wall.

'Your prepared statement said none of this, Miss McKenzie.'

'I know. I'm sorry – I was acting on the advice of my solicitor, but if someone's life is in danger . . .'

Armstrong nodded gently, then shrugged. 'Of course, this could be an excellent play on your part. Divert attention. You and this Jase might well be in it together and this was your plan all along.' He gave a half-smile, then left.

Isla realised everything she said might go against her. Desperate people reverted to desperate measures and the detective clearly thought it was what she was doing right now. She felt confident they would check out her theory, though. It would look bad on them if they chose to ignore the information and then it turned out she'd been right about Zach harming Jase.

It was going to feel like forever while waiting for news. If they would even update her. She was a murder suspect after all. They would drag her back in for questioning if they found something relevant, though. So, one way or another she'd find out.

Alone again with her thoughts, Isla mulled over her theory. If she was right about Jase, then who had slit Zach's throat? Had Simon realised what had happened, come to the house to confront him – and found out how he was about to be framed for murder – so killed Zach and took the evidence? The missing bag was niggling her. It made little sense Simon would take evidence that would've ultimately proven Zach to be the one who'd attacked her.

Someone had done it, though – and removed all the evidence. Someone had blood on their hands.

Isla was confident she wouldn't be charged with murder – she had no blood on her . . . Oh, wait. She *would* have Zach's blood on her because she used the knitting needle she'd stabbed into his side to pick the lock and escape the room. But forensics would confirm that amount of blood wasn't enough, or in the right pattern, to have come from opening up Zach's carotid artery. That blood pumped and squirted. She'd seen it pulsating from the wound. Meaning, it hadn't long happened. She'd just missed Zach's killer.

Why hadn't they killed her?

Obviously, she'd been spared purely so she'd be the one arrested for the murder.

Her one phone call she'd been allowed had been made to her mam. And in it, she'd asked Rowan to contact Christie's Crime Addicts. At least they had the file of evidence they'd been collecting – they'd be able to corroborate what she'd told Armstrong. They were her only hope of getting out of here.

Unless, of course, her theory Jase had followed Zach and had been somehow overpowered and hurt was totally wrong. The alternative, less favourable theory she kept coming back to was that it was Jase who'd done this to Zach. Her head throbbed. She couldn't bear to even consider this as an option, but given his knowledge of events, she had to. In which case, the Christie's team wouldn't be helping her at all. They might even be the ones happy to see her framed for it, if it meant looking after one of their own.

Chapter Sixty-Nine

Within the hour, the door to Isla's cell opened. *Shit, that was too quick.* Either they'd totally ignored her and hadn't even left the station, or they'd immediately found something. Found Jase. Tears pricked her eyes. Having dragged him into her mess she wouldn't be able to cope with the guilt had he come to harm. It would destroy her. Also, without Jase, her case wasn't as strong. Isla's breaths came rapidly as she was once again shown into the interview room.

Trinity had already read out her prepared statement, and Isla had since been advised to respond with 'no comment' to all further questions. Now, having spoken to DS Armstrong in her cell without her solicitor present, Trinity Canmore sat in stony silence, with a face that suggested she was not happy. Sucking lemons came to mind.

'Miss McKenzie, you offered up some information earlier,' DS Armstrong's eyes bored into hers. 'Interesting theory . . .'

He was toying with her. Isla began to hyperventilate.

'Breathe slowly. We need you conscious for this,' he said. There was a hint of compassion in his voice.

She did as instructed, regaining composure enough to ask if they'd found Jase.

'All in good time.'

Was he for real? Isla looked to Trinity. She merely shrugged and Isla had an urge to dismiss her there and then.

'Even if you feel compelled to respond, don't,' Trinity said instead. 'Even if it seems like a simple question, don't answer. Understand?' Her voice was tight; her previously calm, cool expression had slipped slightly, and Isla caught an air of frustration hanging between them.

Isla nodded, muted; silenced. Suddenly afraid.

If only she were lying on her sofa, a coffee and some snacks to hand, watching this all play out for someone else. It'd been entertaining, intriguing – *fun* to play armchair detective. Safe in her bubble. Within a few weeks, her life had tipped upside down, the landscape forever altered. Zach was guilty of attacking her, attempting to kill her, yet here she was accused of *his* murder. The logical part of her mind knew she couldn't be charged nor convicted of this. The irrational side was panicking because it wasn't unheard of for an innocent person to be convicted.

She'd been absolutely livid when she'd watched a recent documentary where a teenager had been charged and convicted for murder on what the programme had shown to be weak evidence. The forensic data in particular had been lacking. He'd served eighteen years. Was still in prison, having lost countless appeals. The thought this could conceivably happen to her filled her with a sense of impending doom.

Isla wiped the back of her hand over her cheeks where tears had dampened the skin. She looked at the broken, battered plaster on her wrist. A reminder of how she'd managed to be strong, think quickly and take action in order to preserve her life.

She had to do the same now.

'You confirmed you'd been the only other person in the house at the time of Zachary Price's murder—'

'No,' Isla said, her eyes narrowed. 'I said I believed at the time I had been, but clearly I wasn't.'

'Isla, please,' Trinity said. 'No comment, remember?'

'You were adamant we should be looking for Jase – full name Jason Turner – as he was your "partner in crime".'

'This line of questioning is uncalled for. If you have enough evidence to charge my client, I suggest you get on with it.'

Isla shot Trinity a worrying glance. What was she doing?

Isla didn't like the direction this was taking. Sod this. She was going to go against her solicitor's advice. She had to put up a fight, here and now. She wasn't prepared to leave her fate in this woman's hands, as good a solicitor she might be. If she messed everything up, Isla would have to live with the consequences. And she couldn't, *wouldn't*, die on this hill.

'In your statement you said you had been at Zachary Price's house – at his parents' – then went to his studio in the grounds. Is that correct?' Armstrong said.

'You know it is. That's what I said.' Isla frowned.

'I advise you to return a no-comment response, Isla,' Trinity said, her voice loud and stern.

'Sorry. But I'm not having this,' Isla said, turning her head to Trinity then back to DS Armstrong. He had a smug look on his face – the air of someone who was chuffed with himself.

'Did you want to add anything to that?' he said.

'There was someone in the house, with Kenneth Biggins. Someone other than his wife, I mean. They must've heard my conversation with him.'

'Which entailed what, exactly?'

'I'd been informed about an incident that resulted in Zach receiving a restraining order. He'd been violent towards the new boyfriend of his ex. So, I confronted Kenneth with this knowledge. I showed my cards, I suppose. I was confident I could prove Zach had form, and that I knew there was something off about his alibi for the night of my attack. Kenneth knew it. And whoever was listening knew it.'

'You're going off the point, Miss McKenzie. You've been arrested for Zachary's murder. He's not the one under suspicion here – you are.'

'I'm giving you context. Zach had form.' Isla paused, remembering Zach's confession to her about the Polish student, Magdalena. If she brought this up now, it might confuse the issue; cause more harm than good at this point in time. She had to keep it as simple as possible, focus on one situation. She had plenty of time to offer her information later, and maybe she would speak to Trinity about it first anyway. She continued, ensuring she maintained eye contact. 'He had a motive, the means and the opportunity,' Isla said.

She caught DS Armstrong's eye-roll, but carried on unperturbed. 'What I'm saying is, he was responsible for my attack, then attempted murder – as that's exactly what his intention was last night – and that yes, in self-defence, as a means to escape, I plunged a knitting needle into his side. But I did *not* then go on to slit his throat. Someone else was in the house, and they finished him.'

Isla waited a beat to see if her words were sinking in. Was Armstrong buying it? 'I'm thinking it was the same person who'd been at Kenneth Biggins's place.' Isla sat back hard in the chair. She was exhausted, yet felt somewhat triumphant, as if she'd single-handedly solved the case.

'And say I believe this *theory* of yours, Miss McKenzie. Why didn't you mention it earlier? You seem to change your story – drop other names in – when it suits. I thought you said you were sure Jase had gone to your house? Now you're suddenly sure someone else was at the Bigginses' house and *they* had followed you back to your property? Hardly consistent . . .'

Isla opened her mouth to hit back. Trinity threw an arm across Isla as a warning not to continue speaking. Isla knew she'd gone past the point of no return in that regard. She almost felt sorry for the woman who'd had no alternative but to provide counsel for her. Isla hadn't made her job easy. Glancing at Trinity, then focusing back on DS Armstrong, Isla launched into a speech justifying her actions.

The solicitor's shoulders slumped, her pen scrawling noisily over her note pad as Isla rattled off everything she knew so far: how her ex-boyfriend, Lance Walker, had been identified as the body on the beach and how during his attempt to kill her, Zach confessed *he'd* been the one responsible for his death. Not only that, but he'd also killed a woman, a Polish student named Magdalena. 'I can't remember her surname, but look it up,' she said.

DS Armstrong's eyebrows were raised, his eyes wide as he listened. Isla didn't know if what she was saying made sense to the detectives, or if she was even being taken seriously. The other, horrifying thought was whether she was incriminating herself further. Isla had no idea what Armstrong was thinking – for all she knew, he could be considering this new information from the opposite angle. That she herself had killed her ex *and* her new boyfriend and was now trying her best to pin it all on the dead guy, adding in detail about another dead girl purely to make her story sound credible. The back of Isla's nose tingled with threatening tears. She hadn't meant to mention Magdalena at all yet. She hoped she hadn't just ruined everything.

A sharp rap on the interview room door prevented Armstrong from responding.

'Yes,' he called.

The door opened and a young officer popped his head around. 'You need to come here, Guv.'

Instantly, Isla sensed a change in atmosphere.

This interruption was significant.

Isla could barely swallow her own saliva as she silently watched DS Armstrong rise from his chair.

Chapter Seventy

Isla fiddled with a loose thread on the grey jogging bottoms. How many others had worn these before her? They were clean, she presumed, but still – they smelt funny, and they weren't hers. Her mind drifted – had her own clothes offered any answers under their forensic analysis yet? Would the swabs, blood, hair and fibre samples all confirm her innocence? She'd never felt so guilty for something she hadn't done.

'Interview suspended at twelve-fifty-eight,' Armstrong said, before nodding to the other DS to stop the recording. 'Stay here a moment.'

Time stood still in the stuffy room. Seconds were like hours and Isla was stuck in a loop of being positive, then negative about the reason for the interruption. She drummed the nails of one hand on the table – the resulting tapping noises eerily loud. And by the expression on Trinity's and the remaining detective's face, very annoying. It was all she could do to release the tension, though.

DS Armstrong burst back into the room, and without looking at Isla indicated for the solicitor to approach him. He took Trinity to one side, muttered something, then he left. The door slammed behind him. Isla looked to Trinity, poised to ask her what was happening, but another officer came in, taking Isla by the arm. She was led out, back down the corridor to the custody suite.

What was going on? 'Hello? You going to inform me what the hell is happening? I need to see my solicitor, please. Where did she go?' Isla frantically turned this way and that, hoping to spot Trinity. She must've followed Armstrong. They'd found something key to the investigation. It was the only conclusion Isla could draw from the abrupt end to the interview. She dared to hope it was positive, and that Jase was safe. Prayed he wasn't the one who'd killed Zach.

Sitting in the cell, Isla allowed herself to think about the past twenty-four hours, replaying the events in her head. She could understand Zach's fear of being caught embezzling from Kenneth's company, but going to such great lengths to cover his tracks was extraordinary. And learning that he'd been jealous of Lance to the point of killing him was so extreme, she found it hard to process. Zach had said it was to ensure he didn't get in the way of his plans to be with her – so would he have done the same to the next man who came into her life? If she hadn't chosen to go out with him when she did, someone else might've suffered from Zach's obsessive and deranged actions.

Zach clearly had trust issues, feelings of inadequacy – and this went a long way back and had resulted in him attacking and killing someone before Isla; before Lance. His issues were obviously deep-rooted, ingrained from childhood, and he'd been a dangerous man. Whoever took him out of this world had done it a favour.

Kenneth hadn't seemed shocked when Isla mentioned the restraining order – only by the fact she knew about it in the first place. Had he warned Zach that Isla had been asking questions? If he had, it would explain why he was ready for her when she walked through the front door. She'd had the feeling someone else had been at the Bigginses' house – the two whisky glasses in Kenneth's study had been testament to that. He'd had company before she interrupted his evening. She'd initially thought it was Zach, but now hoped it had been someone else. Telling DS Armstrong 'someone' else was there hadn't helped; she should've given a name – it would've added weight to her assertion. And the only other person she thought would likely be drinking with Kenneth, was Graham.

She now knew for certain Graham hadn't been the one to attack her. But he had left the party at the same time as her, even walking in the same direction. Despite him not being the one to carry it out, had he been involved in organising it? She couldn't see it. He had no reason to. Unless he was coerced.

Being alone with her thoughts and theories was destructive. Being left to stew, mull over the fact DS Armstrong had been summoned from the interview room, was increasing her stress to an unbearable level. She wished she were on the outside, able to seek the answers to all the questions herself. The lack of control she had over her own future was terrifying.

Isla leaped from the bench as the door opened. It'd easily been an hour since she'd been bundled back in here. *Please don't drag me back into the interview room.* She looked hopefully as the figure of DS Armstrong, followed closely by Trinity, entered her cell. The space immediately shrunk in size and Isla's chest tightened. She looked from one to the other, the anticipation of what was to come like a hot, acidic liquid in her stomach.

'Isla McKenzie,' Armstrong boomed. Isla felt her legs give. Shit. She was about to be charged with murder. She collapsed onto the bench, her head dropping forwards. 'You're free to go.'

'What?' Isla's head snapped up.

'You aren't being charged, Isla,' Trinity added helpfully.

She wrestled with the feeling of euphoria over one of mistrust. 'You found who did it.' She felt a coldness creep through her like a slow-moving, deadly frostbite.

'We have been made aware of new evidence and this, together with a significant development, means you're off the hook,' Armstrong stated in a cool voice.

'Are you going to expand?' Isla felt a rush of emotions, the overwhelming sense of relief was quickly overtaken by fear again. What had they uncovered?

'Your solicitor will fill you in on what we can divulge.' He went to leave, then hesitated, turning back towards her. 'We will need to speak with you again. You're still key to this investigation.'

So, despite being told she was free to go, she wasn't entirely free; there were conditions. She was still involved. 'Can you at least tell me if Jase is alive . . .' Isla was shocked to hear the wobble in her voice; tears sprang to her eyes. 'Please,' she whispered.

DS Armstrong gave a curt nod. 'He is alive, Miss McKenzie.' He left the cell, leaving the door wide open for Isla to exit.

Chapter Seventy-One

Trinity Canmore took Isla to a different room off the main corridor. This one was comfortable with soft furnishings and cheerful, sunny yellow walls and an outlook of the sea on the horizon. Although more relaxed than she had been, Isla was still on high alert, anxiety gripping her insides.

'Well?' Isla asked, as soon as the door closed.

'You've not been the easiest client, Isla,' she said, exasperation clear by her furrowed brow. 'But, your information did help. Maybe, in this case, staying quiet wasn't the best option for you.'

While Isla was pleased to be praised, albeit backhandedly, she was more concerned about hearing *why* she'd been released. 'Where's Jase?'

'The only information I can disclose to you at this time is that your information, together with a file handed to the investigating team, resulted in further arrests.'

Arrests, plural. 'Okaaay.' Isla didn't like the sound of this. It was too vague, and *further arrests* didn't sound conclusive enough. She couldn't feel confident the police knew for sure who had done it. And why hadn't Trinity given a direct answer about where Jase was? Had *he* been one of those arrested?

Please, no. She'd placed her entire trust in him, he'd helped her and she couldn't have misread him – his intentions. The realisation that prior to all of this, she could just as easily have been referring to Zach made her question herself. 'You're not answering me. Is that literally all you can say? I'm free to go, apparently, so I'm guessing no one is even slightly concerned for my welfare. They must be pretty certain at least one of those arrested is the right person – that I'm not in danger if I go back home?'

'As I said, the evidence they are now in possession of appears solid and they're happy you're not at risk. Although, I'm afraid you aren't able to return to your home address. It's still an ongoing scene of investigation.'

'Fine. I'll go to see Jase, then. If you're not giving me any more info, I'll find him at the Christie's team office and he'll have the answers.' If Jase had been arrested, or had been found injured, Trinity would have to tell her now. Though Isla needed to know, she found herself fearing what words were going to come from Trinity's mouth. In the car immediately prior to her going into Kenneth Biggins's place, Jase had told her about his misspent youth. And he'd been in the army, so would've been trained well, which surely meant it was unlikely he'd come to harm at Zach's hands. Which left Isla drawing the conclusion it'd been Jase who'd inflicted the harm. Her heart beat furiously as she stared at Trinity, awaiting the verdict.

'Sure.' She smiled. Nodded. Stuck her hand out. 'Good to meet you, Isla. Good luck.'

That was all Trinity was going to say? 'But DS Armstrong said he'd want to talk with me again.' Isla shot her a confused look.

'Here's my card. If you need a solicitor, don't hesitate. But I have a feeling you'll not be requiring me. Or anyone else.' She gave a short laugh. 'Seems pointless if you just ignore our advice, eh?'

'Sorry. I did appreciate your help.' Isla's mind whirred. Trinity had neatly sidestepped Isla's mention of Jase and she was left with more uncertainty than before. 'Do you know if they're going to look into the murder of the Polish student again now?' It had been playing on Isla's mind – the fact she'd brushed over the details of what Zach had told her purely because she was afraid it wouldn't help her own case. She needed to put that right, make sure justice was done, even if her killer was now dead and wouldn't serve time. Magdalena's family deserved to know what had happened.

'The case has been reopened, yes. And your information is being treated as fresh evidence. As DS Armstrong said, he'll need to speak with you again at some point.'

'Okay. That's good.' Isla was so tired, her eyes heavy.

'I suggest you rest now. Find a nearby hotel, or go to a friend's place for a while, Isla. Contact DS Armstrong to give him the address as soon as you decide.' Trinity smiled warmly. 'You should go where you feel safe.'

'I'm not even sure where that is,' Isla said.

Trinity raised one perfectly sculpted eyebrow. 'I think you'll find there are a few loved ones who are desperate to hear from you. One in particular,' she said.

Chapter Seventy-Two

The taxi dropped Isla off in Torquay town centre. She walked, her legs trembling, to the building housing the Christie's team headquarters. It had been barely a week since she'd made the first brave step to go outside alone and seek their help. With nerves fluttering wildly in her stomach, she pressed the bell. Her whole body shook with apprehension, scared of who would answer. Afraid it wouldn't be Jase. Afraid the team would deny her entry. She had no idea what had gone on, why Jase had left her alone at the Bigginses' place. She was in the dark about all the events to have unfolded since her arrest.

What could she expect now?

Isla heard the click of the lock releasing. The door opened.

She closed her eyes, trying to keep the tears inside her lids. The pressure of anticipation pushed hard against her ribs.

'Thank God they let you out!'

Isla's eyes sprang open at the sound of Jase's voice, relief washing through her like a tidal wave. Her words stuck in her throat. All she could do was stare at him. Questions swam in her mind, but not one word escaped her mouth. She stood, frozen to the spot, and cried.

*

Holding a hot mug of coffee, Isla perched on the red two-seater sofa, eight pairs of eyes trained on her.

'This might be a tad overwhelming, guys,' Jase said, raising his eyebrows at the other Christie's members. Getting the message, Doug, Ed and Christie stood up.

'When you're ready, we'll help fill you in,' Christie said, laying a hand on Isla's shoulder before retreating out of the room. The others offered smiles, a few encouraging words, then followed Christie out.

'Thank you,' Isla said to Jase. She took a few more sips of coffee, then looked him in the eyes. One of them was red, watery – the other exhibited an earthy palette of colours: shades of browns blending with greens and a deep purple. 'Who did that?'

Jase touched a fingertip to his eye. 'My ego is bruised far more,' he said. He gave a hollow laugh then directed the conversation away from his eye. 'I'm so, so sorry I left you. After the fuss I made when you said you wanted to go to Bigginses' place, too. I feel such an idiot.' He looked away from her. 'But more importantly, I feel ashamed I let you down.'

Isla pressed her lips together tightly, willing herself not to cry again. The way Jase was speaking seemed heartfelt; his concern was coming across as more than she'd expect if he was thinking of her in a little sis kind of way. She hoped she wasn't misreading the underlying meaning again as she'd assumed she had when they were in the car. 'I wouldn't say you let me down,' Isla said simply, being careful not to jump the gun this time. 'But then, I'm not really sure what you *did* do yet, so . . .'

'Fair point.'

Jase moved to sit next to Isla. Part of her wanted to shift up, and away from him; the other part wanted nothing more than for him to take her in his arms. She stayed still.

'God, I must look such a state,' she said, indicating to the dodgy-looking clothes. 'I don't think the police buy their clothes from ASOS.' She gave a nervous giggle.

'I've still got the bag you packed – it's here. You can change in a sec.'

Isla smiled. Of course, she'd forgotten. 'That's a relief. I don't suppose you have showering facilities here, too?'

'As it happens, yes, we do. Look,' he said, taking her hands in his, 'before you sort yourself out, I really want to explain.'

Isla tensed, the words Zach uttered flying through her mind. She prayed Jase's explanation wasn't about to leave her in tatters as his had. 'Go on,' she said. The warmth of his hands penetrated her skin. She could even feel it through her cast – although that might've been her imagination. In any case, she felt safe, comfortable, as Jase began to retell the events from the previous night from his perspective.

He'd left because he'd received a call about potential evidence retrieved from CCTV footage belonging to a bar on the route Isla had taken the night of the attack. But, Jase explained, it wasn't that night's footage offering up interesting evidence. From what Isla had told them about first meeting Lance at Cedars Bar, and then him ghosting her, together with the recent news confirming the identity of the body on the beach as Lance Walker, they'd been able to form a timeline of what they thought were his last movements.

Jase had been informed how the landlord had spotted something relevant on the bar's CCTV tapes – ones he'd presumed had been deleted because they usually only kept thirty days' worth. With the potential to gain valuable evidence, Jase left the road near the Bigginses' residence to drive to the bar a few streets away, assuming he'd be back by the time Isla left the mansion. Once at the bar he'd watched the black and white images of Lance leaving the premises, closely followed by a

331

male figure who he could clearly identify as Zach, and a scuffle ensued. Jase said he'd felt certain if he took that to police, they could make a link to Lance's murder. Excited by his findings, he rushed back to the mansion and waited for Isla. Only he was too late.

After Jase had finished his story, Isla told him hers. Including the confession Zach had made regarding killing Magdalena. After an hour of talking, they sat in silence. There was so much more to tell, he said, but there was plenty of time. Isla, although keen to learn every last detail, was drained, and all of a sudden felt she could sleep right where she was. She leaned in against Jase, his presence comforting. Now she knew he was safe and he was no longer a suspect in Zach's murder, she was glad to have involved him. Thankful she'd put her trust in him. It turned out she wasn't altogether useless at judging character.

Chapter Seventy-Three

Isla spent a few nights at Jase's, recovering from the immediate effects of the ordeal. His flat was in Babbacombe, just a twenty-minute walk from Isla's. She learned he was separated, with no children and had plans to sell his flat and buy a two-bedroom house. He couldn't afford the prices in that area of Torquay, though, he said – so was looking at the outskirts. He was kind enough to drive her to Derriford to have her plaster removed fully – her attempts with the scissors had freed her fingers, but she hadn't gone any further. She popped into Burrator ward while she was there and was lucky to find Heather as she was finishing her shift. She was shocked to hear about what had happened, but delighted Isla was now safe. They asserted they'd stay in touch, and Isla was pleased she might have found a more trustworthy friend.

After being filled in on all available facts by the rest of the Christie's team, Isla made one last visit before packing a suitcase ready for Glasgow. She walked through Cary Park, a large bunch of flowers cradled in one arm. She stopped at the edge of a small, square grassed area and looked at the rectangular, bronze plaque with its simple inscription: In memory of

Magdalena Kaminski. There were no other details. She knelt down, laying the flowers on the grass.

DS Armstrong had taken a further statement from Isla and assured her things were progressing with Magdalena's, Lance's, *and* Zach's murder cases. When she came to Devon, she never expected it to be a place where multiple murders could happen. It was rare, of course, but when such a shocking crime touched you in that way, it was all-consuming. Maybe, the fact one person was responsible for two of those murders, and the culprit himself was the third victim at the hands of someone close to him, offered an element of hope. Not everyone she met was capable of harming another human. These had been 'isolated incidents', Armstrong had reassured her.

'Sleep tight, Magdalena,' she said. Isla knew she'd been the lucky one – the two attempts on her life had failed. All she could wish for now, was for Magdalena's family to have closure – a form of justice – and for Magdalena to rest in peace.

Isla was sitting in a forward-facing seat in the first-class carriage of the train to Glasgow. It was her first time travelling in such comfort, and it was expensive. But, she couldn't bear to think of spending nine hours sitting in a standard carriage, possibly jammed next to people who'd make the journey seem even longer. A flight to Glasgow was a fraction of the time and cost – but she didn't find flying at all relaxing, and actually, she needed the extra hours to think – it would be beneficial. Maybe by the time she reached home and set eyes on her mam, her head would be far clearer.

The complimentary newspaper she'd been handed lay flat on the table, the deep-purple face of Kenneth Biggins adorning the front page. The attention-grabbing headline was one she'd never expected to see. Of course, Jase and the rest of Christie's Crime Addicts had told her everything, so it wasn't a surprise now; she'd been adequately prepared. All the same, seeing it all in black and white made her stomach lurch.

Local award-winning businessman
Kenneth Biggins hauled in for questioning
over his son's murder

At the foot of the front page it stated the story 'continued on page 2'. Isla turned to see the double-paged spread, with more photos of Kenneth, this time being arrested at his home at Ilsham Marine Drive. When she first learned of his arrest, Isla was dumbfounded. While it was true Kenneth wasn't the most pleasant man, nor a particularly good father by all accounts, to have killed his own son was abhorrent. How could anyone take the life of their only child, let alone in such a brutal way? It didn't bear thinking about. She'd questioned it over and over – concluding he and Zach were bad, damaged people both putting their own needs above anything else. Then Jase had offered further insight leading her to believe Zach had inherited his father's cold-blooded-killer tendencies.

Isla spotted the shocked, white face of Viola in the background of the photo. There was no indication from police, or the article, of her being involved in any way in what had gone down, but Isla felt certain Viola Biggins must've known at least part of it. She would've had to have buried her head six feet underground to not have realised what her son and husband were like. What they were capable of.

There was a subheading stating an additional arrest had been made. Isla felt her breathing become shallow as she looked at the rounded face of Graham Vaughan. It turned out that he *had* followed her when she'd left the party. She wondered what his intentions had been – she'd probably never know now. All that Jase had been able to find out was that Graham had apparently witnessed Zach's attack on her. He'd done nothing to stop it. But he had relayed what he'd seen to Kenneth, who'd then made the call to the hospital to find out the extent of his son's violence. Whether Isla was dead, alive and conscious, or alive but unconscious, would've no doubt been key in the subsequent course of action that they decided to take. It was then that things took a different turn – none of which was to do with Isla – the part she'd played had merely acted as a catalyst. Her knowledge of Zach's embezzlement had actually been worth nothing – Graham and Kenneth uncovered that themselves following Graham's earth-shattering revelation. Zach had been wrong about Graham being too lazy to dig around.

All the time she was trying to uncover the truth of who had attacked her, Kenneth and Graham already knew. But they'd chosen to keep it to themselves. For reasons that became shockingly clear to Isla when Jase explained everything. The things he'd found out when he'd left Isla at the mansion, and the evidence he'd been armed with when he'd gone back to find her, meant he'd been at risk too. He'd no idea if he was being watched, whether Zach had suspected he was involved and needed to be taken out of the equation. Having knowledge of the lengths Zach would go to in order to get rid of people who stood in his way hadn't filled him with a lot of confidence.

He'd waited for an hour after returning to the street where he'd dropped Isla, but when she hadn't materialised, he'd panicked. That was when he thought Isla must've left and he'd missed her. He'd gone to find her, not realising the occupants of the mansion had had the same idea, but for very different reasons. Kenneth and Graham waited for events to play out, knowing full well Isla's life was in danger. They wanted Zach to carry out her murder, because that got rid of the loose end. The risky factor. Without Isla, no one would find out about Zach's illegal activity in the firm, thereby enabling Biggins & Co to save face; keep the business going without fear of retribution. The family business was everything to Kenneth; he wouldn't allow it to fall into disrepute. And certainly not by his only son – the supposed heir to the business. Kenneth Biggins could not allow Zach to bring shame to the family name. He wouldn't stand by and wait to be humiliated by his useless, good-for-nothing son. He'd rather ensure the business was left in the capable hands of the man he trusted, the one person who'd been at his side, faithfully, loyally since the beginning.

Zach's death was inevitable.

And ensuring Isla was the only one in the house at the time of his death gave them the perfect scapegoat. But they hadn't anticipated Isla's strength. Her determination to live and put up a fight to make sure she wasn't framed for her boyfriend's murder. It looked as though she and Zach had something in common after all. They'd both been underestimated by the almighty Mr Big; Scrooge.

The train slowed into a station. Isla checked her phone for the travel information. They were four stops from Newcastle, where she had to make a change. Going back to Glasgow was going to be strange, it'd been so long since she left in search of a career, a life away from the confines of her childhood home. She didn't think she'd missed it particularly. The dull-ness, the midges, the bleakness. The scenery could be so dramatic, but she didn't find comfort in it like she did the Devon coastline. At this moment, though, she longed to be there, in the home she'd grown up in, being fussed and bothered over by Rowan. As much as she'd found warmth and friendship with Jase, there was nothing quite like your mother when things were rough. It was worth travelling the length of the United Kingdom for a hug from her mam.

As instructed, Isla had informed DS Armstrong of her intention to stay with her family in Scotland for two weeks. Luckily, he was happy as long as he had all the relevant contact details. She wasn't under any suspicion, but he wanted to know where she was so he could gather further information as and when he required it, as they put together a case for the crown prosecution.

Reflecting on what had happened, how she was so much stronger now, Isla knew she could face anything. Given a new chance to make the most of her life – stop waiting for people to hand her opportunities – she knew she must seek them herself. Make things happen for her.

Once settled on the new train, the one taking her to Glasgow Central where Fraser was going to pick her up, she made a phone call to Nicci. It was one of the hardest calls she'd ever made.

'I'm so, so sorry, Isla,' Nicci said, the minute the call connected. Isla heard the tears immediately. She wrestled with the urge to rant at her, allowing her the time to say what she had to say. 'I was so blind to what was happening. What an utter twat I am.'

'Oh, I wouldn't go *quite* that far,' Isla said softly. She was aware her voice might carry back into the first-class carriage and this was one conversation she didn't want anyone to overhear. It was probably as well she'd made the call here, now, because it meant she had to remain calm.

'Can you forgive me?' Nicci's strained voice cracked in her ear.

Could she? Nicci hadn't made forgiveness easy. She'd gone behind Isla's back and stolen her job, lied to her, helped Zach keep tabs on her and slept with the boss, glossing over the underhand stuff that was going on right in front of her. All for what? Forgiveness wasn't something Isla thought she could genuinely offer her ex-friend. If she'd learned anything, it was trust had to be earned; it was a two-way affair. Nicci wasn't in the position for that to be possible right now. If ever.

'Honestly, Nicci? I don't think it's going to be easy. I really don't want to hold on to any negative feelings of resentment, or bitterness towards you, so in that respect, I'll find a way to let go, move on. Our friendship won't survive this, though.' Isla almost added, *I'm sorry*, but she bit her tongue. She refused to be sorry for others' actions anymore. She knew Nicci had suffered and didn't want to make her feel any worse than she suspected she already did. Biggins & Co was no more, with the boss and his second in command both on remand accused of murder and Zach dead, there was very little hope of the company surviving.

Viola may well step into his shoes at some point; however, even if she did, Nicci wouldn't retain her position there. Nicci's own actions had come to light, her affair with Kenneth known to Viola and the wider public, so Isla doubted her life was going to be plain sailing for quite some time. Not to mention how she'd allegedly altered records to implicate Simon, thereby ensuring the finger of blame didn't point at Zach, a detail Isla hadn't divulged to anyone, and that spelled the end of any friendship with Nicci. Isla alluded to her knowledge of this now, and heard a sharp inhalation.

'Oh, Isla.' More tears. Isla waited, wondering how to best end the call. But she didn't need to. 'I understand what you're saying. I'm glad you're okay,' Nicci said. 'Bye, mate.' And she hung up.

They weren't well matched as friends anyway, and Isla never did quite trust what was behind those eyes. She needed to rely on her instincts more. Same with Zach – although a part of her felt sorry for him; for how things had ended – God knows what he'd been subjected to in his childhood, but it'd had such awful consequences. When she had children, she'd be sure to bring them up with unconditional love – and be proud of their every achievement, however small. No one should be made to feel inadequate, inconsequential. Who knew what damage that caused a growing, developing child.

Chapter Seventy-Four

Christie's Crime Addicts – True Crime Podcast

Excerpt from Episode 165 – *The Couple on Maple Drive*

[DOUG] We're bringing a conclusion, albeit a temporary one, to the case of The Couple on Maple Drive – whose names were confirmed as being Isla McKenzie and Zachary Price. As we know, Isla was arrested at the property for the murder of her boyfriend, Zachary. But, following this, evidence gathered by our very own Jase meant police were given additional information that led to her release and the subsequent arrest of local businessman Kenneth Biggins and his loyal second in command, Graham Vaughan.

Jase, from the beginning you were involved in this case, and as a team, we were all helping gather information. At the time the report came into us that there was a possible murder on our doorstep, Christie, Ed and I were unaware that what was occurring was in fact related to Isla McKenzie. She'd approached the team to ask for our help, and you, Jase, took the lead. Do you want to tell our listeners exactly what happened?

[JASE] Sure. Well, as you say, Isla sought us out because she was a fan of our podcast – she'd been listening to the episodes while recovering from what was thought to be a random, violent mugging. Following a head injury sustained during the attack, Isla was affected by retrograde amnesia and had no recollection of the events immediately before and after the incident. Slowly, her memories began to return, and she started to suspect that her boyfriend, Zach – who'd moved in following her attack to help her – was in fact the one responsible for it.

[DOUG] That's a pretty huge revelation, Jase. Why didn't she ask him to move out? Or leave herself? Seems mad to keep living with someone who you suspected had hurt you, almost killed you.

[JASE] It was my concern, too. Right from the off I believed Isla's account detailing the run-up to the attack, and felt she was right to be suspicious of Zach. But, at that time she had no evidence, just a hunch, and she decided she was better placed to stay put and watch his every move, gathering as much info as she could about him and the company they both worked for. As listeners know, Zach was the son of Kenneth Biggins, a local businessman who has since been arrested in relation to Zach's murder.

[CHRISTIE] About that, Jase. The story went from Isla thinking Zach was her assailant, to Zach having his throat cut in the matter of a week. Can you take us through the steps leading up to Zach's murder?

[JASE] Isla gathered evidence to prove Zach had been embezzling money from his father's business and this was the motive for him attacking her. She'd also begun to find items of spyware he'd downloaded onto her phone, with additional trackers and recording devices discovered in household items. She knew he was listening to her conversations and following where she'd been going. With my help, she attached her own tracker to Zach's briefcase so we knew where he was at any given time. I wanted to see if the places he visited gave an indication of what he was up to and added weight to our investigation.

[ED] And did it?

[JASE] At one point it showed Zach to be at his parents' property in Ilsham Marine Drive, and Isla was keen to go there and confront Kenneth Biggins – the hope being that she'd be able to lay the foundation of doubt in Kenneth's mind about Zach's involvement in her attack, given Kenneth was the one who had supposedly asked Zach to stay late at work the night of Isla's attack – thereby giving Zach his alibi.

[CHRISTIE] But before you went – because you'd convinced Isla to allow you to drive her there and wait for her – you'd told her the news about her ex-boyfriend. Is that right?

[JASE] Ah, yes. The catalyst if you like, for Isla's decision to act, came after I informed her that the name of the previously unidentified body on the beach was Lance Walker. The man Isla had been seeing a year earlier but who she'd believed had simply ghosted her. And while I was waiting in the car for her to speak with Kenneth Biggins, I was given another piece of information, CCTV from a bar in Wellswood, offering the much-needed evidence to link Zach with Lance. When I got back to where I'd dropped Isla, I waited but she didn't show up. Realising she must have gone back to her house, I left, driving straight there.

[DOUG] Which is where you were intercepted by Kenneth and his sidekick, Graham.

[JASE] Precisely. Stupidly, I let my guard down. I was blindsided.

[ED] And by blindsided, you mean knocked unconscious and dragged to the rear of the property.

[JASE] Yep. Don't even start me on that, Ed. You'd think an ex-army bloke would be prepared, wouldn't you? I guess my fear for Isla's safety overwhelmed me and I didn't think straight. Took the hit and was out cold for a while, and when I came to, I found I'd been gagged and tied up. The police found me at around midday the following day in the neighbouring house's shed.

[DOUG] Why do you think you were left alive?

[JASE] I think it was all to do with plausibility and one dead man blamed on a young woman was believable, given the circumstances, but two? Not so much. They'd attacked me from behind, I wouldn't have been able to identify them, so I suppose they'd incapacitated me for as long as they needed to do the deed.

[DOUG] The deed being, of course, killing Zach.

[JASE] Hard to believe, isn't it? A man murdering his own son purely to save his business?

[CHRISTIE] According to the prosecution, though, Kenneth hadn't been the one to deliver the fatal wound?

[JASE] No, apparently not. Graham Vaughan had entered the property with a key he'd had cut, and once inside he'd waited for the perfect opportunity to attack. Because Isla had stabbed Zach with a knitting needle in her attempt to escape him, Zach was an easier target. Graham reportedly wore a paper suit, like those worn by crime scene investigators, and approached Zach undetected from behind. He swiped the knife from left to right, severing the carotid artery in Zach's throat. Within seconds Graham had left the property, taking the evidence linking Zach to Isla's attack with him.

[ED] That evidence being the iPhone and handbag stolen during the attack on Isla, which she had found in Zach's studio in the grounds of the Bigginses' estate, together with the bag Zach himself had taken to Isla's house in view of killing her?

[JASE] Yep, and then he fled in the waiting car, driven by Kenneth Biggins. In the meantime, Isla had escaped the locked bedroom and came down to find the bloodied body of Zach slumped at the kitchen table. Police were on the scene moments later, with the only person alive in the house immediately suspected of being the killer.

[CHRISTIE] I was on the scene when the body was stretchered out. It seemed like a cut-and-dried case once a woman was arrested at the scene. Of course, without you to hand, Jase, we hadn't realised we were at the house of the woman we'd been helping. It was one of the onlookers who named the couple, and believe me, shock didn't come close to what I felt. Witnessing Isla McKenzie being brought out handcuffed was both horrifying and a relief. If it had been her who'd been the one killed . . .

[ED] Doesn't bear thinking about.

[JASE] Thanks to the evidence gathered by Isla and Christie's Crime Addicts, plus the incriminating items found in Kenneth Biggins's possession, the right people have been arrested and will be brought to justice. The prosecution team have plenty of evidence – and it looks most likely that Graham was doing Biggins's dirty work – eradicating Zach and the evidence pointing to his involvement in murder and embezzlement, so he wouldn't bring shame onto the family. It's widely reported how Graham Vaughan had been a long-time friend and employee of Kenneth's, helping him build the business from scratch. Others from the company, who preferred not to be named, told us Graham always referred to himself as the 'second in command', making it clear he believed Kenneth would favour him over his own son when it came to handing over control of the company. Having learned about his son's degrading actions on top of the illegal activities within the business, Kenneth had asked Graham to commit the ultimate act of loyalty.

It's not exactly a happy ending – one innocent man lost his life and an innocent woman almost lost hers twice. Additional evidence also came to light during this investigation, which is linked to a cold case, and we'll be bringing you up to date with that in a later podcast. But, for this current case, the outcome for Isla is freedom and closure, and now she can get on with her new life.

[CHRISTIE] Yes, and watch this space, crime addicts, we'll have exciting news about that soon.

[DOUG] Thanks for listening in today. We'll be back with more tomorrow. In the meantime, Christie's Crime Addicts wish you a safe day in the bay.

Epilogue

Isla watched the orange flames licking at the edges of the fire-place. It wasn't especially cold out, but Rowan had lit the fire to make it cosy. And it did just that. There was a childhood feeling of safety at home with her mam. *Murder, She Wrote* was on the telly and Bruce, her mam's ageing cat, was purring on her lap. She stroked him with one hand while holding a crystal tumbler of whisky in the other. Isla glanced at her nails, the French manicure she'd promised herself was pretty and there was no lasting damage where the cast had been. Her wrist was a little slimmer than her other, but it was strong, and it was great to be free of the restriction at last. She had to be thankful for it, in a way; the cast had offered her the housing for the one thing that had ultimately saved her life.

'You should avoid all the nastiness from now on, love,' Rowan said, her Glaswegian accent one of the things Isla hadn't realised she'd missed until hearing it in person rather than just on the phone. Her mam was trying to convince her to stop reading or watching anything crime-related: books, news, magazines – and especially telly. 'You shouldnae be watching that stuff. It's not natural,' she said, her eyes filled with concern. Isla's obsession had become a worry for her mother. The night she'd been attacked for the second time, she also promised herself she wouldn't view, or listen to, any real-life crime in the future. Now, though, she realised it was her fear talking – a part of her hadn't expected to live past that situation, locked in her bedroom waiting for Zach to kill her, so she'd made a silent promise in the heat of the moment. But Isla didn't want to shy away from those things; didn't want to be put off due to her experience. If anything, she wanted to use it. In a positive way.

Which was why she now slowly and calmly explained to Rowan how she had a new future – a new career in the pipeline. With Jase. After long conversations with him, then Christie, Doug and Ed, it was decided Isla would join Christie's Crime Addicts and together, they were not only going to tackle true crime stories and report on investigations in the area, they were also starting up self-defence classes using Jase's military background. And they'd be travelling around schools offering an education package, speaking to children about positive self-image, how to treat others with respect, and tackle issues around consent and boundaries.

Isla's plan was to travel back to Torquay once she'd spent some quality time with her mam and brother, recuperating from her ordeal. It would be a different place – no Biggins & Co, no Nicci. Her phone call to her ex-colleague had acted as a Band-Aid – it wasn't enough to enable them to be friends again, but was adequate so neither of them would feel completely awkward if they were to bump into each other around town. Nicci'd been burned too, in the end. Few had come out of the experience unscathed.

Isla was going to remain in her rented house on Maple Drive for the time being, despite the memories there, awaiting her return. But she was already searching estate agents having made a decision to buy her own flat in the bay. There was a strong possibility Jase would be part of her personal life as well as her working one – with mention of them buying a place together – and as much as it was a lovely thought, for the time being Isla wanted her independence. There would be time enough to build upon their relationship and she wanted to see where it would lead naturally.

Isla smiled, and as the music denoted the end of another episode where Jessica Fletcher had caught the culprit, she and Rowan whistled along to the theme tune while the credits rolled impossibly quickly. There was a comfort in its predictability. A predictability that wasn't echoed in real life – and, finally, Isla felt just fine about that.

ACKNOWLEDGEMENTS

I owe massive thanks to my editor, Katie Loughnane. I'm truly grateful for all your support and for the way in which you've championed me and each of my books. It's been an absolute joy to work with you. This, sadly, marks the last book we will have worked together on at Avon. We've had a fantastic run and I wish you well in your new role – I couldn't be more delighted for you, and I know you have a bright future in publishing.

Thank you to Team Avon, HarperCollins – it's been a challenging year for all, and there have been a few changes meaning I have yet to meet some of you in person, but thanks to Zoom I have at least seen you on screen! I look forward to continuing to work with you all. Your enthusiasm, professionalism and hard work, a lot of which often goes on behind the scenes, is greatly appreciated. I'm incredibly lucky to be part of the team.

Thanks to my agent, Anne. There are many ups and downs in this business and you're right there, helping me navigate the journey and guiding me on my career path. My thanks also to Kate Hordern, of KHLA, and to Rosie and Jessica at The Buckman Agency.

Huge thanks to: Doug for continuing to support me and ply me with prosecco when the going gets tough; to Louis for coming up with the brilliant *Christie's Crime Addicts* name – you're always so full of genius (and sometimes wacky) ideas; to Nathaniel, for help with anything related to tech – I know I can be exasperating, especially when things have to be explained to me multiple times; to Danika for ensuring I have a distraction when required – and Isaac for being THE best distraction of all. Grammy loves you.

I am thankful for the continued support from my sister, Ce, and brother-in-law, Pete – I know you are proud of my accomplishments and that means a lot. And thanks to Josh, Emily, and my wider family who support me by buying and reading my books!

Thank you to my writing buddies – Libby Carpenter, Caroline England and Carolyn Gillis – we speak almost every day, and I couldn't do any of this (writing, or life in general) without your friendship and support. Your good humour, compassion and advice keep me going.

Thanks to friends, J and San – our Wednesday nights are BACK (following a drought during COVID restrictions) – our evenings give me the much-needed escape from my own head. Also, thanks to Nicci, for your friendship and support. I stole your name for this book, but I didn't steal your personality. You are a loyal friend and are gorgeous inside and out; I trust you implicitly! I consider myself privileged to have an amazingly supportive circle of fabulous friends – I thank each of you for being in my life.

I'd like to thank the wonderful blogging community. I'm so grateful for your enthusiasm and commitment. Sharing what you've read on social media really helps promote authors and I consider myself lucky in knowing some super bloggers who are always willing to read, review and recommend my books.

Special shoutout to Cathryn Northfield – you've been so supportive, thank you! We've got to know each other quite well over the past year or so and not only do we share a love of books, but we are both addicted to jigsaw puzzles! Hopefully, we will soon get to meet in real life!

As ever, I want to thank my readers. I can't tell you how wonderful it is to receive messages saying how my books have kept you hooked, or how you've loved the suspense, or a twist. After all, that is the ultimate goal when I sit down to write these stories.

Thank you for picking up this book. I very much hope you've enjoyed spending time with *The Couple on Maple Drive*.

Other novels by Sam Carrington...

All available in paperback, ebook and audiobook now.